Faking Normal

Also by Courtney C. Stevens

The Lies About Truth

Faking Normal

Courtney C. Stevens

HARPER TEEN

An Imprint of HarperCollins*Publishers*

HarperTeen is an imprint of HarperCollins Publishers.

Faking Normal
Copyright © 2014 by Courtney C. Stevens
All rights reserved. Printed in the United States of America.
No part of this book may be used or reproduced in any manner whatsoever
without written permission except in the case of brief quotations embodied
in critical articles and reviews. For information address HarperCollins
Children's Books, a division of HarperCollins Publishers, 195 Broadway, New
York, NY 10007.
www.epicreads.com

Library of Congress Control Number: 2013951716
ISBN 978-0-06-224539-7

Typography by Andrea Vandergrift
15 16 17 18 19 CG/RRDH 10 9 8 7 6 5 4 3 2 1
❖
First paperback edition, 2015

For my mom, who held my hand with every word;
and my dad, who prayed over every word;
and my brother, who taught me to make up characters;
and for every girl or guy who has needed a Bodee.
Ephesians 3:14–21.

chapter 1

BLACK funeral dress. Black heels. Black headband in my hair. Death has a style all its own. I'm glad I don't have to wear it very often.

My dress, which I found after rummaging in the back of my closet, still smells vaguely of summer and chlorine. The smell is probably just a memory.

"Alexi, slide in closer so Craig can sit with Kayla." My mother's voice pulls me from my misery and back to the funeral.

Mom makes room for me to shift down the pew toward her, and I slide obediently into the crook of her arm as Kayla's boyfriend joins our family. Even though I don't tell Mom, it feels good when her arm loops over my shoulder, and her hand gives me a little squeeze-pat that means she loves me. If we weren't at a funeral, I'd probably shrug her off. But that would be sort of selfish, since Mrs. Lennox was in Mom's prayer group all that time.

"How's Bodee doing?" Mom asks.

"I don't really know him," I answer.

"You've been in school together for eleven years."

I shrug. "He's the Kool-Aid Kid." Why do adults always think kids should be friends just because their mothers are? Sharing homeroom and next-door lockers doesn't mean you know a person beyond his label. Across the church aisle from me is Rachel Tate, the girl whose mom did Principal James on Bus 32. I'm Kayla Littrell's carbon-copy little sister. Before this week, Bodee was the Kool-Aid Kid. Now, he'll be the kid whose dad murdered his mom. That label will pass from ear to ear whenever Bodee walks down the hall. But now it's a pity-whisper instead of a spite-whisper.

"It would be nice if you reached out to him." I can tell Mom wants to say more, but the music changes and she faces the front.

There are no words to the music, and that makes me sad. Every song deserves lyrics. Deserves a story to tell. Mrs. Lennox's story is over, so maybe she doesn't need words, but Bodee might. Reaching out to him is one of those Christian things my mom talks about, but you can't share a closet and a stack of old football cards with someone you hardly know. So I say a prayer and hope he'll find a place of his own to hide.

But this'll probably always be what he goes back to. Mom. No Mom.

That's a forever change. I never understood life could be so dramatically sectioned, but it can. And is. There is only after. And before.

My moment was by the pool; Bodee's is by the casket. Or wherever he was when he found out about his mom.

Kayla leans away from Craig and asks, "Alexi, is he in your grade?"

I nod and wish Kayla would lower her voice.

"Lord, he's homely," she adds.

"His mom's dead," I say. I inch even closer to Mom, which isn't exactly possible. Kayla's wrong, anyway. He's not homely; he's unkempt, and there's a difference.

I'd rather sit with Liz and Heather, but all the parents have their kids clumped around them like they're trying to share one umbrella in a rainstorm. I love my family, but it seems that I'm always with people I don't know how to talk to when I feel the saddest. With Kayla, and Craig, her appendage. Or Dad, and Mom the teacher.

"Who does he run around with?" Kayla persists.

"No one."

Mom gives Kayla the eye, and we both stare at our programs.

I repeat Psalm 23 with the rest of the crowd and wonder if God ever considered writing the psalm in the past tense, since so many ministers read it during funerals. "Yea, though I walked through the valley of the shadow of death" is more accurate for Mrs. Lennox.

"And now," the pastor says, "we're going to hear from Jean's two sons, Ben and Bodee."

Ben strides forward, never looking up. He removes a piece of paper from his pocket. The room is quiet, and I can hear the page crinkle as he flattens it against the podium. He twists his sealed lips this way and that, and then opens his mouth and sings—half reading, half crying—part of a hymn. The song is beautiful, and I wonder if music is the real language of grief.

"Mom always sang that when she worked in the kitchen." Ben stares at the ceiling as he says, "I don't know how to make it without you, Mom."

His pain and fear pass through the air like electricity. I don't know how they're going to make it either.

"Thank you, Ben," the pastor says. "Bodee, come on up here, son."

All eyes look to the left, where Bodee rises from his seat in the family section.

Bodee's hair is blond today. I'd thought his Kool-Aid-colored locks were intended to disguise his misfit jeans and generic white T-shirts. Make him look artistic instead of just poor, but now I'm not so sure.

Mom moves her arm from my shoulder to crumple a tissue in her hand and dab at her tears. "Oh, this is just awful."

I can't take my eyes off Bodee. His shoulders bend like

the wire hanger in my closet that sags under the weight of my winter coat. I want to put my hand in the center of his back, force him upright. His sluggish shuffle is as sad as his shoulders.

"I think he's wearing Craig's old khakis," Kayla says. "See the faded ring on the back pocket?"

"Half the guys at Rickman chew," I say. But Kayla's right about Craig's khakis; I've seen those same threads spoon and fork and maybe even tongue around Kayla on our couch.

"Well, they're somebody's khakis." There's sympathy in her voice. "Maybe *you* should take him shopping."

Even though it's the kindest thing Kayla's said, I whisper, "Why don't *you* take him shopping?"

"Maybe I will."

Craig rolls his eyes at me, because he knows as well as I do that the last thing Bodee needs is to become one of Kayla's pet projects.

Now Bodee's at the podium, and Mom's not the only one who needs a tissue. While the room sucks and snorts and wipes, he grips the knot on his tie like it's a lap bar on a roller coaster.

He doesn't look at any of us. The microphone broadcasts his short breaths into the room.

Come on, Bodee. Say something.

But he just breathes and tugs at the tie again with one hand and wedges the other into the pocket of Craig's old pair of pants. I pull at the folds of my dress. Kayla does the same.

Mom squeezes Dad's hand. The rest of the room shifts in their discomfort for Bodee.

"That poor, poor boy," Mom whispers.

Lyrics drift into my head as I watch Bodee drown.

Alone.
Before this crowd.
Alone, in this terrible dream.
Who am I in this visible silence?
Can they hear me scream?

I wonder if Bodee knows that song. Doubtful. I toy with the idea of writing the lyrics on the back of the program. I could drop it in his locker on Monday. But he might take that the wrong way.

My mysterious desk guy wouldn't take it the wrong way, though. He penciled those same lyrics on my desk the first week of school. August 8. Nineteen days after my life changed.

I don't think random lyrics are going to help Bodee.

He's not going to talk.

It's like there's a muzzle over his mouth. A word-thief at work.

Bodee bolts from the podium and out the side door.

"Go," Mom says.

For once our instincts are the same. My knee collides with the hymnal holder on the pew in front of us. The crack announces my movement to the room and effectively ends the silence that Bodee started. Craig steadies me as I climb over him and Kayla.

"Good idea," Craig says as I exit.

I'm not going because Mom told me to or because Craig thinks someone should. I know what it's like to face the silence alone.

Bodee's in the back garden. I'm out of breath when I reach him, which is fine because this is awkward already. All this empathy, or whatever it is, will be gone by the 7:55 bell Monday morning. The school hallway is a war of differences, and Bodee and I have plenty. Accepted; rejected. Shops at the mall; doesn't shop at all. Quiet except with friends; quiet everywhere. But today we have something in common besides last names that start with *L*.

We've both lost something we're never going to get back.

The little concrete bench wobbles as I add my weight to his. He only glances at me long enough to register who I am. There's no surprise on his face that I have followed him to this outdoor hiding place, nor does he send me an *I want to be alone* look.

Time would speed up if I spoke, but I don't care if time is slow. I do wonder what Liz and Heather think about my scramble from the pew, and if everyone in there believes I'll reemerge with a repaired, talking Bodee.

But I don't tell him to go back inside or that everything will be fine. I just sit beside him and let the inch between my thigh and his remain. He cracks his knuckles compulsively, and I stare at a break in the concrete where a little green weed lives.

When the funeral director finds us, I finally speak. "See you Monday?"

"Yeah."

And that's it. I leave Bodee on the bench. The space between us is elastic now, stretching from an inch into yards.

When I reach my mom, she kisses my forehead. "Lex, I love you," she says.

"I love you, too." And as I say it, I think, No one will say that to Bodee anymore.

chapter 2

LIFE starts during fourth period.

It's not because of AP Psych or the fact that this is the one class I have with Heather or that lunch is next. It's all about the desk and the lyrics. And since it's Monday, I get to start them.

What should I write about today? The funeral? Girls who talk to boys they don't really know? Sex? Girls' fear of sex? No. I'll keep the illusion intact, since most guys would rather believe girls are just as horny as they are. This flirty masquerade with Desk Guy is like reading a romance novel. Love in pencil is safer than love in life. So I settle on a piece of pop culture that describes my entire weekend after the funeral.

Do you have a minute?
Can I invite you in
To take control?

Heather leans over to read my words. "There's no way Desk Guy'll get that. And if he does, it's totally some girl jerking your chain."

"It's not a girl. I asked already."

"You can't count on a desk to be honest," Heather says. "Mine has 'Mark loves Lisa' carved on it, underlined. And, uh, everyone knows the only person Mark loves is Mark."

Heather's desk sucks, but I do count on my desk to be honest.

"Dang," Heather says when she sees my face. "If you want it to be a guy that bad, it's a guy. I'm sure Captain Lyric will totally complete you like he does those pretty little verses you write each other. But just in case he doesn't, Dane's going to the soccer game with us tomorrow."

I erase the word *minute* in my lyric and rewrite it so it's easier to read.

"Why do you always do this to me?" I say. "I don't even know Dane."

"Well, he's Collie's cousin, and I've given you almost two months to manage a date with Captain Lyric here. Since you haven't even tried to figure out who he is, I'm in charge of your social calendar. There's a ladder to climb, sweetheart, and you're standing still. At least he's cute."

"Just because you have Collie doesn't mean the rest of us want what you do."

"It's a soccer game, not a proposal," she says.

"Thank God."

"Oh, you know you want what Collie and I have."

"Uh, no. I don't." The idea of anything resembling a relationship gives me hives. First dates are pretty safe, because any guy who wants to mess around on the first date's a jerk. But a guy who's been dating you for six months and who doesn't want to mess around has orientation issues. At least that's what Kayla says.

"You and Collie still talk?"

Heather knows the answer is no, since it's hard to peel the two of them apart, much less for him to have a conversation without her knowing. But she's still fishing for an answer to the lull in Collie's and my childhood friendship.

"Not since summer," I answer honestly.

"Weird," she says, but accepts my answer with a shake of her head. "Something wrong?"

"No. Just nothing to talk about lately."

"You could talk about me."

"That's all we ever did," I say.

"So you don't want a boyfriend, but you want Captain Lyric."

"I don't even know who he is," I say. "School's boring, and this desk stuff's the only thing that keeps my curiosity aroused."

I blush even before Heather says, "I'd say it keeps more than your curiosity aroused."

"Ladies in the back of the room," Mrs. Tindell, our substitute, interrupts. "Could you please keep your voices to a dull roar? Other groups are trying to work."

"Yes, ma'am," I say.

Heather writes WORK? in big letters on her notebook and then raises it to cover her grin. Only two brown braids are visible behind the book, and she looks a little bit like Heidi at the library. I put my head down to keep from giggling at her antics.

Heather inches her desk closer to mine, and it screeches like a hoot owl. We both duck behind books and wait for Mrs. Tindell to look down. "You might not like Dane yet, but you've got to do something to recover from your funeral rescue mission of Bodee Lennox. Trust me, you hook up with Dane and nobody will remember a thing."

I stare at her hard enough to re-part her braids.

Heather rolls her eyes. "Hookin' up means kissing, Lex. I know you're all virgi-terrified."

"I am not." Mechanically, I lower my voice as Mrs. Tindell goes fish-eyes on us again. I make the first excuse that's believable. "I just want it with the right guy. You know? Too many guys running around Rickman with the crawlers."

"Man, you and Liz are gonna be ancient before I can talk to you about this stuff."

"Liz is not gonna sleep with a Rickman, Tennessee, boy."

Heather adds, "Thus sayeth the Lord."

Liz has a pile of blond curls, a collection of vintage T-shirts, and a desire to *wait*. Heather doesn't go to church with us, so she hasn't been privy to all the stuff about waiting rings and promises. She thinks even the people who wear the rings slip them on and off as if they're coated in butter. But Liz is the real thing. She has convictions in all the places I've got fears.

"I'm sorry," Heather says. "I'm not being fair. I wouldn't want you to do it with someone you don't love. I just wish I had someone to talk to." Her eyes waver between rainy and cloudy, and I realize we're having a moment. "Collie and I have come pretty close," she says.

Heather doesn't take her mask off very often. She's the verbal beast of our threesome, but under all those bold, sexy words, evidently there's still a virgin. I try not to sound too surprised. "If you both want to, then why haven't you?" I ask.

Heather is barely audible. "I'm afraid he'll move on."

"Then why are you still with him?" I know the answer before Heather says it.

"Because I hate being alone."

Heather's beautiful where I'm ordinary. She could find someone else in a minute who would love her, but Collie's her flypaper; she's been stuck on him for years. "Alone isn't terrible."

"I don't know." She sighs. "I wish I could talk to Liz about this, but she doesn't get it."

second-place friend, so I say, "She gets it. You
r."

dles her own name and then Collie's on a
sheet of paper. "Is that what you do? Call Liz?"

"No." I put on an exasperated face. "As you pointed out
earlier, I'm not even on the social ladder. So there's nothing
to say."

Sucks to be Heather. Her best friend is a teetotaling virgin,
and her second-best friend is on lockdown.

"But there could be," she says.

From the way she's winking, I know she's thinking about
Dane. And me. Being all sexually deviant. I can't think that
way about Dane. Or anyone. But I can't tell her that.

"No, you don't get it," I say.

"You're the one who is never going to get *it*. And I'm
not either."

She sounds exasperated with both of us. But Heather doesn't
understand. Even if I got up the nerve to tell her everything
about why I'm not interested in going to Victoria's Secret, or
talking porn, or dreaming of Dane wearing only his socks, it
wouldn't help.

He would still be in the hallway, and I'd still have to pass
him. He'd still be a part of my life. Which would only change
for the worse if I told them.

Because then they'd know, and you can't un-know
something.

"Maybe someday you'll meet Captain Lyric and you'll be

ready," Heather says. "And when that day comes, you have to promise to tell me everything."

"Of course."

"You mean it? 'Cause it would make me feel so much better if I knew I wasn't the only one."

My heart pounds as I choose my phrase. "I promise I'll call you first."

A wicked little smile plays on Heather's lips, and just like that, her uncertainty disappears. "Even if it's Bodee Lennox."

"Even if." The piece of paper Mrs. Tindell gave us at the beginning of class is still blank, so I say, "Hey, we'd better do this."

"I'll do one to five if you'll do six to ten."

I nod and open the book to the right page. This plan has gotten us As so far. When our regular teacher, Mrs. Tomlin, returns from maternity leave, this worksheet crap will finally end. I read this chapter over the weekend, so my answers take only a few minutes. I'm left with ten free minutes to consider Captain Lyric, Dane, and Bodee.

Soul mate. Date. Question mark. In that order. None of them would want me if they knew the truth. And I don't really want them, either.

I know I'll make myself go out with Dane tomorrow night to keep Heather happy. Liz takes some martial arts class I can't pronounce on Tuesday nights, so I can't count on her to help. Damn her Karate Kid skills.

"What should I wear?" I whisper.

"Something that shows your boobs."

"What boobs?"

"Just wear that bra I got you for your birthday and a tight shirt. Maybe that red one with the snappy buttons."

I don't have that bra anymore, but I shake my head. Maybe I'll ask Liz what to wear.

This dating thing is a problem. What if Captain Lyric knows who I am? He might think I'm into Dane. Then what if he stops finishing my lyrics on the desk? This date with Dane could ruin the one thing that's getting me through junior year. It could mean Captain Lyric never confesses he wanted to be a priest until the day he saw me in the hallway, and I never get the chance to assure him his call to celibacy suits me just fine. Because I wouldn't let that keep us apart.

I'm more like Heather than she knows. Scared shitless and hoping a boy will love me someday even though I'm a mess. And Dane's probably not looking for love.

Besides considering how mad Heather will be if I find a way to blow Dane off, I'm stuck on what I ought to do about Bodee. If anything.

Mom said it perfectly when she said, "Oh, that poor boy." People have poor boy–ed him all day today. Rumor is that somebody on the football team even asked him after homeroom if he wanted to eat lunch at their table. And I overheard a teacher say she picked him up for school today. I figure he's got maybe a week of grace before he goes back to being the Kool-Aid Kid and everyone at school moves on to the next tragedy.

Turned out today was a blue hair day. Fitting, I'd thought, during our conversation this morning. Which made me part of the pity party Rickman High is throwing for him.

I'd said, "Hey."

He'd said, "Hey."

Then I'd said, "See you around."

And he'd said, "Thanks for, uh, you know."

Then I'd snapped my locker shut and walked away.

Bodee's like this tall dead tree among a forest of green. Or an evergreen in winter surrounded by oaks. I can hardly ignore him anymore, because he's like those trees. You notice them first.

After sharing that slab of concrete on Saturday, I've started wondering about all the things I don't know about him. And that's a long list.

I don't even know what color his eyes are, since Bodee doesn't really look at anyone. Green? Blue? Brown, like mine? Funny how people value eyes, when really, their colors are super limited. I doubt anyone would enjoy a new box of crayons if they came only in eye-color shades. And maybe his teeth are jacked up, because on rare occasions when he smiles, his mouth stays shut.

Besides pain, what's under that mop of Kool-Aid blue?

Across from me I notice the absence of pencil sounds when

Heather stops scribbling. She says, "Do you read these lessons ahead of time or something?"

Of course I do, which is why I always finish before she does. I can't help it; my mom's a teacher. But I say, "No." Because I'm not admitting to this level of responsibility.

And because the homework distractions help keep me out of the closet.

The closet is both my curse and my sanctuary. For at least an hour every day, I hide there. Folded and tucked. Arms wrapped around my knees while I will my mind not to live in whacked-out "before and after" mode. Which is hopeless. Because hiding behind my comics, football cards, stuffed animals, or my old copy of *Superfudge* never really works.

"You thinking about Dane?"

"Can't stop," I answer.

The bell rings, and Heather tosses her folder into her overlarge purse. "Yay, lunchtime. Pizza or prepackaged?"

Prepackaged food is generally safer, but my stomach can't handle a bag of Heather's favorite white cheddar popcorn. "Pizza."

"See you in there." Heather splits while I take the time to straighten my desk. Tomorrow, if the universe hasn't forsaken me, his handwriting will appear below mine. Then I'll have fifty-three minutes to escape from reality into his words.

I walk the hallway with my head down and earbuds in and don't stop until I get to my locker. Too many people drop trays when they try to carry both books and food, so I'd rather unload my stuff and then deal with the long lunch line.

I notice that Bodee's not at his locker.

Maybe he doesn't have my lunch period, or maybe he's already enjoying his new status as the football player's friend. Then again, if it was my mom who died, I'd be in the bathroom crying off my mascara.

Knowing Bodee's location is not my job, but somehow the silence we shared on the bench connected us, and I find myself wanting to know if he's okay.

Or only pretending to be okay.

Bodee is really none of my business. But I did follow him out of the funeral. And as I ask myself why I did, or why I'm thinking about him now, I know the answer.

Because I'm pretending too.

chapter 3

MY alarm clock screams, *It's a school day!* and jerks me out of the few hours of sleep I managed. It wasn't one of my better nights.

I'm in the shower when Kayla pounds on the door.

"Lex, hurry up. Craig's gotta pee."

"Why can't he use your bathroom?" I yell.

"'Cause Dad's in there. Hurry up or Craig'll be late to school."

Why is he even here at six forty-five in the morning? He has a house down the street. And his own bathroom. Can they seriously not make it without seeing each other before he goes to teach and she goes to work?

"Out in a minute," I yell.

Showers keep me sane. And bring me peace. This morning

it looks as if both are already in short supply.

But it's better to avoid an argument with Kayla, so I swallow my frustration at being rushed by Craig (Rickman High's favorite PE teacher) and swap the shower for my closet.

Among the familiar clothes and shoes and bits and pieces of things from my childhood, and Binky the Elephant pressed to my stomach, I am marginally better. With my pink notebook filled with scribbles from junior high. My old Etch A Sketch. The jumpsuit from Space Camp. These things have no purpose except comfort, so I keep them.

Just like I keep my secret.

This morning the secret has claws. And it's climbing the walls of my stomach, twisting my gut, quivering and rolling and burning. Red-hot acid in the back of my throat. Ready to explode.

And I have to stop it before it spews all over my life.

But I wonder why I even try to control it. *I* should be angry at *him*.

I should want to rip off his balls and serve them to him on a silver platter. "Your manhood, you bastard," my imaginary self says.

But I don't say this. Or dream up any more evil castration fantasies. In fact, I'm usually nice to him when we talk. He probably thinks I don't care that it happened. Given that later on, the one time we discussed it, I dismissed the whole thing. I said all sorts of crap like "It's okay," and "I understand," and "It could have happened to anyone," so he probably thinks he's given me the gift of experience.

The problem is, I'm not angry at *him*. I'm not angry with my parents. Or Kayla. Or my friends. And it's not the school's fault.

It's mine.

"You're the stupid idiot. You let him. You let him." Now my nails come out. Tearing the vulnerable skin on the back of my neck.

"You let him." The scabs that needed a night to heal are under my nails again.

It doesn't matter how hard I dig, the words keep going and going in my head.

Blood smears into the collar of my shirt. It'll never go into the hamper for Mom to wash. "You let him. You let him." God, I wish I could bleed him out of my life.

If only I could make the outside hurt more than the inside.

To keep myself from scratching deeper, I push open the door a sliver and stare at my bedroom ceiling. My breath leaves me, and the numbers start automatically. The compulsion is overwhelming. I have to count.

One. Two. Three. Four. Five. Six. Seven. Eight. Nine.

Don't blink. My eyes start to burn.

Ten. Eleven. Twelve. Thirteen. Fourteen. Fifteen. I can't blink. I'm almost there.

Sixteen. Seventeen. Eighteen. Nineteen.

Blink.

Dammit.

No matter. I'll start over and try again to reach twenty-three.

Sometimes I stand on my bed and run my hand over the metal air-vent slits as if they're a weird form of Braille. Those openings breathe cold air on me. Twenty-two holes of darkness. Twenty-three spaces of light. It's hard to count them at night after they blur into a flat black hole.

Now I understand all the girls in my school who cut. I used to think of them as idiots who didn't know how to cope. Now, I realize they *are* coping. Just not as well as I do.

No one knows about my counting, and no one has noticed my neck. Not even my mom, and she's pretty observant. I hope my pain is invisible. I don't want anyone calling in the "crazy" squad. Teachers, parents, doctors, therapists. When the squad arrives, the friends disappear. I've seen it before.

And I already hang on to Heather and Liz by a thin cord.

My parents would understand my pain, but oh God, the complications. There'd be crying and rants and more crying. Pity. Then when we're all dried out and prayed up, the lessons on forgiveness would start.

Which I already know by heart.

I hear their voices in my head. "Alexi, understand the place of pain he was in to lash out at you like that. It will eat away at you if you don't forgive him." Then they'd watch me like a hawk. Further ruining my life.

I don't need anything, and I've already forgiven him—well, moved on—so I use my fingernails. I stare at the vent and count. And I keep my mouth shut.

Heather will be here any minute, and I'm not ready for school. I still can't count higher than twenty on the vent without blinking, but I give myself one more minute of peace in the closet.

Sixty seconds later, I use baby wipes to blot away the blood. My neck is angry and red, but a polo shirt covers most of the damage.

"Lex, Heather's here. Toast is out," Mom yells.

My Dane-date shirt, though not the red one Heather suggested, is already in my backpack. I close my closet door and grab my bags on the way out of my room.

"Sleep okay?" Mom asks as I arrive in the kitchen.

"Counted all my sheep," I say. The air vent has a new name. I shove a bite of toast into my mouth. "Don't forget I've got the soccer game. Should be home by eight o'clock."

"You've got a ride?" She fishes through the bowl on the counter, and I know she's lost her reading glasses again.

"They're by your chair," I say. "Yeah, I've got a ride."

Mom kisses my forehead like she does every morning. "Have fun at the game. Hey, family meeting tonight when you get home."

I pop the rest of the toast in my mouth so I don't have to speak.

"Stop scrunching your nose at me."

Her tone's playful enough that I know I can talk back. "I'll stop scrunching when we stop having family meetings."

Mom tosses the plastic glass I left on the island last night into the sink. "Would you rather we never asked your opinion?"

"It doesn't count if you never take it," I say.

"We will this time." There are tears in her eyes. Which isn't all that unusual, but this has the makings of something bad. Kayla and I have a list of things that make Mom cry. It's seven pages, front and back, and we bring it out occasionally to tease her.

Heather's horn blares.

"Go. You'll be late. And neither of us is dying. I know how you think."

I open the back door and hide behind it. "Promise it's not bad."

She stares past me but says, "It's not bad."

Liz lets me into the backseat of Heather's Malibu.

"Another day in Littrell-topia?" Heather asks.

I snap my seat belt into place. "Family meeting tonight."

Heather raises her sunglasses to glare at me through the rearview. "You are not using that as an excuse to get out of the game."

"I wish," I tease. "No, it's after. She says it's not bad."

"Then I'm sure it's not," Liz says sympathetically. "Your mom wouldn't lie to you. So what do you think about this Dane thing? Heather told me all about it on the phone."

"So y'all talked boys last night?" I ask.

Heather's not glaring now. She's giving me the *We didn't talk about sex* look.

"Yeah," Liz says. "Well, mostly we talked about you and Dane."

"Great. Did you tell her I don't need a boyfriend?" I say.

"Yep." Liz pops Heather on the thigh and says, "You know we can feel you bitch-staring at us, right?"

Heather laughs like a hyena in heat. I bounce against the seat belt as we jerk between the white dotted line and the rumble strip. Heather's got a great laugh.

"Bitch-staring. I can't believe you said that. Alexi, call your Brother guy and tell him about our friend, the potty mouth."

"I'm sure Brother Jacob wouldn't be all that shocked," Liz says, but her face is red.

"Whatevs," Heather says.

"Whatevs," Liz and I say together.

I feel guilty about cussing too. But I only do it when I'm really upset. And even then I wish there were other words for *fuck* or *damn* or *shit*, but if those other words existed, I'd feel just as guilty about using them, too.

"Bitch-staring," Heather says to herself again. "I am the queen of bitch-staring."

She is, and we all know it, so we laugh again.

The Malibu is faithful. We're at school with enough time to go to our lockers before homeroom.

Our laughter walks down the hallway with me. There's a smile on my face, and I share it with Bodee.

He's still got the blue hair, but I think it's left over from yesterday. In fact, he looks like he's left over from yesterday.

But how can you tell with a guy who wears the exact same clothes every day? I wonder if they really are the same ones or just a look-alike set.

He smiles back.

It's an audible smile, almost a happy sigh.

"Hey," he says.

Oh boy, we're back to the heys. I bend down to open my locker. "Hey," I say. "Hair's still blue."

"Yeah." His locker door, which is just above mine, doesn't make a sound as he shuts it. But he actually looks at me. "Neck's still red," he says.

My mouth falls open, and my hands go to work smoothing and patting my already straight hair against my neck so no one else sees the little wounds. "It happens in my sleep," I say.

"Mine too," he says. "I wake up and it's a different color."

Bodee tosses his hair in a way that is neither mean nor a joke. His voice is soft, sort of like my dad's. It keeps my own voice calm as I say, "Don't tell anyone."

Those are zombie words. I immediately wish I hadn't said to Bodee what was said to me.

He smiles again. But this time, thanks to the hair toss, I can see his eyes. They're brown.

"No one to tell," he says.

We walk to homeroom beside each other but with enough distance to drive Craig's golf cart between us. While I've logged one fact about Bodee, brown eyes, he's collected a piece of information I haven't shared with my closest friends yet.

That's a game changer. Because what do I have on him? Day-old blue hair.

There's absolutely no reason to assume he won't tell someone. Maybe he'll tell his new football friend, and that friend will tell Ray at practice, and Ray will tell Liz on the phone, and Liz will tell Heather, and the two of them will go to my parents. Would they do that?

Or maybe Bodee has already told someone. Told his mom before she died, and she told my mom at prayer group.

Oh God, my parents know.

That's what the family meeting is about. It's not *bad* like cancer; it's good like *We'll get you the help you need.*

I can hear it now.

Shit. Shit.

Homeroom is full already. Bodee takes his assigned desk to the left of mine and is back to his old mute self. His cheek lies against the desk with two handfuls of blue locks to hide behind. There's no hope of trying to guess what he's thinking.

My heart's racing on its own track now, putting roller coasters to shame. And black diamond ski slopes. And airplanes falling out of the sky.

There's a tap on my shoulder. "Alexi."

My head is spinning. If I twist around to see Maggie, I'll throw up.

"Lex?"

Maggie Lister sits in the chair directly behind mine. But she must be in the wrong seat today, because she sounds a long, long way away.

"Are you going out with Dane?" she persists.

She taps again, but I'm frozen.

"Hey," Bodee says.

His voice snaps me out of my stupor. "Hey," I say.

There's nothing audible, but I can read his lips. "Even if I had someone to tell, I promise I wouldn't."

I breathe. And nod. Either he's as good at lying as I am or this is the truth. Since I've only basically exchanged one-word sentences with him, I'm not sure I can judge. But he has color in his cheeks, and I must look as white as snow. And one step up from a coma.

Maggie's spazzing. My cookies don't feel as tossed as they did a minute ago, so I risk swiveling in my seat to face her.

"Sorry." I think fast for an excuse to explain my dazed and confused state. "I just realized we have a test in psych today. That I forgot."

"Oh, crap. Do we? I thought that was next Tuesday." She sifts frantically through her purse until she finds a memo pad. "Yeah, I have it right here. October second. Next Tuesday."

"Whew. Thank goodness. I almost totally flipped."

"Me too," she says as she tosses the memo pad back into the abyss she calls a purse. "You gotta tell me about Dane."

I shrug.

"Girl, you can't be going out with Dane Winters and have nothing to tell."

Bodee lies on the other cheek. He's facing me, but he looks asleep and uninterested. "Heather set it up," I say to Maggie. "We're going to the soccer game, and we're not dating."

"So there's nothing between . . ." Her eyes dart between Bodee and me.

I give her my best *Do I know what 4,678 times 7,543 is?* look.

"Good. O-kay. Awkward," she says, drawing her own conclusion.

Maybe there is something between Bodee and me. I just don't know what it is.

And it totally freaks me out.

School happens for the next three hours without my noticing. That psych test I invented in homeroom was prophetic: pop quiz on post-traumatic stress disorder. But I pass with flying colors. Finally, my personal knowledge of stress is useful.

The desk is my saving grace.

There, below my neat handwriting from yesterday, is the tight script of his I've been waiting twenty-four hours to see.

HOLD ON TIGHT
AS I LOSE MYSELF AGAIN

Then, a couple of spaces down, I see he's printed today's new lyrical challenge.

CAN YOU SEE ME ON THIS WALL? A FAIRY TALE ABOUT TO FALL

I feel warm all over as I grip my pencil. He got mine right, and this new one is easy. No research required.

"I guess he's on it," Heather says, seeing my smile.

"Oh, yeah."

"What did he leave you? Sinatra?"

"That was last week." I take out my phone and show her last Friday's picture of the desk before the custodian cleaned it, pointing to a section on Old Blue Eyes. "He's gone more folk this time."

Nice genre switch. I'm humming as I write.

Won't be horses
Won't be men
Put my soul back again

"Maybe you two do deserve each other," Heather says. "'Cause that's crazy. I've never even heard that song."

"Do you think Dane can do this?" I ask.

"Nobody can do that. At least not without the internet."

I'm between a lyric high and a Bodee low for the rest of the day. Dane barely registers on my radar. He doesn't even bleep the screen until I'm in the bathroom of our local pizza place and I realize I'm not wearing the right bra for my date shirt.

"What's taking you so long? The boys are already at the field," Heather says.

Forgoing the bra is not an option. Kayla will be at the game, since Craig helps the soccer coach on nights there is no football. She'll pitch a fit if I show up in a "Heather" outfit when I could have shopped in her closet.

And I might need her on my side tonight at the family meeting.

Heather pounds the stall door. "Alexi, it can't be that bad. Let me see."

There's no choice. I can't wear a black bra under my white shirt. I'll have to wear the polo I wore to school. Time to face Heather.

"Not what I suggested," she says. "But it might get chilly in that." She points to the discarded peasant shirt.

"Yeah, that's what I was worried about."

Sometimes the lies I tell Heather aren't little and white. They're a dab of honey-beige foundation applied to the blemishes of my life.

The upside of this night with Dane is that I don't have to pay for the soccer game. The downside is his hair. He's got all these corkscrew curls that fuzz. Most of the girls think they make him look hot, but I can't get serious about a dark-headed Annie guy.

"You want a popcorn or something before we sit down?" he asks.

I've never actually seen his hands out of his pockets, so I'm tempted to say yes. The guy likes to use girls to carry his books instead of a backpack. Which begs the question: since he can have any of the giggly chicks, why did he decide to go out with me?

"Thanks, but I'm not hungry."

"Are you sure? I don't mind paying," Dane says.

The offer is nice, but I shake my head. Maybe the next two hours won't be so terrible.

"Suit yourself," he says.

Then he spends twenty-four dollars on concession-stand food for himself. I carry two hot dogs and the popcorn so he can carry his nachos and an energy drink. Which he chugs before we get to our seats.

"Man, you're handy to have around," he says, and nudges my shoulder. Then he adds, "That's what she said," like he's cracked the best joke of the century.

Collie drags one finger across his neck, giving his cousin the cutoff sign, and says, "Alexi hates 'that's what she said' jokes."

"No, I don't," I argue, even though he's right. I start wishing the Seventh Circle of Hell would open wide enough to suck in the entire Rickman County soccer field. Even Heather looks embarrassed by Dane's lameness.

"So do you like music?" she asks Dane.

The rest of hot dog number two goes into his mouth, but he still answers. "Yeah. I love rap. What do you listen to?" he asks me.

"Everything. Nothing in particular. I like words," I say, trying not to watch him eat.

"Rap's got words."

There's no good way to respond to that. Yes, genius: rap has words. I think I can eliminate Dane as the potential Captain Lyric.

Dane takes a long sip of Collie's drink. "For a girl who likes words, you don't talk much."

He holds up one finger. I don't breathe as he lays it across my lips. "Shhh," he says playfully.

I am silent.

Frozen.

Remembering.

Another finger on my lips. Another "Shhh" followed by "Don't tell anyone." Hands on my hips. Against my skin.

"Please don't," I say, but I'm so scared, and "don't" dies in the evening air. He thinks I'm begging for more. That's when the demon enters, binding my lips and tying my hands and laying me down in choking silence.

That terrifies me and excites him.

The referee blows his whistle, and I come to myself. My cheeks are wet with tears, and Heather says, "Alexi?"

"I have to leave," I tell her.

"Sure." Miffed but clearly worried, she adds, "Should I go or stay?"

"Stay. I'll catch a ride." I lean over to her and whisper,

"Sorry. My granddad used to do that to me."

"Aw, I'm sorry, Lex."

I leave them on the bleachers. But I hear Dane grumble, "Damn, she wants to talk, let her talk. I was just messing with her."

"Shut up, asshole," Heather says. "Her granddad used to do that."

I keep walking. My granddad never shushed me a day in my life.

chapter 4

WHEN Heather arrives at the Malibu after the game, I'm sitting in her parking space, propped against the passenger-side tire.

I turn off my music as she says, "I thought you were catching a ride."

"Decided to wait. I didn't want to go home crying and have to explain," I say.

"I could go home naked and not have to explain."

I'm not sure if Heather is bragging or complaining. She unlocks the doors while I stretch. The hour and a half on the pavement has been as hard on my butt as on my mental health. Thinking sucks. I wish I could be an android. Or have an on-off switch installed in my head. Flip on: Lexi is able to do homework, pick a college, plan a spring break trip with friends. Acts normal. Flip off: Lexi lives in a thoughtless world of stars and music and puppies. Feels nothing.

Heather's fingers coil around the luggage rack; she stares at me across the roof. "We won. Dane asked about you."

"Asked if I'm crazy?"

"He didn't understand the freak-out, but he still thinks you're cute."

"Then I can die happy," I say.

Heather leaves her side of the car and reappears beside me. She's got longer arms and legs than a runway model, so when she hugs me it's like death by boa constrictor.

"I'm sorry you had a rough night," she says.

My arms hang limply to the side, but I allow myself to rest my head below her shoulder.

"You've been a little weird lately, and I'm worried about you."

"You're being weird right now. Since when do we hug?"

Heather's arms loosen and she surveys me again. "Liz is worried about you too."

"Is this an intervention? Because I've got a family meeting I'd rather be at," I say.

"No. I'm just reminding you that we're here if you need us."

Great. My two best friends are talking about me. And I really thought, minus tonight, I'd been pulling off the act. Time to ratchet up the efforts. "I might want to talk sometime. It's nothing big, just lost inside my head. I've got a bunch of questions about God."

"Oh." Heather retreats.

It's not fair that I know her well enough to push the button that makes her shrivel. But it's the perfect distraction. She'll tell Liz on the phone tonight, and all my actions will make perfect sense through Liz's spiritually tinted lens.

"So this is sorta what Liz went through last year after that little kid got hit by the car?"

I nod. And now all my weirdness is logical. I just bought myself at least another month before they ask again.

"Questions like that suck. I'm sorry," Heather says.

"Thanks," I say, and mean it. "And thanks for the hug."

The Malibu is a dance party from the school to my house. Evidently this is Heather's solution to the big questions of life. Which means we sing and there is no need to talk.

"See you tomorrow," she says before she pulls away.

Now it's time to face the real music: the family meeting.

Inside, I slip off my shoes at the back door and grab a water from the fridge before my mom hears me.

"We're in the living room," she yells.

The hardwood groans as I move slowly down the hallway. My mind is like old bones that creak along with the boards. This could be life-changing. I might not be able to lie my way out of it. How else can I explain the scratches?

Fight with Kayla. No, she'll be here, and she lies better than I do.

Fight at school. No, Mom would know.

In my sleep.

That option gives me a degree of deniability. It's really the only choice. But it's sort of like choosing between a boat with a hole and a raft with a leak. I still sink.

I lean around the door for a quick view of the living room. And my knees go so weak I could dissolve into a puddle on the floor.

Bodee is on the center cushion of our couch with my parents flanking him on either side. He doesn't look up, but my dad does.

Won't tell anyone. Jerk. He didn't even wait a day.

Dad waves me into the room. "Come on in, Alexi. Kayla and Craig just called. They'll be here any minute."

"Craig's coming?"

"Honey, they're practically engaged," Mom says. "Plus, you know how good he is at helping Kayla make decisions." Mom winks, a code that reminds me of our private Kayla Debates. After a half gallon of ice cream and two spoons a year ago, we'd emerged with a strategy to use Craig to curb the worst of Kayla's hotheaded behavior. She's easier to deal with when he's around.

Dad looks out the front window. "They're here."

Bodee is uncomfortable. The way he is at school, slumped shoulders and tucked chin, when he's forced to speak to a teacher. Of course, his face is hidden behind his hair, so the fact that I'm giving him the death stare is totally ineffective.

"We're here. Start the party," Kayla yells before we see her bounce into the room with Craig in tow.

At the sight of Bodee, she shoots me a little body language easily identifiable as WTF. I shrug as she and Craig take the love seat. And swing my legs sideways over my chair arm, which my dad hates and probably recognizes as a show of anger.

Dad wants to start in on the abuse of furniture, but Mom's first out of the starting gate.

"Well, I'm sure you all know Bodee Lennox." Her eyes get teary as she says his name. "And you know that his mom and I were friends."

We nod and she continues, "I've had a chance to talk to Bodee several times over the last few days. Which led to some conversations between your dad and me." Dad smiles and pats Mom's hand.

I scan the kids' section of the family meeting for some clue of what's about to go down. Kayla is puzzled; Craig has a small frown between his brows. Bodee is doing what Bodee does: nothing. My toes start flexing, my calf cramps, and I shift positions. Fingers drumming on my knee, itching to get to my neck. But I can't. I can't. Not here. Breathe.

"Now, Alexi," Mom says. I jerk my eyes away from my hands. "This is going to affect you more than Kayla or Craig." My parents exchange another compassionate look. Bodee still looks like a broken bobblehead.

Oh God, I need a miracle. Please. Heal my neck, I pray, and I promise I'll never lie again. A tremor I'm sure everyone can feel moves from my head to my toes, so I dig my fingernails into my palms and pray some more.

God's not buying my lie.

"We've talked to the counselor at school and a lawyer."

Over on the love seat, Kayla shifts closer to Craig, and they both give me an anxious look.

It's worse than I thought. My whole family is going to have me committed. For scratching my neck. A few times. Not fair. Not effing fair. My gut twists as I vow to take every cutter with me. If I go down, all the long-sleeve girls at Rickman are going with me.

"And . . ."

My breath stops on that *and*.

"We think Bodee would be better off living here for the rest of the school year instead of at his brother's house."

All the air I've stored up rushes out in a gust of relief. Neither Kayla nor I speak. I am so happy that this is about Bodee and not me that I don't care where he lives. Hell, he can move into my room if he wants.

Now my dad speaks. "We didn't come to this conclusion lightly. It's a big deal to add someone else to our household. We've given it a lot of prayer and consideration, but Mom and I believe our family is supposed to do this."

"Bodee's brother has three jobs and a lot to . . . to handle right now." Mom's voice falters a little as we think about why his brother has so much to do. "It's not that Bodee isn't welcome there, but Ben agrees with us that our home may be a better option."

"Now," my dad picks up where Mom leaves off, "we won't ask either of you girls to give up your rooms. We'll set up a bed for him in the bonus room over the garage. He's here tonight because we assured him you girls would be on board with our decision. Don't you think we can make this work?"

"Why are you asking us if you've already come to a conclusion?" Kayla tosses her head at Bodee.

"We're a family," Mom says.

Craig squeezes her shoulder, and Kayla starts again with a different tone. "What I mean is, if you think this is the right thing, then it probably is."

"I knew you would understand, Kayla. If something happened to the two of us, wouldn't you be thankful if Liz's mom offered to help you with Alexi?"

Kayla looks taken aback. But she and Craig both nod.

Mom and Dad are slick to have Bodee right here in the room. Brilliant plan. We can hardly vote "no" in front of him. The guy's already been through hell. And we all know it.

Not that he's showing a reaction.

"Lex, you're awfully quiet," Mom says. "We want to hear from you, too."

"I trust you guys. He needs a room. We have an extra one. It's perfect."

The bobblehead comes to life. Our eyes meet, and Bodee's lips twitch. Did he just mouth *thanks* at me?

"I knew you'd understand." Mom practically bursts with pride, and Dad nudges my feet off the chair. Evidently, my compliance means it's now okay for him to correct me.

"Bodee, I know we can't replace your family, but we hope you'll agree to stay with us. We'll all do everything we can to make you comfortable. I think it's what . . . your mother would want."

"Thank you, Mrs. Littrell." Bodee's polite tone sounds automated, the way Mom's second graders recite math facts. He nods at my dad.

"Well"—Mom pats Bodee's knee as if everything in the world has been settled—"I'll go get some sheets for the couch. We'll set up the bed tomorrow after we get your stuff from the house."

And then my family follows Mom from the room. Dad to his office. Craig and Kayla to the driveway. The Littrells add a new family member and that's it?

No one has anything more to say.

Done.

Meeting adjourned.

Bodee doesn't move off the couch, so I put my feet back over the side of the chair. Not out of anger. Because I can't walk away from him.

"So you live here now," I say.

"I guess." He brushes the blue away from his eyes.

There'll be Kool-Aid stains in my shower.

White tees in my laundry hamper.

Presents for Bodee under my Christmas tree. . . .

Will we have conversations around the Sunday dinner

table where "hey" is not the primary word?

Weird.

But Mom's right. Holy hell. If something happened to my parents, I could never live with Craig and Kayla. I'd take Liz and the Pullman family any day of the week and twice on Sunday over that option.

"You okay with it?" he asks.

"You could have told me at school today," I say.

"I promised your mom I wouldn't."

Honest, promise-keeping Bodee. I'm a slug.

"I'm okay with it."

chapter 5

LAST night I played the blame game for hours. This routine is pretty well established. There's only one contestant: me. Then the flashbacks. Then the compulsive counting. And hovering in the background, the knowledge that morning will arrive way too soon.

And I'm right. Four hours of sleep pass like a gunshot.

Awake, but not alert, I stumble toward the hall bathroom.

"Get a move on, Lex. You're going to be late," Mom yells from the kitchen.

I lock the bathroom door, lift the hair off my neck, and twist to check the mirror. Dang, I went to town last night. The shower's going to burn like crazy.

"You've got to stop," I tell the girl in the mirror.

She gives me a blank look. Like I don't know what I'm asking.

Only when I see the used towel folded neatly over the shower curtain do I remember Bodee.

We share a bathroom. Of course we do. He can't use Mom and Dad's, and Kayla's is at the other end of the house. Ripping back the curtain, I check the shower for leftover colored powder. There's nothing. Maybe he's going back to blond. He's been here, but he's gone about the invasion of house and bathroom as silently as he goes about life.

Out of necessity, I get ready in ten minutes. It's a wet hair, curly-scrunch day, and that means I dress in jeans, ballet flats, and a T-shirt I've had since fifth grade. Snug, but not too tight.

"Lex!"

"I'm here," I say as I enter the kitchen.

Mom evaluates my outfit before she bends toward me for a forehead kiss. "You look cute, hon. I like it when you wear your hair that way."

Nearly all her evaluations are encouraging and Mom-like. I shrug. "No time for anything else."

"Bodee, help out, please. My daughter is the world's worst self-critic."

Bodee's hair is red with just a touch of blue left over at the roots. He looks like a Rocket Pop. And uncomfortable at my mom's obvious attempt to include him in our conversation.

"Yes, Mrs. Littrell." He twists a coffee mug in his hand and stares at the black liquid. "Alexi, you look nice."

"Now, see? Very nice. Bodee and I agree."

"Mom." The woman is oblivious to how awkward this is for both of us. Bodee's shoulders cave, and he turns away to sip his coffee. Poor guy. Mom just shellacked the shell he lives in.

Heather's horn blows, and it occurs to me that this is a new frontier. We're going to the same place. Do I ask him to ride with us? I would, but I haven't given Heather and Liz a heads-up about the new family mission Mom and Dad have going.

"Well, that's my ride." Please, woman, say something. My eyebrows become one with my hairline as I pray for God to open up a telepathic route between Mom and me.

She's clueless.

But Bodee gets the message loud and clear. He stands up from the table and looks at my mom. "Mrs. Littrell, could you drop me at school today?"

Split-second decisions suck. There's no time to weigh how strange this trip will be against the feelings of the boy who had to ask my mom for a ride to school. "You can come with us," I say, and hand him the second Pop-Tart from my package.

Mom smiles. I see her proud-of-me look, which means "Thanks, Lex."

"Perfect," she says in a chirpy voice. "We'll figure out all these details by tomorrow."

As soon as we're out the door, Bodee says, "I can walk."

"Don't be stupid. You'll be late."

There's a glare on the windshield, but I can still see Heather's and Liz's expressions. Either they've just had a close encounter with aliens or Bodee Lennox is the last person in the universe they expect to see come out my back door.

"You guys know Bodee," I say after we're in the backseat together. "He's staying at our house for a while."

"Cool," Liz says after half a heartbeat.

"Yeah, cool," Heather says. But her face in the rearview mirror tells me a different story. She thinks this is whacked. And it is.

The car makes more sounds than we do for the next two miles. By the time we arrive, I feel terrible for Bodee. He's a foreign exchange student among us, except we all went to kindergarten together. I want to remind Heather that he speaks English and understands all the hand signals she's using.

Bodee and I leave Heather and Liz in the hallway and turn left toward our lockers. "See ya later," I say over my shoulder.

"Okay," Liz says. Heather is still staring at me like I've brought a pet crocodile to school with me.

"Jeez, that sucked. Sorry," I say. "I should have called them last night."

"Can't blame them. I'll walk to your house after school."

Your house. Man, a dull knitting needle is stabbing my heart. The guy doesn't even have a home anymore, and he doesn't sound bitter or angry with me that my friends are selfish jerks.

"You can't do that." I swap a few books in my bag for the ones in my locker. "That's dumb."

"I'm used to walking, Alexi."

And he walks away. Without me.

I plug in some tunes on my iPhone, lean against my locker, and consider my options. I'm not so important in the social hierarchy at Rickman that my friend choices carry any punishment. Liz, who is on the student council, has friends in every circle. And Heather is Heather: loved by boys, despised by (most) girls. But other than our fourth-period class together and to-and-from school rides, most of her time is occupied by Collie. And Liz.

There's no personal risk to befriending Bodee. It's more of a risk not to. He knows too much.

Craig interrupts my thoughts. "You're going to be late to homeroom."

"Oh, shut up, Craig."

"Hey. It's Mr. Tanner at school."

"Okay. Shut up, Mr. Tanner."

Craig overlooks my sarcasm. "You okay with your parents' decision about Bodee?" He lightly punches my shoulder. A school-approved quasi-hug from my almost brother-in-law. "I told Kayla last night we ought to check on you, but she said you'd be fine."

I have to laugh. As long as I have all my limbs, Kayla will think I'm fine. "I am fine, *Mr. Tanner.*"

The bell rings. Craig pushes his hands into his khakis and sounds sheepish. "Go on before it's too late. Tell your homeroom teacher it's my fault."

"Will do," I say, and zip toward homeroom.

The teacher raises her eyebrows as I slide into my desk, but she doesn't say anything. I'm not normally late, and she's pretty cool.

Bodee's tucked into his usual ignore-the-world posture. I tap him on the shoulder and lean toward him. The coffee on his breath is from a cup in my kitchen; the shampoo in his hair is from the bottle in my shower.

Weird. Just as weird as what I say.

"I'm walking with you this afternoon."

He sighs, but maybe he sounds okay with it. "Your friends'll think you've flipped."

"So what? They probably think I flipped, like, two months ago. What's a walk gonna do?"

"I'll be at my locker," he says, and his head disappears back into the crook of his arm.

"I'll be there."

I can tell long before I see the desk in fourth period; it's going to be a rock-and-roll day. The beat's pounding in my head until I can hardly sit still. Not one song, but hundreds marching along my veins. Sad. Angry. Happy ones, even.

So when fourth period finally comes, why can't I decide on a single song or choose even a few lyrics to express my mood?

But he can.

YOUR HAND COVERS MY HEART
WE STEP OUT INTO THIS YEAR

How does he do that? Every day he picks something that haunts me, words that echo the sorrows and joys in my life. I print the next two lines on the desk before Mrs. Tindell passes out our group work.

Surviving, we stand for once
Drive away these fears

"Your turn to leave him hanging, right?" Heather asks.

"Yeah." I spin the pencil in my hand.

"There's a million zillion songs. Just write something."

"I can't just write *something*."

"Huh. Just as you obviously can't *tell* your two best friends the biggest thing going on in your life?"

I cringe. She doesn't know the half of it. "I didn't find out until late last night."

"I have a phone," she snaps.

"You have Collie," I say back.

"Ladies. Worksheet," Mrs. Tindell says.

Under the guise of checking an answer, I lean in close and whisper, "I'm sorry."

"Lex, I had to corner Craig, *Mr. Tanner*, in third period to get the story. You should have told us."

"It's not that big of a deal."

"Oh, really." She doodles on my desk. Which I promptly erase. "I'd say Kool-Aid Boy moving in with you is a freakin' big deal."

"He hasn't moved in with me. He's moved in with my family. Actually, he's slept on the couch for one night. We haven't adopted him or anything. And anyway, I knew y'all would make a huge issue of it. Like you did about me talking to him at his mom's funeral."

Heather looks totally justified. "Well, yeah. And I was right, too. I knew something was up."

"Nothing's up. Our moms were close friends. They were in a prayer group together for years. No way Bodee's mother didn't share crap about her marriage. My mom feels responsible now that her friend's gone. Guilty, even. That's all." I meant to divert Heather's attention from me, but I realize that what I've said is probably the truth.

Heather takes out a pen and writes upside-down on my desk before I can stop her. *You're gonna end up FRIENDS with him.*

I spit-wash the words, but they are still visible. Like an accusation. Like prophecy. "Go write on your own desk," I say. "And who cares if I end up friends with Bodee Lennox? He needs a friend. I need more friends."

"You have friends. You could have Dane Winters, too."

"I have *two* friends. And I don't want Dane Winters." Or Bodee, I remind myself. "So I'm thinking that since I have to share a house with Bodee, what's wrong with being friends with him too?"

"But he's the Kool-Aid Kid."

"So?" I say. "You're all about Captain Lyric, but we don't

have a clue who he is either. He could be anybody. That boy who farts and snorts in gym. Or the guy who always wears his shop helmet even when he's not in shop."

This is not a thing I want to say out loud. Or even think about. Because the unknown Captain Lyric has to be sweet and sensitive. And sexy. And love me. He's a special, one-of-a-kind guy who will wait forever and a day for me.

And not pressure me for sex.

"I guess you're right," Heather says. "Still, you have to admit. The idea of Captain Lyric is just so totally much better than Bodee Lennox."

"They aren't in a competition," I snap. "Bodee lives at my house. He might be my friend someday, but he's not Captain Lyric. I don't even think he listens to music."

Mrs. Tindell drifts down the aisle toward us. "One of these days, I'm going to separate you two."

I slide my folder over the desk lyrics from this week and show her my completed paper. "We're finished, Mrs. Tindell."

"Dull roar," she reminds us, and drifts back to her desk.

Heather looks wowed. "How do you do that? I haven't answered a single question."

"I can think and talk at the same time."

She draws a frowny face on my desk and says, "Stop bitch-staring at me."

We both snicker. That phrase is going to stick.

"Okay, be friends with Bodee if you want. Just don't go drinkin' the Kool-Aid. If you know what I mean."

"I won't." Things are square, so I tell her, "I'm going to walk home with him after school today. You talk to Liz, and maybe tomorrow, we can all be nicer to him."

"Oh, all right." Heather sighs. "If he gets you, he gets us, too."

"Thanks." I slip my worksheet onto her desk. "You wanna copy my answers?"

"Thought you'd never ask."

Now it's just me and the desk. Time to rock the lyrics for the Captain himself.

> Dance to forget yourself. Dance to forgive
> Let your body and your mind agree

I imagine tomorrow's response in his strong, heavy strokes.

> IF ONLY FOR THIS BREATH RIGHT NOW
> DANCE LIKE YOU'RE FREE

And then I make the mistake of thinking about Bodee. And for the rest of the day until I meet him at our lockers after school, I wonder how long he'll be a member of my family.

"Hey," he says.

"You know any other words?"

Bodee runs his fingers through his Rocket Pop hair. His eyes are sad. Or happy. I can't tell.

"Yeah. You know. Not a lot of practice," he says.

"Well, since we're gonna share a bathroom, I think we could move on to sentences."

We walk down the hall, and for a while, he doesn't say anything.

"Alexi . . . I know . . . I don't know you well enough to ask, but . . . could you, I mean, would you maybe . . . help me with something on the way to your house?"

The starts and stops, the painstaking precision of words, and the sheer length of time it takes him to ask make it clear that this boy never asks anyone for help.

Bring out the dull knitting needles, stabbing my heart, again.

"Sure," I say.

"I need to stop at my house."

"Okay."

"Can you . . . go inside?"

"Sure," I say without thinking.

He's silent again. We're outside on the school sidewalk before I really understand what he wants me to do. *Oh.*

"You haven't been in, have you? Since . . ." I don't finish the sentence.

"No." He long-steps to avoid a crack in the sidewalk, and I'm sure we're both thinking about what broke his mother's back. "Most of my stuff's in the tent, but there's something in the house I need."

The tent. Had he been living outside? I don't ask, but I shiver thinking about it. I'll know soon enough.

The walk to his house takes twenty-five minutes. We don't talk, but now I'm more comfortable with our silence. It's like autumn is speaking for us. We watch the wind swirl the dust and pollen and urge the turning leaves to let go. A cool breeze makes me shiver, and I wish I'd thrown a hoodie in my backpack.

And then I shiver for a different reason.

A wad of crime scene tape, meant for the trash. Left behind.

My mind wraps the same yellow tape around the pool in our backyard.

What if I had called the police? What if everyone knew a crime had been committed? Everything would be different. Everything is different—even without the yellow tape.

I throw up in the grass.

"Alexi."

Bodee holds my hair back when round two seizes me. If it had been anyone else, I'd have jerked away. But he already knows about the scabs on my neck. I sit back and wipe my mouth, and Bodee's hand drops to his side.

"Sorry," I say. Tears spill down my cheeks. Throw-up tears; the kind you can't stop.

"I shouldn't have asked you to—"

"I'm okay," I say.

His fingers are on my elbow, urging me toward the road. "No. Let's go back to your house."

"I'm fine. This is important."

He rocks back and forth on his heels. Bodee in motion is

like a silent film. Words without the words.

"I'm not asking you to go in there," he says.

"Too bad. I'm going." Channeling brave. "Tell me what you need, or I'll go in there and rummage around until I find something."

Bodee shouldn't know me well enough to understand he's lost the argument, but he caves. "Okay. A diamond earring. My mother's. It should be in the bathroom beyond the kitchen." The key he takes out of his pocket is warm, like he's had it in his palm all day.

"You got it."

The back steps bend with my weight. I focus only on the lock. I've got my closet if I need to retreat from thoughts about me. This is about Bodee and his one request.

The door opens and I walk into their small kitchen.

"Oh, Jesus," I say.

It's a prayer, not a curse. This is *the* crime scene. There's no blood. Mr. Lennox squeezed the life out of his wife. But as I take in the broken dishes, the spilled food and turned-over furniture, there's no doubt that she put up one hell of a fight.

I tiptoe through the broken room and wonder if this kitchen ever served up happiness. Toast with peanut butter. Waffles and syrup. Hamburgers. Mac and cheese.

Probably not, I think, and swallow the bile in my mouth.

The bathroom is small. There's no jewelry box among the soap and toothbrushes on the vanity. I don't suppose monsters dote on their wives enough to buy them special things. Mr.

Lennox probably never bothered.

The metal medicine cabinet squeaks as I force its hinges. My heart, which has been racing, jerks with pain. The shelves are practically bare. Two bottles of aspirin, a small bottle of Midol, some antiseptic, bandages of various sizes. A few odds and ends of makeup: foundation, some powder, a nearly empty tube of concealer. A pill organizer.

Oh God, this is her cover-up kit.

These few items kept her secret and hid her lies. They were her Binky the Elephant and her football cards. Her air vent in the bedroom ceiling.

Don't throw up. Don't throw up, I pray.

Instinct screams at me to shut the cabinet and get out of the house, but I have to find the earring. I touch the items and slide them around. And feel I am vandalizing the soul of Mrs. Lennox. I open the pill organizer and hope the earring is in one of the daily compartments. But there's nothing. Where could I hide something so Mr. Lennox wouldn't find it? I twist the lid off the bottle of Midol and see a sparkle.

"Thank God."

The earring is in my pocket, and I'm back in the kitchen in a flash. I am almost through the door when I see the little boxes. They come with me. Bodee needs them as much as he needs the earring.

Outside, Bodee's stuffing a tent into a nylon bag. He has a sleeping bag and an extra duffel.

"I got all my stuff," he says without looking up.

All his stuff? Wow.

I could make a list a mile long of what he will need but doesn't have. Like a jacket. A hat. Boots.

His mother.

"I found the earring. And I got you these from the kitchen." I hold out the five little boxes of Kool-Aid.

And Bodee smiles.

Really smiles. Teeth and all. (They're straight.)

And even though I have thrown up, walked through a crime scene, and rooted through the remainder of Mrs. Lennox's life, I smile too.

chapter 6

WHEN Bodee and I reach the house, towing his tent and everything he owns like we're Tom and Huck, Kayla and Craig are sitting in the front porch swing.

"Y'all walk?" Kayla asks.

"Nope," I say.

"Always so sarcastic."

"Learned from the best," I say, and give her a smile.

She nods and pats herself on the back and gives me a little bow. "Thank you. Thank you," she says. "Hey, where are Heather and Liz?"

I put on my best psychic pose and answer, "Heather just called Collie and asked him to make out with her at Freeman Lake, and Liz is practicing her ninja moves."

"Oh, shut up." Kayla tosses a pebble from the potted plant

in my direction and then kisses Craig.

Craig's face can't contain his smile.

"You look like one of those clowns who sell porn on the side. A little too happy," I tell him.

"Bodee, tell her to be nice," Kayla says. "A girl only has this kind of day once in her life. Guess what's happened?"

Bodee doesn't exactly look full of guesses, but I decide he needs a full dose of Littrell sister reality. "Okay, let's see. You got the gas pump to stop on exactly forty dollars again, Kay? Or the Sik Purse is carrying your shade of lipstick now?" I say only the letters that light up on the sign at Kayla's favorite Rickman boutique. "Wait; I know—"

"You're such a beast." Kayla untangles her body from Craig's to sit up in the swing. "This is why you never keep a boyfriend longer than a day."

"I don't need a boyfriend."

"Every girl needs a boyfriend. Especially in Rickman," Kayla says.

"The only girls who need boyfriends in Rickman are the ones who never want to leave," I say. My mother and grandmother were bound to the ground on which they were born because of boys. That won't be me. I'll find another zip code to live in someday.

"You wouldn't know what you needed if it bit you in both ass cheeks. What kind of girl blows off Dane Winters?"

"Kayla," Craig says.

"Don't Kayla me," she says. "She's the one who got snippy."

Craig kisses her ear and whispers just loud enough for me to hear. "Babe, she's just jerking your chain. Let it go."

Kayla pouts and gets another kiss and grope. Bodee will stare a third hole in his sneakers before I can get him inside. Time to give her what she wants. "Come on, KayKay. Tell us what amazing thing happened today." I overdo the enthusiasm, but she doesn't notice.

"You really wanna know?" she asks. Man. It's like the previous argument happened on a different day or a different planet. It's one of Kayla's charms. She's bitchy, but only for minutes at a time. After which she seems unable to recall she was ever bitchy. I love this about my sister, in fact, and wish I had a little dose of it myself. Unfortunately, I recall all the crappy stuff I do. And the little ghosts of words I've said return to haunt me.

And the ones I didn't say.

"Y'all like this all the time?" Bodee mumbles.

I nod, as Craig, still wearing the freaky smile, asks, "Can you keep a secret?"

"Pretty sure I can," I say.

But then I understand before either of them answers. Just from the expression on Craig's face, I know.

Because Craig is looking at Kayla the same way he did when he arrived to escort my sister to their first homecoming dance. (I was six.) Like he did when he came to pick her up for prom. (Seven.) Like the day he left for college to play football and she stayed behind at Rickman Community College to work at the bank with Dad. (Eight. Nine. Ten. Eleven.) And when he moved back after grad school to take a teaching job. (Fourteen.) So, for the better part of my life, Craig has looked at Kayla as if she has the power to take the Big Dipper right out of the night sky and insert those same stars in his eyes.

He loves her.

Kayla squeals the words I already know, "We're engaged!" She and Craig skip down the steps, and she wraps me in a hard hug that makes me gasp.

"You'll stand up with me. Right next to me, Lex."

Suddenly, there's a lump in my throat. "Okay." I peel myself away from Kayla and say, "Tell us the whole story."

And then they do. Except there isn't one really.

Because couples don't get engaged on Wednesdays. (Unless Valentine's Day or Christmas happens to fall on Wednesday, which makes an engagement perfectly acceptable.) A guy shouldn't pop the question at Mr. Hoback's Apple Festival and Corn Maze right after he's bought a candied apple with extra nuts. Usually there's a story. A romantic one.

There are rules for this sort of thing. Expectations. Every girl in Rickman knows them, and every guy should too.

Except, it appears, Kayla and Craig.

Lame.

Even lamer, their nonstory is absolutely precious. And simply Rickman County. Like them.

"So it was just time to make it official?" I say, after Kayla rattles on about the hay wagon and the candied apple.

"Yeah." She strokes Craig's chest, and I swear he purrs. "We decided we can't wait another minute to be engaged."

Craig looks like his football team has won the state championship. "So, uh, Lex, do we have your blessing?"

"Blessings are for dads," I say. "I'm just glad you have to replace that promise ring. Kayla's finger is permanently green." I laugh.

"Hey, not fair. I was eighteen, and it was all I could afford." Craig gives me a shoulder punch, his favorite form of affection, and looks down at Kayla with adoring eyes. "She'll have a real ring as soon as we talk to your parents."

"Well, shouldn't be a prob for you." I repeat the words Mom uses all the time, "You're practically family."

"He is. Isn't he?" Kayla beams.

My sister is radiant. The thought is like a flaming brand applied to my heart. I'm not jealous of her thick, dark hair that's always straight and the eyelashes she seems to have in triplicate. I'm especially not jealous of her relationship with Craig. I don't want to be Kayla, and I don't want what she has. But I wish she wasn't the physical standard by which I measure myself.

"Bodee, we'll soon be saying the same thing about you, man," Craig says.

"What does that mean?" I snap.

"I only meant he lives here now, Lex. You know how your mom and dad are. That makes him practically family." Craig gives Bodee an easy smile. "This is like the best family in the world. Don't you think?" Craig asks him.

Bodee drops his tent in the driveway and scratches behind his ear. A blue strand of hair hidden behind a bold stripe of red is now visible. He doesn't bother to fix it. His hairstyle doesn't matter to him, and a week ago it didn't matter to me. But now, I want to smooth it down for him. Want to offer him words so they don't look so painful on his lips. Want to give him lyrics the way I do with the Captain.

"I had a family," Bodee says.

And then there's nothing to say.

Bodee lifts the tent, swipes the gravel dust off, and slips into the house like a ghost. Even the front door, which usually squeaks, is quiet. Bodee's loss is so unimaginable that it squeezes my heart. And from the looks of it, Craig and Kayla are disturbed too.

"Craig, you have to help him," Kayla says.

"I don't think he's ready for help yet, Kay. It hasn't even been a week. But maybe I can do something," Craig says.

"Don't. Please," I say to both of them. "You can't buy him some new wardrobe or cut his hair and make it all happy. His mom's dead. His dad killed her. No matter how badly you want it, there's no magical cure that makes it go away. Sometimes life just sucks." At some point, maybe I forget the speech is about Bodee. "So do Bodee a favor and get on with your giddy little love story and leave him alone. He doesn't need fixing."

I leave the newly engaged couple, slack-jawed and wide-eyed with astonishment, and contrast Bodee's quiet entrance by slamming the front door. Stomping the entire way, I climb the steps to the bonus room.

Bodee's room.

He's sitting on the edge of the twin bed, which Dad has decked out with the only available twin linens in our house. Mom will be horrified when she realizes Dad has rummaged in the attic and found my old Cinderella comforter. Bodee sleeping beneath the yellow princess is almost more than I can bear.

"I was rude," he says.

"Stand up," I tell him.

He stands, and in one motion I flip Cinderella over so the plain yellow plaid side is faceup. "Better. And you are never rude."

Bodee Lennox is never really anything. I'll bet most kids in our class didn't know his name before the murder. And yet his face is not expressionless the way I once thought. That slight twitch of lips, a little half grin, says more than Heather does in a week. But the full-teeth smile, the one I saw today at his house, is like a work of Tolstoy.

He's not smiling now. "I shouldn't have left like that. Mr. Tanner was being nice."

"Yeah, but *Mr. Tanner* should have thought before he said something so insensitive. Bodee, you know we're not trying to replace your family. Mom and Dad know they can't fix this for you. I know it. We just want . . . I just want this year to be . . . easier from here."

He is silent for a moment, and then he nods. "I want that . . . for you, too."

There's so much to say in return. Like telling him my pain is nothing compared to his. Like asking how he sees things about me when no one else can. But words will only make me more vulnerable, so I say, "Me too," and leave it at that.

I'd hug Bodee if I could. A friendly hug. And maybe if he wasn't hibernating in a den of grief, he'd hug me back. As I stand there not hugging him, I think if we were normal teenagers we'd probably squeeze each other and sigh, and let our hands roam around until we had a knockin' boots of a one-afternoon-stand before supper and then never speak of it again.

But we're not normal. At least I'm not, and I'd bet on the ponies he's not either. And I don't feel the urge to touch his fuzzy, can't-grow-a-real-beard face. Or run my hands through his Kool-Aid hair. But I like him in this room. Like him in my house.

Instead I say, "I can help you put your stuff away."

Bodee nods; it's his typical wordless assent.

I stack the tent and the sleeping bag in the corner of the closet while Bodee unzips his duffel. This is not a job for two, but I'm not ready to leave.

"Won't take long," he says.

I reach for his worn copy of *Hatchet*. "God, I loved this book. Where do you want it?" I ask.

"Under the pillow," he answers.

Bodee removes his underwear from the bag so quickly the stack tumbles into a disheveled pile. I'm not supposed to have seen, so I hold the book and fumble with his pillow until I'm sure he's finished. It's weird how something as ordinary as white boxers turn a face red.

"I can hang those up," I say when he pulls the khaki slacks from the bag.

The tie, still knotted as I saw it last, a wrinkled white shirt, and pants come to me in a ball. They haven't been washed, and I can smell the earth and sweat of last Saturday on them.

"Why don't I wash these first?"

"I'll do it once I buy detergent."

"You're not buying detergent. It like, well, comes with the house. Like my shower soap and blue shampoo. And dinner."

Bodee tucks the strand of blue hair back, the one that's been driving me crazy, and says, "And rides to school?"

"Yes, and rides to school. And anything else you need."

An indeterminable number of white T-shirts, three pair of jeans, some socks, and the five boxes of Kool-Aid from the kitchen counter are the only other items he removes from the bag before shoving it under the bed.

"That's it," he says. "Told you it wouldn't take long."

Guilt doesn't stab at me, but it pokes at a place between my ribs.

I want to see him smile again.

"So"—I scroll my finger down the boxes of Kool-Aid he's

balanced on the windowsill— "what shade you going with tomorrow?"

"Sugar-free grape."

"You ever wear the lemonade?"

"Nah, too much like the natural," he says. "That was for drinking."

"Your mom bought them for you?"

This time there's no nod, but there are tears in his eyes. "She was . . . the best."

Now there are tears in my eyes. "I'll make you a promise, Bodee. Long as you're with my family, you won't run out of Kool-Aid."

He blinks up at me. "And I promise you, I'll stop *whoever's* hurting you."

I stand there barely breathing, and he says something that sounds like, "Even if it's you," but the words are mumbled, and I can't be sure I've heard them right.

If he were Heather or Liz, I'd deny this completely. But I can't lie to him. Not after today and his kitchen and the Kool-Aid on the counter and his tent and the stack of tumbled-over underwear on the bonus room floor. We're already more than the sum of my lies. So I just breathe and look away, trying not to lie with my face, but to stand in the presence of the truth.

It hurts.

There's complete silence until I say, "See you at dinner."

"Okay."

"Make a pile and I'll throw your clothes in to wash," I say.

"Okay."

"I'll have Dad take us to the store tomorrow in case you need something."

"Okay."

"And don't say anything about Kayla and Craig and the engagement." This reminder is pointless, since he rarely speaks unless spoken to.

"Okay."

"Okay" has become the new *hey*, I realize, as I leave him with wrong-side-up Cinderella.

chapter 7

I have to stop scratching my neck or I'll never be able to pull my hair up for the wedding.

And the wedding's official now that my parents know. There were happy tears in the mashed potatoes tonight. And hugs. I imagine there will be plenty more, too, before their *Christmas* wedding. Holy moly, that's quick. They've done everything else slowly. Why do they have to do this so fast?

I don't know if there's time for my neck to heal.

And . . . I'll need to be happy.

I'm fresh out of happy.

The air vent's slivers of darkness reel me in; my one way to cope that doesn't involve digging at my neck. One. Two. Three. Four. Five. I am up to nineteen before I blink and ruin the count. I start again because sleep hates me. Again and again until my brain gives in and allows the numbers to take me to dreamland.

In dreamland there's a pool.

Not our pool, because there's no wooden fence around the patio, but it looks like ours. A bunch of guys are there, sitting on the edge, swinging their feet and looking lazy, and kicking up little splashes of water.

"Hey. Okay. Hey. Okay. Hey. Okay," they chant. Automated and eerie, like the cry of a bobcat. I want to rip at the scabs on my neck.

The guys all have on black goggles that mask their faces. One minute they're all the same guy, but the next minute each individual face is different, and I know them: Dad; Collie; Dane Winters; Bodee; two boys from homeroom I've known since preschool; Matt from church; Craig; Hayden from our lunch table; and the band director, who has more hair on his chest than a shedding dog. There's Liz's on-again, off-again boyfriend, Ray, and then a guy I don't know whose face is painted up like Captain America. I'm pretty sure there are more, but they're too blurry to identify.

The painted-up guy must be Captain Lyric. I stare at him because I have to know who he is. But he shimmers in and out of focus until his face is like all the rest.

"Alexi. Alexi. Alexi." My name on their lips is hypnotic.

"I'm lonely," they say together. Now they're splashing a fountain of big fat drops of water to the center of the pool. "We're lonely. Lonely. All so lonely."

The guys on the right side speak. "You understand lonely."

I can't wake my brain enough to recognize I'm dreaming. And I'm paralyzed with fear. And mute.

Then it's not like a dream anymore. I know this pool. Know these guys.

And one of them knows me too well.

My eyes lock on his. I try to scream, *Stop!* It's more of a wheeze than a word.

Everything is wrong. A hand covers my mouth, but it's not mine. I don't have any hands. Or arms. This mutant isn't me, but it is.

The guys on the left side of the pool say, "She always understands."

"She didn't understand me," Dane says.

"Or me," Collie says.

"Or me," Matt from church says.

Another kick-splash. "But she won't tell," they all say.

"She never tells," Bodee says.

"And we're practically family," Craig says. "Families know everything."

I want to scream, *Families don't know everything!* but I can't.

"I don't know anything," my dad says.

"He doesn't know anything," the rest of them say as laughter sparks around the pool.

"It all happened on his patio," Hayden says. "But he doesn't know anything."

It's like a memorized script as the rest of them chime in.

But then something changes. Their hands reach toward my face before I can turn away. Each one claws at a side of my mouth. They jerk, and I scream and taste the pillow as my skin rips, and tears spurt from my eyes at the pain.

And then I'm awake. Sweating and shivering and dry-mouthed, the taste of blood on my tongue.

Before my alarm. And I don't want to think about the dream.

I sleepwalk through the day until fourth period.

Heather's in a chatty mood. "We were nice to Bodee in the car," she says as if they deserve an award.

"You were," I agree, though I barely remember the ride to school.

"So, tell me. What do y'all do at night?"

"Do? Bodee and me? We don't do anything." My voice rises, and I check to see if Mrs. Tindell notices, but she's buried her nose in a novel. "It's not like we're the only ones there. Last night we sat at the table with the fam for two whole hours while Kayla and Craig talked wedding details."

"You don't seem super excited for them. Jeez, if my sister was marrying a guy like Craig, you know, like with a job and no kids or jail time, I'd be flipping. But Hallie's got this thing for the gutter, so I doubt that's gonna happen."

"Sorry I'm not all rose petals and 'Canon in D.' I slept like crap last night. My head feels like it got run over by a tractor." Not a lie. "And anyway, they've been together so long that it's not like this was big news. Sort of like Collie saying he likes your boobs. Heard it a million times."

Heather rolls her eyes. "He doesn't say that. Not a million times."

"Kidding," I say, knowing Collie mentioned Heather's boobs to me only once. And it was after he'd had a couple of beers.

"He is sort of horny," she admits.

"I don't want to hear this," I say.

Heather's voice is unusually whiny as she says, "You said I could talk to you about him."

"Not today. I'm too exhausted to discuss your sex life."

"Yeah, my nonexistent sex life. Do you think he's getting it somewhere else?"

I fold my head into the crook of my arm, a disappearing technique I've learned from watching Bodee. "Not today, Heather."

"Fine. Sit over there and brood."

"I'm not brooding. I'm thinking. You should try it." I don't lift my head.

"You don't have to be pissy. Are you too tired for Captain Lyric?"

"No." I show her the desk.

After yesterday's lines are the new ones I wrote today before Heather arrived in class.

Nothing is sure but you
Nothing is safe but you
Nothing's left in this world
Only you

"Great. A power ballad."

"Hush. I'm just thinking about the wedding," I say, because I know what lines come next. *Promise me a wedding day. That you'll stay—forever. And ever. Only you.* Will the Captain write them as my end-of-the-week lyrics?

"You're lucky Mr. Wixon likes you," Heather says.

"I made a deal with him," I say, knowing that our old custodian, Mr. Wixon, may wear overalls to work, but he's a starry-eyed man at heart.

"Of course you did."

"We write in pencil, and we erase them on Friday. He Cloroxes the desks over the weekend. We're not hurting anything," I say.

Heather smiles. "Hey! Does he know who else writes them?"

"I didn't ask. I'm not ready to ruin this."

"You're so weird. I can't believe the suspense isn't killing you," she says, shaking her head.

I'm operating under the assumption that I am as much of an enigma to him as he is to me. It's romantic (and tragically stupid?), but this is the perfect way to reveal myself. Everybody at Rickman has heard by now that Kayla and Craig changed their status to Engaged. If the Captain is half-awake, he'll know. And make the leap that it's just logical for Kayla's little sister to write lyrics about a wedding. Right?

Maybe I should erase this clue. This constant ping-pong between wanting to know him and wanting to keep it all on the desk, safe and distant, bangs around in my head.

I leave the lyrics. Channeling brave. Looking forward instead of behind.

"You should be thinking about the homecoming dance," Heather says. "He's the person you should ask. Just leave him a little question out to the side of the last lyric."

"I am not asking him." But dang, the temptation . . . it's intoxicating. And paralyzing.

"Well, then, what would you say to Hayden if he asked you?"

"No. And he hasn't. Asked."

"Well." Heather chews her bottom lip. "Maybe we talked about it. And maybe I told him that you liked him."

"Heather."

"Lex, I knew you'd never ask Captain Lyric, so something had to be done. The dance is next week," she says.

Mrs. Tindell is up and on the roam. Heather looks expectantly at me, and I slide the completed worksheet from my folder.

"Finished already?" Mrs. Tindell asks when she reaches us.

"Yes, ma'am."

Satisfied, she circulates to the next group, and I exhale.

"I know you don't already have a date," Heather whispers, while keeping an eye on Mrs. Tindell's retreating back.

"No." The homecoming football game and the dance afterward is a big deal. But I can go group stag. Lots of girls go together and dance way more than if they have dates. But if I want to go with Heather and Liz, I have to have a boy who is picture-ific and just mine.

I do want to be with them.

And I don't.

Being with Heather and Collie on a date is like watching low-grade porn with my mom in the room. Heavy breathing. Hands in the places they shouldn't be in public. Awkward.

Seeing them makes me remember . . . what I'm trying to forget.

Liz and Ray are the opposite. They're together because they believe they're *called* to be together. Until they don't feel called anymore. So then they break up . . . until they're called again. What the hell? They treat each other like a lion and an antelope bungee-corded together.

Maybe they're lonely and too complacent to find someone else.

Heather raises a brow. I know what her question is before she asks. "No, I'm not going to the dance with Bodee," I say.

"I was afraid that might be part of *being nice* to him," she says.

"Not hardly." The truth is I *would* go to the dance with Bodee. And I wouldn't go just to be nice. But that's too close. Too soon. Right now we're both yard sales of emotions. A penny for pain. A dime for bitterness. A quarter for grief. A dollar for silence. It binds us together, but I don't want him to pay the price for the parts of me that are used and broken. And that's what the dance would be.

Besides, we live together. In the same house.

"That's a relief. Hayden really likes you."

"Hayden doesn't know me," I say.

Heather copies the last section of my worksheet and says, "He will after homecoming. Seriously, Lex, he's a good guy."

"That's what Craig says too," I say. According to Craig, there are only a few guys on the football team I'm allowed to date. Hayden's one of them. Ever-protective, opinionated, determined-to-have-his-way *Mr. Tanner*. I want to tell him to shut up and leave me alone. I'm a big girl, and I can choose my own dates, even if they aren't on his list. But he'd warn Kayla if I wanted to date some *bad seed*. And she'd tell Mom and Dad.

What does *bad* even mean anymore? Everyone is bad in some way. Except for Bodee.

"Well, there you go. If Craig believes it, then it's true," she says. "I think Hayden even goes to some church like you and Liz."

"Well, gosh, Heather, now you've convinced me." I flash fake googly-eyes at her. "Any guy who goes to church is bound to be Mr. Perfect."

"Oh, you know what I mean. He's got, like, a good soul or something, I think. And he'll ask you himself if you want."

"Wow. Thank you, date doctor."

I want to tell her I don't need her pity hookups, but she knows I won't take the initiative to flirt enough to snag a date. Her efforts mean I matter to her, and that's kind of nice, so it's only fair that I show her some appreciation. And the benefit of going to homecoming with a football player is that you barely see them until the dance. Basically, I'll be in the stands all night with Heather and Liz (and Ray). It's doable.

"I'm sure I'm going to regret this, but why not? Tell him I'll go if he asks," I say.

The pent-up squeal Heather lets out just as the bell rings is loud enough for Alaskan wolves to hear. And we're a long way from Alaska. "*Perfect.* See you at the table," she says, stacking her books and grabbing her purse. She's clearly trying to leave before I can change my mind.

I pick up our completed worksheets and speak to her empty desk. "No problem, I'll just turn this in for you."

Until tomorrow, Captain Lyric.

The hallway is crowded enough to give Times Square some competition. Hot and thankful for a lunch break, I put my shoulders down like a linebacker and barrel toward my locker. Next year when I'm a senior, the waters will part and I'll walk like a queen of the high school empire, but for now, I feel like a freshman. In the way.

Bodee's leaning against his locker, so I wave at him from down the hall. He's not the waving kind, but he gives me a lime-green hair toss.

I remember that he's usually not at his locker during this break.

"Got a question," he says as I reach him.

God, I hope it's about laundry or toothbrushes or even new

boxers. Please don't ask me to go back to the crime scene again after school. "Sure. Let me dump my books," I say, spinning the combination on my locker.

There's a tap on my shoulder.

"Hang on, Bodee," I say.

"Uh, Alexi."

The tapper is not Bodee. I know this without turning around, because Bodee's voice isn't that deep. Three books fall out of my locker as I cram my bag inside. Bodee squats beside me and helps me stack the books.

"An admirer," he murmurs.

An admirer who didn't help pick up my books. I slam my locker door and turn around.

Hayden: Collie's friend. One of Craig's football players. Sits at the lunch table. Deep voice. Dated Janna Fields all last year. And according to Heather, goes to some church. That's all I know beyond the obvious. He's picture-ific.

And probably here to ask me to homecoming.

Heather has wasted no time.

"Uh, Alexi," he says again now that he has my attention. "I was talking to Heather about the dance."

"Yeah, she told me in psych," I say, wishing I had something to fiddle with. Where do you put your hands when a guy asks you out?

"Well, I was wondering if you'd like to go with me."

"Um, okay. Yes, that would be nice," I say. Hayden may or may not be all the things Heather says, but add direct to the list. He's clearly no fan of chitchat or the get-to-know-you crap. He asked what he wanted—well, what Heather wanted, and I gave it to him. Done.

"Cool. Guess I'll see you at lunch then," he says.

"Yep."

He walks away with a satisfied look on his face. No details about plans or times. Not even an exchange of numbers. He'll see me at lunch; and this might be easier than I thought. Hayden strikes me as a guy who won't think about me again until ten p.m. next Friday night. That's fine by me. Because I won't think about him, either.

Except to worry.

The warning bell rings, and I turn back to Bodee. Heat stings my cheeks, because he's wearing my whole exchange with Hayden on his face. I've never seen him at a dance or at any after-school event, but something in his eyes suggests he might have had plans for this one.

"What'd you wanna ask?" I say.

"Nothing important," he says, and walks down the hallway away from the cafeteria. Why does that make me feel like he's just lost his mother all over again?

chapter 8

BODEE is silent for the next four days.

He speaks only when he has to and says only what is necessary. At the store when we buy a few things. At the dinner table or in the house with my parents. But in the car with Heather and Liz, he says nothing at all. Even at church, which is a mandatory outing at Littrell-topia. Bodee has a way of making his silence feel ordinary, like it's not a weapon, so I can't tell if he's mad at me or if he just has nothing to say.

Heather and Liz double-date the weekend away while I do homework in the closet and make new playlists for the week. Mostly grunge, but ironically, a whole list of classical songs, too. The genres don't usually make a good mix, but my brain needs both the ache and the peace.

Classical stuff makes me miss being in band. When I turned

in my saxophone at the beginning of the year, my mom was the only one who argued.

"Mom, I'm not going to Juilliard," I said, and then added some excuse about how I needed more time for homework with my AP class load. Total bullcrap. School's easy and I love music, but I can't spend that many hours in marching band. Too near the football field.

"Your call," Mom said, but I know it worried her for me to give up something I'd enjoyed doing for so long.

All weekend, I don't scratch my neck. Not once.

But I don't sleep. And that makes me look like hell. In fact, that Monday morning before Bodee and I leave for school, my mom asks, "Lex, you feeling okay?"

"Yeah. I'm not sleeping so well," I say. Better the truth on this one, since I have purple-as-a-plum circles under my eyes. She gives me a Mom look and tries for casual in her voice.

"Why, do you think?" She hands me and then Bodee a hot piece of toast.

"A lot on my mind, I guess. The wedding. Not practicing driving enough. The dance this weekend. You know, stuff." I butter the toast and do a quick check of Bodee's expression. It's unreadable.

"Well"—Mom pats my cheek—"maybe you and I need some time away from the house. We could do some shopping in Nashville. I know you're borrowing one of Kayla's fancy outfits for homecoming, but we could maybe take some girl time. What do you think? Spoil ourselves a little before we have to get so busy with the wedding and the holidays."

"Sure," I say. Mom probably thinks I'm fretting over the changes in our household. Bodee moving in; Kayla moving out.

"Are you going to the dance this weekend, Bodee?" Mom asks.

"No, ma'am."

"'Cause you can, you know. John and I want you to feel free to do whatever you like, to go out some or have friends in. Alexi's borrowing Kayla's stuff; I'm sure Craig wouldn't mind if you borrowed something too. Y'all are about the same size."

Are they? I've never thought of Bodee as anywhere near Craig's size, but now that Mom says it, I see they're closer than I thought. I figured Craig's khakis were belted on Bodee pretty good at the funeral, but maybe not.

"Thank you, ma'am, but I don't plan to go."

"Shame. I'm sure it'll be a lot of fun. John and I had so much fun at those dances when we were at Rickman. But oh, that was a million years ago now. Things have probably changed."

"Yeah, Mom, like dinosaurs no longer roam the earth," I say, and see her grin before heading to the door. "Come on, Bodee, there's Heather pulling in."

"Have a good day," Mom says.

Before I close the door behind us, I know from the look on Mom's face that she's happily reliving Rickman High School homecoming, circa the 1980s or something.

"Please. Shoot me if that's ever me," I say to Bodee on the way to the Malibu.

"I thought you liked dances," he says.

"Hell, no." I point to the front seat and mouth, "I'm only going because of them."

Bodee smiles for the first time in days.

The day-to-day lines added to my desk are the only other highlights during the rest of my week.

Monday:
I'd like to hold you in the mountains
LIKE TO KISS YOU BY THE SEA

Tuesday:
Take you far, far from here
TO A PLACE WHERE YOU FEEL FREE

Wednesday:
'Cause we are safe
WE ARE TRUE

Thursday:
We are going to make it through
CRASHING WORLDS, FALLING STARS

Friday:
Breaking all of who we are
I WANT INFINITY WITH YOU

"This week's weirder than usual," Heather says as she leans over and peers at my desk on Friday. "Y'all didn't say much."

"I think we said more than normal."

Heather twists her braid into a bun and sticks my yellow #2 through the middle. "What will Hayden think when he figures out you're in love with some random guy who writes on your desk?"

"He won't care." I pack my books away. "Not unless it's about football. And I'm not in love."

"You're in somethin' with him. Like you're in somethin' with Bodee. You know we could hear y'all whispering when you got in the car this morning."

I roll my eyes. "Forget it, Heather. Captain Lyric's a figment, and you can't be *in love* with a figment. He exists in this room only."

"So? I've been in love with that guy on MTV since seventh grade, and he only exists on TV. Captain Lyric's a whole lot closer than that." Heather points at the door of our classroom. "He's out there somewhere."

"But I don't know who he is." This is the real issue. That I *could* fall in love with this guy. If I knew who he was.

But all I know about him are the words he chooses from someone else's songs. If it's a love story, it's a short one. "And for your information," I add, "Bodee and I were talking about him *not* going to the dance. Again, let's review: he lives In. My. House. We are *not* in love. *We* aren't anything."

"Huh. That's too bad, 'cause I think he's growing on me."

"You date him then." I regret saying this immediately. Bodee's not a pawn, and he's not mine to give away. Of course, Heather's attached at the hip to Collie, and she's not interested in Bodee. But the thought that she could be gives me the same feeling I have after I find a hair in my nachos.

Heather grins; she's on the verge of letting go with a hyena laugh. We're in class, so she jams a fist in front of her mouth and crosses her eyes. It doesn't help. We're still loud.

"Ms. Littrell, may I please see you at my desk?" Mrs. Tindell asks from the front of the room.

Uh-oh.

Everyone looks up. I'm like one of Mom's second graders as I walk the aisle to our teacher's desk. The rest of the class awaits my punishment.

Mrs. Tindell's voice is so quiet that no one else can hear her. "I know you've already finished your work. Would you mind returning these books to the library for me?"

"Of course not." Sigh of relief. I reach for the books, but she touches my hand.

"So you know, Ms. Littrell. I find this preferable to telling you and Ms. Jackson to . . . keep your traps shut . . . again . . . so everyone else can work. Understand?"

I'd find it preferable if she'd actually teach us something, but I say, "Yes, ma'am. Uh, thank you." I take the books from Mrs. Tindell and leave the classroom with everyone staring holes in my back.

The library is on the other side of the school. By the time I get there and leave the books in the return bin, the bell rings. My stuff is still in psych, but it's hard to be late to lunch. The lines are so long.

On my way down the hallway, someone slides into step with me.

"Hey, Alexi," Hayden says. "You ready for tonight?"

He's wearing the mandatory Friday home-game khakis and red jersey, and it's an understatement to say he looks nice. Some high school guys are like men already. Hayden and Collie both are. Maybe it's their chiseled faces and muscular football bodies, but it's intimidating.

"It'll be fun," I say, trying to drum up some enthusiasm.

"I'm on the homecoming court. Janna's escort. Just wanted to say sorry about that." He huffs and then stops short. "That's not gonna ruin your night or anything, right? I'm not big on drama."

I realize I could get dropped right now if I act pissed, but I say, "Me either. No big deal."

"Thanks. Just wait with Heather outside the locker room. Collie and I'll be out after we shower."

"Um, I know this is stupid, but do you mind meeting my parents first? They don't like me riding in cars with guys they don't know." Is this drama? I hope not.

Hayden shrugs like he's heard this before. Maybe Janna's parents wanted to shake his hand too, back when they first started going out. "Sure," he says. "Lot of parents are like that in Rickman. Pretty crazy, if you ask me. Even a psycho can act normal long enough to do a meet-and-greet." He grins. "I mean, I could be some whacked-out serial killer or rapist, and they'd never know from a handshake. Why even bother?"

I check the ground for blood, because I'm pretty sure mine just drained right out of my face and fell straight down my body.

His big football hands shake my shoulders. "Alexi, you know I'm no serial killer or rapist. God, I'll meet your parents. I was just saying . . ."

"I know you're not," I assure him as I slide my shoulders away from him and think this is the kind of drama that will have me dateless in the blink of an eye. "But somebody did assault a girl over the summer. So you probably shouldn't joke about it."

The words are out of my mouth before I can stop them. They're vague, but it's the first time I've said . . . *anything* like that. Why Hayden? Why now? Maybe because he doesn't matter. We'll have homecoming, and then we'll have nothing. He'll probably take Janna back by this time next week.

"Dang. Where'd you hear about an assault?"

Thinking fast, I say, "The bathroom."

Hayden exhales. "Probably no truth to it. Some girl went all the way with a dude and then felt bad about it. Happens to guys all the time, and it makes me *furious*. Once you're labeled a 'rapist'"—he curls his fingers up to air-quote the word—"you're always a rapist." Another indignant sigh. He gives the impression it's on behalf of the entire football team this time.

There's a nuclear explosion mushrooming inside my head. Fried neurons floating in a vacuum where my brain is supposed to be. The urge to scurry out of his sight like a cockroach is overpowering. "Yeah, um, that's probably it. See you tonight."

I duck into the closest bathroom. Three girls stand at the mirror reapplying makeup—probably freshmen, since I don't recognize them. They're talking about the huge number of calories in school food. I make it to a stall at the end and forgo any thought of sanitary hygiene. Collapsing on the open toilet seat, I sob quietly into my hands.

I am one of those girls Hayden has such contempt for, the ones he thinks are so unfair when they cry "rape."

Because I didn't try to stop him.

He had no indication, absolutely nothing from me that he wasn't doing what I wanted.

Except for the tears. They rolled from my eyes and wet my hair and ran into my ears.

But he never looked at my face. I know because I never blinked. I can't count the slits in the vent without blinking, but that night it was as if my eyelids were wired open. I saw everything. Everything. His eyes were closed when it started, when he reached for me for comfort, and I froze. When he kissed me and I stayed silent. And his eyes were closed while he worked. Because he didn't want to remember I wasn't his girlfriend. He didn't want to realize he was doing to me the things he wanted to do with her.

The end-of-lunch bell rings. I don't move. Even as the bathroom door revolves for girls in need of a pee or a mirror. They hurry in, they hurry out, and no one sees me hiding in the stall.

Bells ring at the beginning and end of fifth period. Technically, I am cutting class. But I simply cannot move.

I hear the bells ring at the start of sixth period and again at the end of sixth period. I still don't move.

Packs of girls end their day in the bathroom. Little snippets of conversation drift under the stall door. Kate Applebee is the favorite for homecoming queen. (I agree.) The Spanish II teacher, Mr. Moore, is gay. (I agree.) Dane Winters has the best ass in the class. (I agree.) The dance will be ballin'. (I don't care.) I want to leave. And I should call out that I'm here and can hear everything they say.

But I can't.

Eventually, the girls are gone. And so is the noise in the hallway.

I have been crouched here with tears running down my cheeks for two and a half hours. The phone in my back pocket vibrates with four messages from Heather and three from Liz. They have my psych book. They're waiting. They're at the car. Still waiting. Where am I?

They're not happy. *Where am I?*

It is the need to lie that wakes me up and gives me the courage to move. I text Heather and Liz.

Don't wait. Sorry. Talking to a teacher about SAT. See you in dresses.

If my fingers can move, so can the rest of my body. I stand up. My legs surprise me by walking out of the stall. Slow, secret tears don't mess with your eyes or ruin makeup the way a gully-washing cry-fest does, so I'm able to dab my face with a paper towel and look mostly normal.

Faking normal is a skill I learned seventy-seven days ago, but tonight it's going to require everything I have.

chapter 9

THERE'S one lone figure slouched against the long brick planter outside the front doors of the school. He has green hair, and he looks up as I push open the doors and walk outside.

"Bodee, you didn't have to wait," I say. The empty parking lot looks like a concrete desert. It is extra hot for October.

"Yes, I did."

I open my mouth to tell him I was talking to a teacher about the SAT, but then I don't say the words.

"Rough day." Bodee isn't asking; he's stating instinctively what he seems to know about me.

"Yeah," I say. There is a silent consensus to head home, so he joins me and we walk toward the street together.

"Thanks for not making something up," he says.

"I guess you'd know if I did," I say.

"You don't want to talk about it."

Again, he's stating a fact. He's opening a door, but he already knows I won't walk through. The power of Bodee is in the way he reads me, sees through me, and then understands the truth behind the facade. He's the guy who can walk straight through the House of Mirrors on the first try. It's almost annoying. No one should ride tragedy like a pro surfer while I drown.

"Not in the mood to talk," I say. Talking will lead to more crying, and more crying will lead to puffy eyes, and puffy eyes will lead to questions from people who aren't as undemanding as Bodee.

"It's Hayden," he says.

"No, not Hayden." I sigh. "Something Hayden said."

"A man is partially made up of his words," Bodee says. After that, we just walk.

Then Bodee boots an acorn, sending it spinning into the grass. We keep walking, and he kicks at the stub of a pencil from someone's backpack. And then he's shuffling his feet left and right. Anything on the sidewalk has to go: more acorns, scattered rocks from a driveway, and candy wrappers and cigarette butts. Trash left by a horde of students when the school day ends. I join in, and together we clean the sidewalk with our emotions.

When the stretch ahead of us is clear, when there's nothing left to kick, Bodee speaks.

"Mom gave me ten dollars before . . . um, you know." He

stops and faces me. "I could go to the dance tonight if you . . . if it'll help."

Dull knitting needles. A dozen of them to the heart. "Oh, Bodee," I say.

I might sob right here and not worry about the puffy eyes. How does it happen that a boy I hardly know has become the only person in the world I trust? Decide fast, Lex. Do I ask him to spend the ten dollars? The little money he has (that his dead mother gave him) for a dance where he'll stand in a corner just to make sure I'm okay? Or do I tell him to keep it and reject one of the sweetest things anyone has ever offered me?

"I won't interrupt your date," he adds.

"I know." I have to accept his offer, but I don't know if it's for him or for me. "Yes, please. Come to the dance."

I want him to hold my hand, and magically he does. Not boyfriend style, and only for a squeeze. But long enough that a tiny seed of hope grows inside me.

"If you come, you have to dance with me," I say. It's only fair. His ten dollars more than earns him one dance.

"What about Hayden? Will he know I'm not trying to date you?"

"I'll explain."

Bodee knows I'm not explaining anything to Hayden. He knows this means I will lie, but he nods.

"I haven't danced with anyone before," he says. Little tinges of pink bloom across his cheeks, and I haven't seen that since the night he stacked up his boxers in front of me.

"Good," I say. "I'm a terrible dancer."

"We *aren't* . . . trying to . . . date each other. Right?"

"Nope. The last thing I need is a boyfriend," I say, and mean it.

"Good." Bodee exhales, and I hear his relief. "You're my . . . first friend, Alexi. Except for my mom. And I don't . . . I'd rather not skip ahead."

"No skipping ahead," I agree.

This thing with Bodee is shaped with expectations, but they're easy. And right. Like when I hold one of my stone carvings or a piece of pottery in progress and can tell I'll like the artwork. Even when it's not quite complete.

Friends.

"I can use the lemonade on my hair." He sends a glance sideways. "Look normal."

"Don't you dare," I say. "I'm dancing with a green-haired guy."

I say a little prayer of thankfulness. Mom and Dad believe they invited Bodee into our home to help him, but the truth is, he's helping me.

"Thanks for waiting," I tell him when we reach the house. "And for tonight."

"That's okay," he says.

And it is.

The two and a half hours in the bathroom are forgotten. The time with Bodee is like a dose of vitamin C. Soul-healing.

I check my watch. It's four o'clock, and I have an hour to get ready before Heather arrives to pick me up. "I gotta go in," I say.

"I know. See you tonight."

After a quick shower, I dress in my favorite of Kayla's black dresses. I'm taller, but she's bigger than I am in places. So I show less boobs and more legs than intended. I'm only moderately pleased with the outfit, so I take extra time with my hair, which means Heather's horn blows before I finish my nails. I paint the last two toes in a hurry, leaving a dab of silver on the carpet, and slide into a pair of heels, stuff my phone into my clutch, and yell "Bye" to Bodee. Mom has to do her mom bit, looking me over and giving me compliments, before sending me out the door.

"Smokin'," Heather says as I wiggle into the front seat of the Malibu.

"You too."

Heather's wearing a strapless, empire-cut teal dress that makes her eyes look like blue fire. Collie will take one look at it, at her, and try to talk her out of it. And this might be his lucky night. She slides huge pink sunglasses over her flames and says, "That dress says you're ready to make memories."

"Absolutely." I'm surprised at my own excitement. This morning the dance was an obligation, but now that Bodee's going and it's safe, I'm happy to put on the swank, glad to wear the bling.

"Love these nights. One reason to tolerate high school. I'm

so glad you quit band. I'd miss you like crazy tonight if you had to sit with them." Heather leans her head against mine and holds a camera out at arm's length to take our self-portrait. We both show our teeth. "The game is going to be awesome. Then the dance. And afterward, there's a party at Dane's. I don't have anywhere to be until Monday morning at seven fifty-five. That's what I call a weekend, baby."

"I'm probably not going to Dane's," I say.

"Buzzkill. Well, we'll see." Heather sounds confident. "You know Hayden will want to go."

"Hayden's just going with me tonight to make Janna jealous. They'll be back together before the end of the dance."

Heather looks over her glasses at me. "I think you're wrong on that one. He likes you."

"We'll see."

We run by Liz's house to take pictures with her before Ray picks her up. Her mom has pizza on the table, and knowing we'll dance the calories off before the night is over, we eat two slices each. As I glance between Heather and Liz, I realize this is why it's worth putting up with Hayden. There's girl energy between us as we stuff our faces and joke and tease one another. And avoid getting grease on our dresses.

"I'm glad we're all going together," Liz says. "We could leave the boys behind, and I'd be okay with it."

"Me too," I agree.

"Uh-uh, not me. Way too much estrogen. I want me some Collie."

"We know," Liz and I say at the same time.

"Pretty sure Collie wants you, too," I say, but no one hears because Ray rings the doorbell.

"Go on or you'll miss the kickoff," Liz says. "We're right behind you."

At the game, the student section is packed with fancy dresses, button-ups and silk ties, and even one powder-blue suit from a donation store. But formality hasn't stolen our school spirit. The cheers are just as loud and the clapping and stomping just as rowdy as any other Friday night. Kayla and Bodee are higher up, one bleacher below the press box, and my parents are with them. Kayla gives me a thumbs-up for the dress and waves me toward her, but I don't have enough ambition to climb all those steps in heels.

"I've hardly seen him in anything but a T-shirt," Heather says as her eyes follow mine.

Heather's right. Bodee's not wearing his usual. I take a second look, and he pops his knuckles and then gives me a little wave. I don't wave back, but I smile. "It's Craig's stuff," I say, wishing we'd gone shopping for something new.

"That's nice," she says.

"Yeah, but I sort of miss the T-shirt." It's funny how things you don't like are the things you miss when they're gone.

"You would." Heather rolls her eyes at me. If rolling your eyes burned up calories, Heather would be skin and bones. "Hey, you're wearing this hot little number"—she eyes the hemline of Kayla's dress—"so let the guy have a dress shirt."

We return the kickoff for a touchdown, and Styrofoam-cup alcohol passes right beneath the blind eyes of parents and teachers. The party has begun.

Heather screams at the top of her lungs in celebration, but then leans down to whisper, "What happened?"

"We scored a touchdown," I say.

"Oh. Okay. That's good."

"Scoot over," Liz says as she and Ray slide in next to us. "What did we miss?"

"We scored a touchdown," Heather says like she's the expert.

"Is it still hard to watch them play?" Liz asks Ray.

Ray touches his knee and says, "Yeah."

Ray'll be back from his ACL tear by next season, and then he'll be the one getting an earful from Craig like number seven is right now.

"Why aren't you down there with the team?" I ask, wishing the night could go on as a girls-only event.

Ray shrugs. "'Cause Alex is a basket case. Number nineteen." He points to a guy in the middle of the huddle. "Coach says I make him nervous, and since I'm not technically on the team right now, he doesn't want me down there messing with his receiver's head."

I understand. I'm tired of a certain someone messing with my head too.

Football games are usually long. Not tonight. Craig and the other coaches mill among our guys, screaming stuff. They scribble on clipboards and wave their arms like they're sending jets off a carrier. I notice Craig pokes number seven right in the numbers on his chest before he sends him back onto the field.

"That was Hayden," Heather says. She doesn't know anything about football, but she totally knows which guy goes with which number.

"I'm glad I'm not Hayden," I say, seeing Craig's red face. I feel a little guilty that I never thought to look up Hayden's number. Down on the field, the players look like red ants scurrying around after a log is turned over.

"Hayden do something wrong?" Liz asks.

"He got sacked. Wonder what Coach said to him," Ray says. "Bet it wasn't good."

Heather giggles. "Craig said, 'You screw with my little sister and I'll be the one knocking the crap outta you.' Just a loose interpretation," she says, and infects everyone around us with laughter.

Including me. But of course, that's not what Craig said. Then again, I wouldn't put it past him—just not during a football game.

"Well, whatever Craig told him must have worked. Hayden just scored," Liz says.

Students we don't know give us high fives while the band cranks out the fight song. I look up and over my shoulder at Kayla. She's giving me two thumbs-up, and it's because my date just scored the touchdown that put us up at halftime. Approval. In Kayla's mind, which is way too easy to read, I now have my best chance at true happiness.

The loudspeaker announces the homecoming court and waits as they arrange themselves on the appropriate yard lines, and every girl who'd normally make a run to the bathroom at halftime waits to hear who will be king and queen for a night.

"Come on, come on; tell us who won. Nobody cares about all this crap," Heather says as they introduce each princess and her escort. But I'm listening to Hayden's little spiel.

"Hayden Harper, representing the junior class, is the seventeen-year-old son of Beth and Don Harper of Horn Branch. Hayden is a member of the varsity football team and was named to the All-Region first team last year. He is also a member of the varsity track team and active on the student council, FCA (Fellowship of Christian Athletes), and FFA (Future Farmers of America). Hayden attends Horn Branch Christian Church."

Liz mimics the announcer's voice. "Hayden Harper stands next to his ex-girlfriend, Janna Fields, while his date, Alexi Littrell, waits in the grandstand and blushes. Alexi is the sixteen-year-old daughter of . . ."

"Shut *up*," I say. Am I blushing? "Besides, I knew he had to be Janna's escort. He told me."

"Too weird," Liz says.

"And I'm calling it now," I say as the announcer continues to rattle on. "Hayden gets back with Janna by the end of the night."

"I'll take that bet. Five dollars says he's kissing you instead of Janna before the last song plays," Heather challenges.

"Make it ten, and you've got a deal." I figure there's more than one way to pay for Bodee's dance ticket.

"Deal."

"This year's Rickman High School Homecoming Queen *and* her king . . ."

The whole stadium is quiet as the announcer pauses and milks the moment. "Kate Applebee and Dane Winters."

Everyone cheers for, like, thirty seconds, and it's over. So much for fifteen minutes of fame. All most girls want now is popcorn, a drink, and to check themselves in the bathroom mirror. Bra straps. Shiny nose. Lipstick. Duplicate dresses. And then to gossip about bra straps, shiny noses, lipstick, and duplicate dresses all over again.

The second half goes faster than the first. The Rickman Raiders remain undefeated, and I'm able to join in the fun, laughing with Heather and Liz most of the time. It's the best I've felt in two months, fourteen days, and twenty hours.

Mom and Dad clomp down the bleacher steps to our seats as the crowd disperses. They're wearing identical red Rickman Raider T-shirts. Not the current ones; these are the ones *they* wore in high school, for God's sake. Kayla and Bodee follow behind Mom and Dad.

Mom hugs me and whispers so Dad can't hear, "You look beautiful, honey."

Dad freaked out when Mom told me I was allowed to start dating. Mom says it's because I'm his baby, but Kayla says he was the same with her. He wouldn't let Craig come to the house when they weren't home the first three months they dated, which meant they sneaked around. And that's funny, because now Craig is at our house all the time with or without Kayla. He and Dad love every sport in the universe, and they love talking about them all the time.

"Thanks, Mom," I whisper back.

Mom nudges my shoulder and says to the group, "Lexi's date sounds like a nice guy. Don't you think so, John?"

I make eyes with Bodee, who is hiding behind Kayla. He scowls at the mention of Hayden and says, "The announcer is hardly going to list their bad traits."

Well, he doesn't say it out loud, but I can read his lips.

"Looks like you're moving up in the dating world," Kayla says, snapping me back to attention. "Date with the future homecoming king last week. Date with a football star tonight. Way to snag them, sis." Before I can smile, she adds, "Even though the football star *did* look awfully happy standing down there by his ex."

I see Bodee's mouth make the word. "Jerk." I guess he's not always soft-spoken.

"Kayla, stop," Mom says.

"Just saying. Sorry," she says, but there's no sign of sorry in her tone. That's Kayla. She gives and she takes away. I'm used to it.

"Well, Heather's in charge of my social calendar," I say, "so you can give her the credit, not me. Oh, and Dad, Hayden said he'd come out to meet you and Mom after he showers."

Liz and Ray say good-bye, and the rest of us drift toward the locker room. Craig comes out first. He's a sweaty mess, but Kayla latches on like he's a tree and she's a sloth.

"Hey, baby." He kisses her and then shakes my dad's hand.

"Great game, Craig," Dad says. "Had me worried the first quarter, but *man*, the second. You musta lit a fire under your guys."

"They're all great when we win," Craig says with a grin. Before he and Dad get into the world of Discussing-the-Game, Craig notices me and does a double take.

He squeezes Kayla's hand and looks all proud of me. "Lex, you're sure growing up on us."

"I know. Happened sometime this last summer," Kayla answers for me.

July 20, to be exact.

Before Craig can say anything else, Kayla leans into him and asks, "You remember me in that dress?"

A hint of red appears on Craig's cheeks as they lock eyes for half a second. He nuzzles her ear like a fool in love. "Like it was yesterday."

O-kay. Pretty *sure* there's a story regarding this dress that neither Craig nor Kayla is about to share, especially not with Mom and Dad standing here. More likely it's Kayla *not* in the dress he's remembering. We all blush a little, because it's obvious what's going on. Even Heather shuffles her feet, and she's hard to embarrass. And now I wish I'd dry-cleaned the dress before I put it on.

My dad has now lost all desire to chat with Craig about the game; in fact, he's fuming. I guess he's just been jerked out of denial about the existence of his older daughter's sex life. And he's *not* a happy camper at the moment. You'd think Kayla would have more sense than to flaunt it in front of Dad, even if they are engaged now.

Just as the silence grows a little too long, Hayden and Collie, smelling of soap and cologne, emerge from the locker room and rescue *Coach Tanner.* Hayden looks only slightly smaller in his suit than in his football pads.

"Mom, Dad, this is Hayden," I say.

He shakes hands with both of them. "Mr. and Mrs. Littrell, nice to meet you."

"You played a great game out there," Dad says to him, and includes Collie in his comment.

"Thank you, sir."

Hayden is good at this. Too good. He's got the confident grin, the handshake, and the Mr. and Mrs. down pat. And the suit doesn't hurt. Because everyone knows high school guys who look this good in a suit don't drink or do drugs. Or have sex. Yeah, I think it's Parental Illusion #552. And what Hayden told me in the hallway this afternoon is true. He could be some kind of psycho and absolutely convince my parents with a handshake that he's a normal, well-mannered guy.

There's some easy chitchat, and then Dad says, "Curfew's at twelve thirty, Alexi."

"Don't worry, Mr. Littrell." Hayden gives me a sweet smile, the of-course-I'll-respect-your-daughter type that all fathers want to see, and says, "I'll make sure she's home safe and sound."

Behind my dad, the shadows shift, and Bodee steps into the light.

Mom moves to include him in our huddle and puts an arm around Bodee's shoulders. "Hayden, you know Bodee, don't you?"

"Not well," Hayden says, but he nods and reaches for Bodee's hand. Like the reaction over the dress, it looks awkward. They grip each other's hand for a bit too long.

"Good game," Bodee says in his usual quiet voice.

Until this moment I haven't thought of Bodee as very tough. He's not as solid and his shoulders aren't as wide as Hayden's, though no one has shoulders like Hayden's. Not even Craig or my dad. Now that I'm looking, Bodee is not the same Bodee. I try not to think it's the borrowed clothes or the ten-dollar dance I promised him. But he has a look I haven't seen before, and whatever it is causes Hayden to take a step back.

And then I realize: Bodee's not hunched over and his

chin isn't tucked in his shirt. His head's back, and his eyes are making direct contact with Hayden's.

Hayden says a quick thanks to Bodee and exchanges a few more words with my parents, then sends me a look that says he wants to cut this short. "You ready to go, Alexi?"

Also escape-minded, Heather and Collie are quick to move toward the gate. I nod, but glance back at Bodee as Hayden offers me his arm. One corner of Bodee's mouth moves. There's neither a smile nor a frown on his face, but I understand. Without words, he's telling me not to worry.

He'll make certain I get home safely tonight.

chapter 10

"WHAT'S the deal with Bodee Lennox?" Hayden asks as soon
as we're out of earshot.

"He lives at my house." I say this as nonchalantly as possible and concentrate on keeping my heels out of the parking
lot divots.

"Oh." Hayden nods to himself, and I see he's working out
the why and how of the situation. "I didn't realize that."

Heather runs her shoulder into mine before she says,
"Yeah, sort of the way I didn't realize you"—she reaches around
me and pokes Hayden in the chest—"were Janna's homecoming escort. You better not be jerking my girl here."

Now, I bump Heather. Uncomfortable. But she doesn't
care; there's a smile on her face that would put a clown to
shame. "Tension" is her second middle name. "Flirt" being her

first. Dear God, I wish the walk between the football stadium and the gym wasn't so long.

"I'm not jerking her around." Two bright pink spots tinge Hayden's cheek. "I told you about Janna, didn't I?" he asks me.

"You did," I agree.

"Careful, man. The girl still wants you," Collie says. "She'll have her hooks out tonight. Lex, you'd better watch her like a hawk."

He hasn't called me Lex in a long time; he notices and so do I.

"Janna's not the only one with hooks," Hayden says. "You see that glare Bodee gave me? Pretty serious."

"Bodee always looks serious. It has nothing to do with me," I say. This lie is easier than it should be because it's half true.

"If you say so." Hayden's not convinced. "But hey, it's not like he's competition."

Hayden and Collie laugh. Their disregard of Bodee grates on my last nerve. Like when Kayla makes a racial slur, but I bite my tongue. This is a turnoff. Somebody (not me) should tell them, when you act like you think you're cute, you're not.

We're all a little shocked when it's Heather who says, "Be nice now. Bodee's harmless."

There won't be a better time to come clean about the dance I promised Bodee before they add any other disparaging remarks. "Look. I'm not gonna lie." *Completely.* "Bodee's a friend. I didn't plan on it when my parents moved him in with us, but now it's hard not to get to know him a little. And I feel—"

"Sorry for him. Yeah, so does the rest of the school. What a whack job! His dad, I mean," Hayden says.

"Yeah. That's why I promised my mom I would dance with him at least once tonight." I use every pitiful expression I know, including an over-the-top sigh. "You know, so he's not completely alone."

Collie shoots me a sly grin. "Does that mean you're gonna let Janna have a dance with my man here?"

"No," I say, because it's what Hayden expects to hear, and I want this night to be drama free. But Hayden's a guy who's been stroked and adored by Janna for a year and a half. They probably have firsts together, and if she wants him back, she'll get him. She's got that conceited *I'm gorgeous* laugh, too. But it means nothing to me. After the dance, she can have him.

In fact, I stand to make ten dollars if she does.

"Janna causes a problem tonight, I'm gonna let Heather tell her where she can go," Hayden says.

"Aww. That sounds like the perfect job for you, honey," Collie says, and squeezes Heather's shoulders.

Jackass; instead of looking at her face as he refers to her, Collie focuses right on *the girls*, as Heather calls them. He didn't used to be that way.

"And she can take a crack at Bodee, if the dude wants more than a dance," Hayden says.

"Y'all always let Heather fight your battles?" I am only semi-teasing.

"Uh, yeah," the guys say together, and bump fists like they're on the football field. Heather laughs like she thinks it's funny too.

I'm starting to think I'll owe Heather ten dollars. Hayden is not sounding like a guy Heather had to talk into going out with me. And I don't get that. Because last year, guys did not form a line to ask me out.

So I have to wonder. Did *he* change me? The image of blue Hawaiian swim trunks rips through my brain. Rips through the peace I've held on to so firmly tonight. Did he . . . *do* something to me that guys can *see* on the outside? Now do they want to do it too?

Craig and Kayla both commented that I'd changed over the summer. All the trauma feels like it's happening inside me, but maybe it's leaking out.

"You know we're kidding about Bodee?" Heather asks with a laugh. "He's the most undatable, nonthreatening guy at Rickman. You're more likely to sleep with Collie than date Bodee Lennox."

"Yeah," I say.

Collie steals a kiss from Heather and quickly says, "Hon, please don't pimp me out."

Even though the night air is warm, I shiver and pull away from Hayden's arm.

"You cold?" Hayden asks. "Because I can warm you up."

"I'm fine." I say it fast, but Hayden is already digging in the inside pocket of his suit coat. He shakes a little metal flask at me and then at Collie.

"All right! Your brother came through," Collie says.

"Doesn't he always?" Hayden says. "It's better than a blanket," he promises me.

"Alexi's a wine cooler girl," Heather tells him with a wink at me.

"Oh," Hayden says. *"Okay."*

Saying I'm a wine cooler girl is like saying Bodee's chatty. But I give Heather an appreciative look for her protective comment. I'm off the hook. Even if I did want to drink tonight, it would definitely not be from Hayden's flask.

"Well, we're gonna have a good time tonight, buddy," Collie says.

"Just don't let Coach Tanner catch you again," Heather warns. "You'd have been suspended last time, if he hadn't agreed to keep your little secret."

"Suspension would have been easier. He ran us the next day at practice till we puked," Hayden says. "That was punishment enough."

"Probably the reason he didn't tell is he did the same thing in high school. Right, Alexi?" Collie asks. "Hayden's older brother says Coach was wild back in the day."

"I don't know," I say, thinking another reason might be that Craig couldn't win without his star football players. "I was, like, seven when he was that age."

That little flask makes me nervous on so many levels. Because it turns an otherwise decent guy into an octopus with eight hands. Or, at the least, an idiot. But I can't say anything. This is my night to act normal. My night to forget. And to remember that I still like guys. Guys who think I'm attractive and want to hold my hand. And buy me dinner. And get cheesy, stupid dance pictures taken with me so my mom can put them in her scrapbook.

"I'll bet Coach has plans with your sister. He won't catch us tonight." Hayden conceals the flask in his large hand like a magic trick. "Our only plan is to celebrate. Just like every other guy on the team. Right, Collie?" Hayden slings an arm around my shoulder. "You don't mind, do you, Alexi?"

There's a pause as Heather, Collie, and Hayden wait to see how I'll respond.

"Long as you don't confuse me with Janna," I say, and think I deserve an Oscar.

Everyone laughs, and Hayden takes a sip while we're still in the shadows of parked cars. From here, I see the open gym doors and hear the music. Dane's probably happy because a popular rap song is blaring out lyrics I'd never dream of writing on the desk.

A nagging sensation, the one whispering that Hayden is a creep who'll try to take advantage of me, is back. Along with the need to tear at my neck. My knuckles are white from gripping my clutch, and I take a deep breath.

"Ready to go in?" I ask, and hope the dark camouflages the panic in my eyes.

"Absolutely," Hayden says.

In we go. Collie and Heather. Hayden and I. And the flask.

As Hayden hands over our tickets, I think about Bodee. Is the ten-dollar bill crisp or wrinkled? Has he kept it wadded up in his pocket since she gave it to him or flattened between the pages of *Hatchet*, where I imagine he stores important things? Will it hurt when he hands it over to Mrs. Ramsey for entry into his first dance? Guilt is a good distraction from my fears. And so is Bodee. He'll be behind us somewhere.

"You want pictures?" Hayden asks.

"Sure," I say, as if I haven't already thought about this.

Hayden smiles and pulls me along toward the tacky photo backdrop. *A Knight to Remember.*

We move closer together at the photographer's insistence.

"Beautiful couple," the old man says, looking at us through the lens.

The camera flashes and he takes one more, promising we'll have our hard-copy memories in a week. Perfect. By then, we won't even care about the dance or the twenty Hayden shelled out to stand by the life-size statue of a black knight made of plastic.

And the girl who is not Janna.

When we leave the lit hallway and step into the gym, it takes my eyes a minute to adjust to the disco ball and strobe lights. My ears beg for a pair of plugs as my heart rate matches the bass from the DJ's speakers. There are nearly six hundred students at Rickman High, but there must be a thousand people here. Well, probably not, but it already smells like a thousand.

"Check the newbies." Hayden points at the edge of the gym. The freshman class is a border of braces and shyness.

"Hey, you were just like that once," I say.

He eyes a boy who's wearing a bow tie with a plaid shirt and says, "I was never like that." And then points to a couple slow-dancing to a fast song and says, "I was a lot more like that."

"You and Janna were sort of legendary," I say.

"It's your job to hide me tonight," he says.

Hide him. Is he kidding? As he pulls me toward the drink table, heads twist around as girls get a look at the football player attached to my side.

"Oh God, there she is," he says.

"Where?" My eyes sweep the room in search of the Janna-monster. I'm only partially looking for her, because I'm Bodee-watching, too. I can barely see the people next to us for the fog machine in this corner. Where is my Kool-Aid friend? Would he stand along the edge with the boy in the plaid or in the corner like the girl wearing a tux?

"Over there." Hayden flips his head toward the entrance.

Janna's top-heavy and bottomed-out, and the girl by the entrance looks a few cup sizes short of Hayden's ex. "You sure that's her?"

"Oh yeah."

The girl turns to the side to talk to a friend, and I can tell Hayden is right. The familiarity between them is something that only comes from spending time together. Across a crowded, dark room, Hayden knows her shape. Will I ever know Captain Lyric that way? Or Bodee?

The Captain's probably here somewhere tonight. Dancing with another girl who doesn't complete him any more than Hayden completes me.

I play the Where Is Captain Lyric Right Now? game. What if he's Janna's date? Now that would be ironic. Or the boy in the plaid? I hope not. Hayden? What if I'm already on a date with my perfect guy?

"Just need enough to take the edge off sharing a room with Janna," Hayden says as we reach the drink table.

I've got an edge like the Grand Canyon, and nothing takes it off. "Whatever," I say. Hayden can't be my Captain. The Captain doesn't drink. Or in my fantasy he doesn't.

Hayden doctors and drains the drink. "Now, I'm ready to dance," he says.

"Me too," I say, hoping to get us away from the drink table.

As I join him on the dance floor, the Captain and Bodee aren't the only thoughts filling my head. My personal silencer is here too. Reminding me Heather was the one who rejected the alcohol, not me. Suggesting that when Hayden's hands want to linger in places they don't belong, I'll let him do whatever he wants.

We dance two fast songs before Collie and Heather and Liz and Ray make our twosome a circle.

"Hey," Heather screams over the music. "We lost you after pictures."

The flask moves between Hayden and Collie. And back again.

Liz rolls her eyes. "Neither of you need that."

Maybe they do, because that's when Janna steps into our circle and puts her mouth up to Hayden's ear and her hands around his waist.

Whatever she says gets an angry look from Hayden. "Where's your date?" he asks, and doesn't sound like himself.

"He left me. Alone on homecoming," Janna says with a pout.

"I can't imagine why," Heather says.

Janna's like a three-year-old who just lost her favorite stuffed animal. I see Hayden soften, and for a moment, I almost feel sorry for her. Almost. Then I think, What a nervy bitch. But I'm not going to tell her off; I'm too curious to see what Hayden will choose.

"Hayden, baby"—there's alcohol in that whine—"dance with me just once for old times' sake. I'm sure Allie won't matter, er, mind."

"Her name's Alexi, *Janie*," Heather snaps.

Hayden leans over to me and says into my ear, "This might be the only way to get rid of her. Any chance you could find Kool-Aid now? We could get these dances over with."

I nod and leave the group as the first slow song begins. Couples bump into me as they sway to the music, their bodies entwined like snakes.

I don't have time to wonder where Bodee is before he taps my shoulder. Like he's been here all along. "Now?" he asks, just loud enough to hear him.

"Yes, please." There are tears on my cheeks as he puts both hands on my hips.

"I don't have to touch you," he says.

"It's not you." I put my hands on his shoulders so he knows I'm telling the truth, but he uses only his index fingers and thumbs to touch me.

"Okay." I see sympathy as the light of the disco ball catches his eyes. "He matters more than you planned?"

"No." I swipe the tears away. "It just sucks not to matter more than that. It took him less than three dances to take Janna back. I didn't think he was anything special, but I thought we'd make it longer than pictures and alcohol."

"I'm sorry." Like a willow in the wind, Bodee bends toward me and says, "Love is awkward sometimes."

"But I don't love Hayden."

"Good." Bodee touches my cheek. Only as he shows me a tear on his finger do I release the breath in my lungs. He smiles, but it's not a happy smile, and says, "I meant you have trouble loving yourself."

"You think?" I ask.

"I do," he says.

God, I wish this song had a million verses.

"Can I stand closer to you?" Bodee asks.

Considering we've locked our arms, and Hayden and Janna and Janna's boobs could fit between us, that sounds like a great idea to me. "Yes."

He moves maybe an inch closer to me. A tiny bend of his elbow. And then he uses the happy, teeth-showing smile. We're close. Closer than Hayden and I were moments ago, and Hayden had been all up in my space.

"I have a secret," Bodee says.

He can tell me anything.

"Yeah?" I ask as a hand wraps around my bicep and tugs me away.

"We're leaving. Now!" Hayden says.

chapter 11

"WHY?" I ask Hayden as I look over my shoulder at Bodee. He's wearing another of his unreadable expressions. Maybe fear. Or even anger.

"Because I can't stand to be in the room with that"— Hayden uses a word for Janna I can't quite hear over the guitar riff that ends the slow dance—"for another minute."

Couples break apart. Ahead of us, people clog the path to the exit, but Hayden's shoulders part the dance crowd the way he dodges through the defensive line. Behind me, there are arms and torsos and blue dresses and gray suits and punch glasses and striped ties. But there's no Bodee.

I plead with Bodee's mind as if we are somehow connected. Follow me. Help me.

"Janna. Ohh. I hate that girl," Hayden says. "She ruins

everything." And that's not all he says, but it's all I listen to as he drags me after him.

I need to stop him before we get to the gym doors. Hayden, angry and tipsy and alone with me, is a nightmare on repeat.

"We barely even danced," I say again, looking for my rescuer's blue shirt. Bodee will come. He promised he would get me home safe. Right?

"No, but at least you got to keep your promise to your mom about Bodee. I'm sure you'll remember that for the rest of your life."

As Hayden snickers about Bodee, I realize the only thing Bodee actually promised me was that he wouldn't interfere with my date. These lies are starting to confuse even me. Sure, Bodee offered to come to the dance, but he only gave me a look after the game. A look I must have misinterpreted because I wanted it to be protective and more than it was.

Hayden nearly runs over a sophomore girl and her date when he looks over his shoulder to say, "We can dance somewhere else. Dane's. The bottoms. Anywhere but here."

Sweet Jesus, he wants to go to the bottoms.

"The bottoms," I mumble to Hayden as the strobe light quits blinking and the twinkle of the disco ball looks like a solid fluorescent bulb. Why did the DJ stop playing music? My mind tilts and spins. Like God used Earth to shoot marbles, and I have to roll dizzily along with it.

"Yeah, that's where the team always goes on Friday nights. You'll love it," he says.

Heather's told me all about the bottoms. Four-wheeling is the only legal thing that happens there on the weekends. The county could put up a little green marker that explains the bottoms as the most popular place for teen drinking, drugs, and sex. Or almost-sex, in Heather's case. I have to stop us. This desire is louder than anything in the dance and yet a mouse squeaks from my lips, "Yeah, okay."

I want to stay here. Want to tell Hayden that Liz and Ray will take me home. Or that Bodee, with no car, will find a way to get me home safe. But no. I'm tethered to Hayden for the night. His fingers are wrapped around mine like a noose, and I go where he wants.

What is wrong with me?

"You don't care about some stupid high school dance, do you?" Hayden asks as he wobbles across the parking lot.

One last look through the double doors of the gym. No Bodee. "I don't care," I tell Hayden.

"Good, you can drive."

"I only have a learner's permit," I say.

"So. It's not like I should drive."

He's right. His speech is normal, but his balance is way off. I have no idea how much he's had of what, but he shouldn't be behind the wheel. Neither should I. I've barely practiced beyond passing the written test. Life has been too crazy for me to drive.

When we reach Hayden's truck, he walks me around to the driver's door. Well, it's more like I walk him. He opens the door. In the pause, while his fingers weave through mine, he kisses me. Minus the whiskey on his breath, it's perfect in a non-important way. Last semester it would have sent me over the Big Dipper and back again. But now, I'm only thinking about what he might want next.

"I've always wanted to do that," he says.

My face flushes; I can practically hear the blood beating in my veins. "Whatever. I know Heather talked you into this."

"No." He brushes the back of his hand over my cheek. "I talked her into it. She said you have some rule about dating football players."

There's a reason for that. I stare at Hayden. He's handsome all over. From his steel-gray eyes to the way his nose flares slightly and his cheeks dimple when he smiles. He's smiling now, and I put on a grin to match as I realize maybe I can stop him before he starts.

"Yeah, I have a rule about dating boys who sleep with half the school." The words roll out of me like a herd of horses.

"Good. 'Cause I have a thing against girls who sleep with a quarter of the school."

"You do?"

"Alexi, we're not all man-whores." He grips the door for balance. "I'd rather have a girl who's hard to get. Like you."

When *his* hands explored beneath my swimsuit or when his body pressed mine into the concrete while I counted the stars instead of kisses, my words were gone. Deleted. Zapped. But here, while there is still breathing space between Hayden and me, I find the courage to delay him. "Very hard to get," I say.

"I got all the time in the world, and I like a challenge," he says as if I'm Saint X, the only team our guys haven't managed to defeat in the last three seasons.

"What about Janna?" Maybe this reminder will put some distance between us.

"You"—he kisses below my ear—"are nothing like Janna."

"I know." Which is why this is a very bad idea. A guy like Hayden was with a girl like Janna for a reason.

"Actually, you're not like anybody I know," he says. "I mean, who dances with Bodee Lennox? The guy's a loser, but you're nice to him. Maybe it's because his family's jacked up, but Janna would shove her heel up her own ass before she'd dance with a guy like that. God knows I'm not perfect, but I'd like to be with someone like you for a while."

"Someone like me." *For a while?* I escape his spider hands that seem to keep me against the truck. Backward, I struggle to climb the running board and sit facing him in the driver's seat. "What's that mean?" I ask.

Hayden's body is a perfect Y as he hangs on to the truck door and the truck to look at me. "I don't know. Nice and stuff."

"You already said that." I grip the wheel and the limp seat belt and think there are huge gaps in what he just said. Like pretty. Or special. Or . . . well, that's the end of the list, but he could have thought of something besides nice. "And I wasn't dancing with Bodee because I'm nice."

"I know. It's because of your mom. Same thing. You, like, promise your mom stuff. Who does that?"

I'm getting ready to say, "No, it's because . . ." even though I don't know what comes after that because Hayden steps up on the running board and slides my knees apart with his hips.

"Someone like you could make me a better guy," he says as Kayla's black dress skims up my thighs. I pull it down. "You *are* hard to get," he says.

This can't happen. Not here. Not again.

"You're not just nice, Alexi." His hand is on my skin; skin that had a dress covering it a moment ago. "You're beautiful."

Then his coat is off and behind the seat. I see the look—it's not evil or forceful, but I know what he wants as he lays me down. Not sex, but something worth bragging about to the football guys. His wide shoulders seem a mile across as they descend toward my chest. "Uh," I say, and wiggle beneath him. Only two layers of fabric separate our skin. And one zipper and some nylon between Hayden's excitement and my terror.

"Um," he says. Or *yum* or some other word that means he's very, very happy. Then his mouth is on mine so hard his lips could be made of concrete.

I owe Heather ten dollars.

I kiss him and the whiskey back because I don't know how to stop him. My hands find his at my thighs and lace us together. He can't touch me if his hands are occupied with mine. "Uh," I try again, hoping it sounds remotely like *stop* or *wait.*

"Alexi," he says back, as if I moaned with pleasure.

Please, stop. Please, stop. *Please.* But thoughts are not words. He doesn't stop.

Hayden's eyes are closed. His hip bones dig into mine as all of his weight smashes my chest against his. My eyes are wide as peach-colored skin and dirty-blond hair blur into a claylike blob. It's not crazy that I hate him and that stupid smile, but it might be insane that I hate myself more. Why can't I rescue myself? Another girl would either do it and like it or tell him to keep his dick in his pants. I'm not either girl; I'm nothing.

Then, he catapults backward, yelling as he goes.

I shove my knees together and sit up as Bodee, who has a handful of Hayden's shirt, swings his fist into Hayden's jaw.

The pop sounds like a firecracker in a jug. Contained, hollow, and forceful.

The guys are at war before I can shut the door and beg them to stop. Hayden's fist is in Bodee's stomach and then both guys are on the ground.

"Don't you ever touch her again," Bodee says. There must be muscles in his arms where before I thought there was only T-shirt. But it's not those muscles that pin Hayden against the ground: it's white-hot fury that's as visible as Hayden's grimace.

"I wasn't hurting her," Hayden says, and twists against Bodee's hold. "I was kissing her."

Bodee sniffs the air and cracks Hayden against the pavement. "You're wasted. You don't know what you were doing with her."

"Hey!" an all-too-familiar voice yells as he pounds the pavement toward us. Craig pulls the guys apart as quickly as Bodee pulled Hayden off me.

Sweat breaks out on my forehead. This is a terrible mess. Craig is the first and last person I want out here.

"What's going on?" Craig asks. And he is much more Mr. Tanner than he is my soon-to-be brother-in-law.

"Kool-Aid's gone crazy. He jumped me," Hayden says.

Bodee has a look I know his father must have worn while he chased his wife around the kitchen, but for a very different reason. "He was hurting Alexi." He licks some blood off his lips.

"I was not," Hayden says. But he doesn't say what we were doing.

Craig collars both guys and turns his concern to me. There's no Coach Tanner now; there's only Craig, who has known me since I was six. Craig, who sat next to Kayla on my bed and read to me by flashlight to make the stories scarier. "Lex, is that true? Did Hayden try to hurt you?"

One pair of puppy-dog gray eyes and one pair of angry muddy browns await my answer. "This is all a huge misunderstanding," I say.

"Is it?" Craig presses. This puts him nose to nose with

Hayden, or rather breath to breath. Disgust is easy to see on Craig's face; the whole stadium saw it in the first quarter of tonight's game before we scored. Hayden can't hide the whiskey now.

"You've been drinking again," Craig says.

"Hayden didn't hurt me, but I can see why Bodee thought he did," I say, trying to keep both guys safe from penalty. Because as much as I dislike Hayden for pushing my boundaries, I didn't say stop, and I don't want everyone to know about this incident. Tamping it down into a nonevent seems safer.

"I guess you planned on her driving, eh?" Craig says, and releases Bodee, who smooths his borrowed shirt and cracks his knuckles without making eye contact.

"I, uh . . . ," I try to explain.

"Lex, stop. You should have come and found me."

Yeah, right. Like I would do that. Craig's anger with Hayden is understandable, but when we left the dance I didn't know this would happen. Now Craig's on a different planet of mad than I've ever seen him with Kayla. Than I've ever seen him with anyone.

"You guys always have to celebrate. Don't you?" Craig says to Hayden. "You should thank Bodee here for misunderstanding, because if you'd had Alexi drive you out of this parking lot because you're drunk, I wouldn't just run you at five a.m. tomorrow, I'd turn your butt in to the principal, and he'd suspend you in a heartbeat. Bodee, get Alexi out of here.

I'll handle the two of you later at the house. I have a few more words to say to Mr. Harper."

Bodee and I don't move.

"Go," Craig says.

And we do. Quickly.

Bodee and his cracking knuckles. Me and my shaking body.

"Was it?" Bodee asks.

"Was it what?"

Bodee puts a hand under my elbow and faces me. "A mis-understanding," he asks tenderly.

All the tension ricochets through my body as I answer, "I guess it all depends on who you ask. Lots of things are misunderstandings."

"Well, just so you know, I'm not sorry I hit him."

My shoulders pop as the shaking twists my upper body into a pretzel knot. "Just so you know, I'm not either."

chapter 12

ONE. Two. Oh God, keep breathing. Three. Keep counting. Is something screwed up in my head? Why am I so weak? Four. Five. Will I always hate this part of me? Six. Seven. Eight. If Bodee hadn't hit Hayden, how far would I have let Hayden go?

Damn you, stupid air vent. Nine. Ten. Eleven. Don't stop counting.

Bodee hit Hayden because of me. Did that really happen?

Twelve. Thirteen. What did Craig do to Hayden after we left? And Kayla? Could I keep her from telling our parents? My friends. What will happen Monday at school? Fourteen. Fifteen. Does Hayden hate me now? Sixteen. Will the football team retaliate against Bodee? Seventeen. Is Bodee safe?

Will I ever be safe from myself?

How far would I have let Hayden go?

Eighteen. How far would I have let Hayden go?

I blink and I don't care that I lose count.

How far would I have let Hayden go?

Of all the questions, this is the only one that matters. It cycles automatically as I stare at the familiar dark slits in my ceiling. I know it cycles because I don't have the answer.

Or maybe because I do.

All the way. I would have let Hayden go all the way.

Because I didn't stop *him*, either.

I tumble neck-first off the scratch-and-tear wagon. My weeklong self-discipline ends as my nails claw at my neck and rip into skin. The pain is comfortable and the counting subsides, but not the reality.

Stopping Hayden felt like trying to halt Earth's orbit.

But *why*?

I don't understand this about myself. This invisible enemy, this inability to say no. I need answers. Isn't there a reason why I'm so afraid to assert myself?

My life has been nothing like Bodee's. I mean, I've never had to live in a tent, and my parents love Kayla and me. They'd never hurt each other or one of us. My mom even listens to my side when we're arguing, so I'm not one of those kids with no voice at home. And as far as I know, no one abused me as a baby. There's never been a traumatic event that would cause . . .

But . . . is that true?

Images, out of sync, from my earliest memories. They're blurring in and out of focus, like cable TV during a thunderstorm, and I struggle to make sense of them.

Something is hiding in my childhood. Something *off.*

My fingernails bite into the palm of my hands, where they leave little U-shaped dents.

Because there *is* something.

I'm scared and I'm wet. And naked. There's a damp, musty smell that clogs my nostrils and closes my throat. I'm maybe three or four years old, a chubby little girl with two dark pigtails.

And I *remember.*

Swimming lessons at the local Y.

"Don't wanna go in there," I say.

"I'm sorry, honey, but Mommy's late and you're missing your lesson. I can't take you into the little girls' bathroom, but you can go in the boys' side. It'll be okay this once."

My dad pushes open the blue metal door and calls out, "Anybody in here?"

Silence.

"See, sweetie, there's no one inside. It's okay."

I shake my pigtails. "Don't *want* to."

But I really have to *go,* so I wait while Dad checks the boys' bathroom.

"See, Lexi?" He kneels down and smiles, squeezing my hand. "It's fine."

"But what if someone comes? A *boy*?" I ask.

"I'll stand out here by the door and make sure no one comes in. And if you need me, you can yell. Okay?"

"Promise?" I say, and my voice is a frightened squeak.

"Promise."

I hurry into the boys' bathroom, past the low sink-looking thing, and enter the first stall because that door is wide open and the other two are closed and scary.

Struggling out of my one-piece swimsuit, I climb on the toilet. Before I can grab it, my suit falls past my knees to the concrete floor. Dripping wet and shivering, I pee.

I'm feeling relieved when there's a rustling and stirring in the next stall.

I'm not alone.

My body locks up, and I'm frozen to the toilet as a bare butt wiggles backward into my stall.

"Wanna play swords?" a boy says as he turns and scrambles upright.

Then his eyes widen until they almost pop out of his head. He's staring at me, and I'm staring at him. His hoo-hoo is right in front of me; hot tears fill my eyes.

"You're not a boy," he says like an accusation. But he doesn't crawl back to his stall, and I'm trapped between his hoo-hoo and the potty.

"I'm Ray," he says. "Who're you?"

My tongue is sticking to my mouth, but I slide off the toilet and I'm all thumbs in my panic as I struggle to pull up my wet swimsuit.

"You okay in there?" Daddy calls from outside the bathroom. "Need some help, Lex?"

I shove past naked Ray and run out to my dad. But I don't say a word about what happened. Not then and not ever.

I push it far back in my mind until it's as if it never happened.

But now the memory is so vivid that I know it's real.

The thing is, why am I remembering it now? Especially since . . . I *know* naked Ray.

He's Ray Johnson.

Liz's Ray.

I roll out of my bed and pad down to the den. The streetlight casts enough light through the half-curtained windows that the couch is visible. Sinking into the cushions, I run my hands over the woven upholstery and cover my lap with the throw pillow. And wish I'd closed my eyes when Ray crawled under my bathroom stall.

Ray Johnson's seen me wet and naked. And I've seen him. We were three, and it shouldn't matter. Doesn't matter. My brain processes the innocence of this memory. Kids don't mind being naked. I've done enough babysitting to know Mrs. Hampton's kids down the street wouldn't wear clothes if she didn't insist. So, this particular memory isn't important. There's a hammer pounding on my brain that says I'm missing something. Have I forgotten other things? Other things that keep me silent?

"Whatcha doing?"

Bodee's whisper causes me to jerk with surprise. He's shirtless, so I look past him into the hallway toward my parents' bedroom door, where snorts and snores assure me they're asleep. Bodee and I could be a herd of elephants, and they wouldn't hear us.

"Trying to figure some things out," I whisper.

"You should sleep," he says.

There's a shadow of a bruise under his rib cage, courtesy of Hayden. Tomorrow it will look black and angry, but I doubt I'll see him without a shirt tomorrow.

"I know. You all right?" I ask.

"If you are." He sits on one side of the couch and puts the other throw pillow in his lap.

"Well, you're not asleep either," I say.

"Weird getting used to a bed."

Whether it's the hard ground and a sleeping bag or a closet and clawing fingernails, the familiar soothes us like a milk shake sliding down a sore throat.

"But are you making it okay?" I ask. It's been only two weeks since his mom died. When my granddad died, I cried for weeks. Bodee's tearless, but I see the pain oozing out of him.

"What's okay?" Bodee's question is rhetorical and not meant for me to answer.

He slides his right leg under him, and I notice the hair on his legs is blond and soft and nearly invisible. I always notice the guys at school who swim or bike because they shave their legs and arms. Very sexy. Body hair usually grosses me out.

But I don't mind Bodee's almost invisible, blond leg hair.

Funny, the things I know about Bodee Lennox that I never

thought I'd know. Or care about.

"You can talk about her if you want," I tell him.

"I will sometime." He twists the pillow by the corner and then lets it spin. "You can talk about *it*," he says.

My heart thumps like a rock inside a coffee can as I ask, "What's *it*?"

"I don't know, but you do. And I know you should tell someone. Even if it's not me."

Whenever I'm with Bodee, it feels as if I'm made of glass. Mascara, blush, and fake smiles never fool him. Maybe it comes from years of seeing his mother hide her fears from the world. But I'm not ready to share.

"There's a place I want to show you tomorrow," I say, hoping the topic will fade away.

"Okay." Bodee stands and holds his hand out to me.

My pastor held his hand out to me during an altar call at a morning service. I didn't hesitate that day, and I don't tonight. Putting my hand in his is for me and has nothing to do with *us*. This is an offer of comfort. An invitation. He traces the lines in my palm and pats me the way my granddad used to.

"You're going to be okay," he says, and squeezes my hand. I watch as he leaves the den and climbs the steps to the bonus room. Maybe Bodee's not really a teenager. Maybe he's an old man trapped in a sixteen-year-old body. Then again, he did knock the shit out of Hayden.

For tonight, at least, I'll trust his words. Instead of going back to bed, I unfold the throw on the back of the couch and curl up beneath it.

It is the smell of bacon tickling my nose that finally wakes me.

"Lex, it's ten thirty. You going to sleep the day away?" Mom plops down beside me and pulls my toes into her lap.

Yawning, I say, "No-oh-o."

"Why'd you sleep in here?" she asks.

I sit up and cover my lie with a big yawn. "I didn't mean to. Just keyed up after the dance, I guess."

Mom removes her reading glasses from the top of her head and tosses them on the table. There's nothing between me and her blue eyes. "Craig told me this morning that Hayden got sick and had to go home early. I'm sorry, sweetie. That's a real bummer."

Out-of-date word alert. *Bummer*. Out-of-touch mom alert. Thank goodness. "Yeah." I go with Craig's lie.

"I thought you got home a little early last night, but I didn't want to pry."

"Hayden was probably just exhausted from the game. No big deal," I say, praying there are no more questions. Bodee and I had waited at Kayla's car until she showed up about eleven forty-five. Besides walking home, which had been impossible in my high heels, my sister had been our only transportation option: something Craig should have remembered when he ordered us to get lost. It wasn't like we could go back to the dance. Everyone would have asked about Hayden, and there was nothing I could say.

Mom's eyes dart toward the stairs leading to Bodee's room. "What do you think about Bodee, Lex? Is he all right? Did girls dance with him last night?"

"I did," I admit. "I'm sure other girls did too."

"Oh, that was sweet of you. I worry about him. Dad's tried to get him to talk, you know, but Bodee says he's 'fine.' But I don't see how." She puts her reading glasses back on and then pushes them onto her head. I've seen her do that a million times when she's thinking. "We checked with the guidance counselor, and Mr. James says Bodee's keeping it together at school. But I don't know. Considering what he's been through and what he's had to do just to survive, he's probably good at faking it with adults."

This makes me giggle with amusement and shudder with regret. Because the very thing she worries about in Bodee, his ability to fake normal, she has dismissed in me. Thank the good Lord. I am *glad* I haven't given her cause to worry over me. "Well, we're gonna hang out today. I'll check on him," I assure her like a good spy.

"Perfect. Dad and I are going to that flea market on Old 48. Kayla and Craig have plans too; I forget now what she said. There's food in the kitchen. Junk food, anyway. I *have* to keep your dad out of the grocery store. The man's addicted to sugar and starch. Oh well." She pats my toes, and then kisses her hand and smacks it to my forehead. "Love you, Boo-Boo."

"Love you back, Coo-Coo," I say so she'll smile again.

My mom is blissfully simple and unsuspecting that any bad thing has ever touched her younger daughter. As she leaves the room, I decide that's my gift to her. I'll keep it that way as long as I can.

Bodee's towel in the bathroom is damp. He's up, but I take my time washing away last night. My neck isn't as bad in the morning light as I thought, so I tuck my wet hair under a baseball cap and set out to find Bodee.

He's on the back deck eating bacon from a paper plate. He has a blue-and-black flannel shirt I've never seen tied around his waist, but other than that he's back to wearing a white T-shirt and jeans.

"You ready to go somewhere?" I snag a piece of bacon and bite into it before he can protest.

"Been ready all morning."

I open the gate of the privacy fence that surrounds our pool without letting my eyes drift to the area near the deep end. "Follow me," I say as we step into the backyard.

There's nothing great about our house; it's just a brick split-level ranch we've added on to three different times. But I love the trees that surround us and make our house an island in the midst of the woods.

"You guys own all this?" Bodee runs a hand back and forth over his hair. It is purple-brown today, and now it's standing up like a forest of its own.

"Yeah." The subdivision ends with our house, and we own

the land behind us all the way to the river. There's still a remnant of my path. Weeds, those little plants I call umbrellas, and fallen trees clutter what was once a well-traveled thorough-fare for my bare feet. I pick my way forward, swinging my arms right and left at the spiderwebs hanging from low branches. If not for spiders (and the fear of snakes), I could navi-gate this path on a starless night.

Craig and Dad must have made a hundred wheelbarrow trips this way. It should have taken fewer trips, but I insisted on riding atop the pile of building supplies each time.

Dad would sing out, "Have you met the Queen of Never Ever Land?" And Craig always went along with him and pretended he couldn't see me. I remember as if it happened this morning instead of eight years ago.

I laugh, and Bodee raises an eyebrow. "This is Never Ever Land," I explain.

"Nice," he says. "Why Never Ever Land?"

"Well, I would have named it Land of the Lost, but I had a lisp," I say, "so Lost sounded like Loth."

"I remember. We had speech together in elementary school."

"We did," I say. And there he is in another memory. In a white T-shirt and jeans, sitting at the desk across from mine.

"We got trapped during that storm too," he says.

"I'd forgotten about that," I say, wondering how I could have forgotten something that wasn't that long ago. June. But it was *before*. And it's like when I whited out the bad, I also whited out the good.

"I didn't." Long pause. "I like your Never Ever Land."

"Thought you would. You could bring your tent out here sometime if you wanted."

"I might," he says.

There's no grass growing under the trees, but everywhere else green is changing into red and yellow and orange. In another month, my fort will be visible from here. But right now, the leaves haven't abandoned their summer homes for the forest floor. One of the smaller creeks we cross is bone dry, so we don't use the plank bridge my dad set up against a huge fallen oak.

"Almost there," I say as I claw my way up the dry bank. I can feel the magic of my old hideout calling me. It's where I played G. I. Joes and Polly Pockets and Hot Wheels. It's where I read stacks of library books. And pretended. My fort became a plane wreck, a log cabin, a space station, a boxcar, and dozens of other stories in Never Ever Land.

"Who built this?" Bodee asks as he gets his first look at my fort.

"Dad and my uncle Tommy. And Craig." The urgency to be inside, to show Bodee my safe place, is overwhelming. I plow through the last part of the trail to reach the four tall poplars Dad used to frame the fort. First, I check the mailbox Craig nailed to the tree. Empty. Well, of *course* it would be.

Even in its golden years, it held only imaginary mail. Then, with one hand on the ladder, I say, "Pretty cool, huh?"

"More than cool."

I wonder if Bodee's thinking that this place is a palace compared to his tent. Two tiers of platforms and real windows and doors have to be better than whatever was in that small nylon bag I put in the closet of the bonus room for him. We climb to the top level, probably twenty feet from the ground, and I open all four windows. I lean out and let the breeze kiss my face and swirl the loose curls that have come untucked from my ball cap. Oh, I've craved this for months without knowing it.

Bodee sticks his head through the window beside me. "Easy to breathe up here."

The sweat I worked up from traipsing out here is cool on my back. I lean my head next to his, our shoulders touch, and we take in the aerial view of the woods. There's plenty to see, but not houses, not subdivisions, not schools. In their place are bird nests and chattering squirrels, trickling creeks and a new growth of evergreens along the southern boundary. Even a deer with its white tail erect and alert before it disappears from our sight.

It's a world away from the world.

We are silent like that for a bit, looking and breathing the magic and feeling easy. Time passes as the sun filters through the canopy and creates shifting shadows below.

"I love this place," I tell Bodee as I extract myself from the window and grab the broom from the corner. Dust motes swim in the air before sinking to the ladder opening.

"Who wouldn't?" Bodee says without turning. "Alexi, there's something I need to ask you."

This makes me nervous, but I say, "Okay."

"Did I scare you last night?" he asks. He backs out of the window opening and sits on the wooden floor.

Tossing the broom in the corner, I sink down beside him. "*Scare* me? No."

"Are you sure? 'Cause it's the last thing I wanna do."

"You were protective." Why won't he look at me? This is the old Bodee, the Bodee he rarely shows me anymore. The guy who slumps his shoulders and buries his head like a turtle. "Hey." I touch his knee. "I promise."

He sighs. "Okay. Hayden said . . . something about me being crazy like my dad."

"You aren't." I stare at the purple top of his head.

"Lex, this'll sound weird, but when I was a kid I believed in monsters. You know, like vampires. Werewolves. Ghosts. And I believed in them because I knew at least one monster existed. He wore a shirt with his name stitched across the pocket. And carried a fifth for a weapon. And sometimes a knife."

Bodee pauses and then cracks his knuckles. Both hands. One at a time.

"He always hated me," Bodee says, "and I don't know why. Must have hated Ben, too, because he enlisted the second he turned eighteen."

"Why didn't your mom leave him?" It's a cheap question that people who don't understand abuse ask. I realize this too late.

He looks up and massages his temple. "She tried to leave once. The earring. Her mom gave her the pair, and she pawned one for our bus tickets. That's why there's only one. But he found out, and she never tried again." Bodee's voice hardens. "'You try to leave me and I'll *kill* you,' he'd say every other day or so, just so she wouldn't forget. And where would she go? Her parents died young. No support. No education. No job and no way to make any money; *he* never let her have a thing in her own name." Bodee's eyes are bright with unshed tears. "And she had me."

Gasping, I say, "I'm sorry."

"Mom tried to get me out of there. I think she even talked to your mom about it once. But I wouldn't leave her. I knew he'd kill her one day. *Knew* it. And I was going to be there to stop him." A tear drops off Bodee's chin and makes a round, wet mark in the old wood. "We worked out the plan for me to camp in the woods at night . . . so when he came home drunk he wouldn't—couldn't—take his anger out on me. In the morning when he was asleep, I'd slip inside and shower and check on Mom. Always at seven a.m. Always."

More tears stain the wood, but this time they're mine. I

cannot imagine this life Bodee's lived.

"Until . . . *that* morning. I woke up early because it was hot. I was fifty feet away from the house when I heard her scream. Fifty feet."

As Bodee speaks, the kitchen in the Lennox house appears in my mind. The sink. The table. The stove. I could put them all in place, and I can see her running, screaming, throwing pots and pans at Bodee's dad. Anything to stall him, to keep him away from her.

"I took off running. He never woke up that early. *Never.* God, Lex, she was screaming like crazy, so I grabbed a broom from the porch. It was the only thing I could find, and I was gonna kill him." Bodee stares past my shoulder and relives it. "She saw me at the door and waved me off and I was just frozen . . . like I'd been Krazy-Glued to the porch. I couldn't go in, and I couldn't leave the way she wanted me to."

I squeeze his knee because I can't bear it, and his hand comes down on top of mine in a death grip.

"Lex, I watched him. I just stood there and watched him kill my mom."

chapter 13

I think first of Bodee's safety. "Does he know you saw him?"

"No. I hid under the porch until he passed out."

Bodee wears shame in the scrunched bridge of his nose and in his clenched jaw. This would look like anger on other guys, but it is too weighty, too painful for anger. It's as if he wants me to say he could have stopped his dad, so he's handing me a whip to beat him. But I won't, because I'm glad he hid. Glad he's beside me instead of six feet under.

"Thank God you did," I say.

He releases me and wraps his hands around the back of his neck. Clenching his fists. Unclenching them. "But I let her die without . . . She was alone and I . . . I *left her.*"

He's silent for a moment while I consider this. He knows his mother waved him off and why she did it. So do I. But these memories are still a cage without a key for him. But I don't say this, because I can tell he is not finished with his confession.

"So last night," he says, "when I saw Hayden leave with you, something in me just unraveled. Maybe he's a decent guy, but anybody could see he was drunk. At least I could."

Bodee unties the flannel shirt from his waist and lays it across my shoulders before I even realize I'm shaking. The shirt swallows me, but I welcome the warmth and the scent of him and slide my arms into the sleeves.

"Then when I got to the parking lot and . . . he was on top of you . . . it was like it happened all over again. I hated Hayden. Like I hate my dad for . . . for everything. Treating my mom like he did, and then . . . you know." Bodee's hands are fidgety. He shapes his hair into a faux hawk and then flattens it before he speaks again. "I guess I lost it."

He doesn't ask me how I felt about Hayden on top of me. Not because it's taboo. I'd probably tell him, but it's as if he already knows. As if he takes it as a given I didn't want Hayden.

"I hit him before I even realized it, but I didn't care. I wanted him *off* you. Knowing where to hit his lower jaw so it wouldn't bruise was automatic. I learned that because of *him*." Bodee is quiet again, and I wait him out, my stomach churning and knotting around a ball of pain. "And if I could do what my dad did so easily, Alexi, maybe I'm not safe to be around."

"You're safe." I say it with confidence. Because Bodee pulls back when other guys his age rush forward. Because his two fingers on my hips while we're dancing and swaying to slow songs don't threaten me.

I *know* he's 100 percent safe.

"But if Mr. Tanner hadn't separated us, I might have—"

"Stop. You're torturing yourself for no reason. I don't know your dad, other than the obvious, but I've gotten to know you pretty well over the last couple weeks, and you are not like him." I don't say it, but I'm thinking, *You can't be.* "I told you last night I wasn't sorry, and I meant it."

An odd feeling niggles at me, though, the way a worm squirms its way through an apple. Maybe I'm a little uneasy about how Bodee's so protective of me, how it speaks through his actions. And the dance: the Hayden stare-down followed by the Hayden smack-down. And how Bodee noticed the scratches on my neck. He's close. Closer than any guy's ever been to me emotionally, and I have a choice right now: reel him in or cast him out. But I can't decide to do either yet, because I can't unravel why Bodee is Bodee.

He doesn't talk. Except to me. Doesn't smile. Except for me. Doesn't go to dances. Except for me. This is the refrain of our song. He's different with me, and yet I know this is the real Bodee. He's not pretending anymore.

Is it because he feels burdened with guilt? Am I only the replacement for the mother he couldn't help and didn't save?

Am I okay with that, or do I want more from him? A relationship? Almost. Maybe. But I've never wanted more with anyone.

Can he give anything to a relationship? Can I?

After what I've been through, I'm like a burnt and crumbly cake that some sly baker covers up with beautiful icing. So even if he likes me on the outside, my inside is tasteless crap.

We're not skipping ahead, I remind myself.

Bodee needs a good friend right now, not some selfish *girl*friend. This guy's life sucks. He's survived worse stuff than anyone I know, and he's still amazing.

"I must be like him or I wouldn't have hit Hayden," Bodee continues as my mind races a million miles per hour.

"Come on, Bodee. Did you hit Hayden for the pleasure of hitting him or because you thought he was hurting me?"

"Because I thought he was hurting you, but—"

"Then you're not like your dad," I say, and squeeze his knee. He stares down at my hand, and then looks up to meet my eyes.

"I'm glad you believe that." He shakes his head. "There's, uh, one more thing."

I close my eyes as he reaches for me, my heart thudding loud enough that anyone a mile away could hear. When nothing happens, I open them and realize he's only fastening the top button of his shirt at my neck. Embarrassed, my face burns and I look away.

"The police know I saw him. When I called it in that morning . . ."

He pauses, and I know he still sees his mom lying on the floor. I can almost see her myself. Lifeless and broken, my imagination says. With thumb-shaped bruises on her neck as purple as Bodee's hair.

I exhale for us both.

"I told the police everything," he says. "And now the lawyers want me to give a deposition before the trial. They say I can make sure he goes away for life."

"You'll do it."

"You saw what happened at the funeral. Here with you . . . I can talk. But that's a first. In a courthouse or some office, with those lawyer people watching me, I'll freeze."

"But if he gets away with it, he might come back and . . . hurt you."

"I know," he says.

I've lived all but two weeks of my life without Bodee. But now, sitting with him in my fort, I know these two weeks have been God walking right into my life like he has flesh and Kool-Aid-colored hair. The gospel according to Bodee Lennox. His safety. His protection. And love.

"Then you know you have to do it," I say. "Testify."

"Yeah. But knowing and doing are two totally different things. You probably think it's easy, since it's just words. I mean, how hard can it be to say, 'I know what he did'?"

"*Very* hard. Almost impossible, but—" My hands grip each other as if they have minds of their own. Minds to scratch and tear at my neck until I really believe what I'm saying. "We'll get you through it," I promise him with more fear than assurance.

"There's a whole lot of *it* going around." He nudges me with his knee. "You need to talk about last night?"

This is an intentional conversation shift. Away from him to me. I should recognize the technique. I've done it to my mom often enough, though she never notices. "My hero showed up, so there's nothing to talk about."

Bodee smiles the teeth smile, and he doesn't press me any further about last night.

"You ready to go back to the house?" I ask.

"Can we come again soon?"

Kayla and Craig and even Mom and Dad were forbidden from entering my sanctuary (unless repairs or improvements were necessary). I've never before wanted to share this special place with anyone. "Anytime," I tell Bodee.

When we get back to the yard, Craig is waiting for us with his Coach Tanner glare. Kayla's propped up in the Adirondack rocker, and she doesn't seem much happier. The cap comes off and my hair falls over my neck as we walk through the gate and around the pool.

"We need to settle up before your mom and dad get home." Craig indicates that we should sit in the glider opposite them.

"Mr. Tanner," Bodee starts.

"You only have to call me that at school." Craig sighs and crosses one ankle over his knee.

Craig's edgy, chewing one side of his mouth. He's wearing his doghouse expression. Something's up and it's not good. Has Kayla broken up with him? Again?

No; Craig usually cries when she does.

I brace for bad news.

"About last night. Both of you—," Craig starts.

"I'm sorry, Mr. Tanner," Bodee says. "I really thought Hayden was hurting Alexi."

"He understands that," Kayla interrupts impatiently. "But you're lucky Craig was the one who found you instead of one of the other chaperones."

Bodee nods. "I'm very sorry."

He's too polite for my taste. "Whatever," I say to Kayla. "I think Craig's the lucky one. He knows his guys can't beat Raxton next Friday without Hayden. He gets suspended from school, he won't be playing that game."

"That is not true." Kayla rolls her eyes at me. "That's not the point anyway. Craig would rather handle things without turning it into a big mess. Now *you* apologize to Craig, just like Bodee did, before I decide to tell Mom and Dad."

"Tell them what?" I throw my hat on the concrete and then pick it back up, twisting it like a rag. "And I don't owe Craig anything."

Craig gives Kayla a warning look as if he thinks that will calm her down.

Kayla's more than ready to argue. "You absolutely do. He totally stopped you from ho-ing it up with Hayden. At the very least, from driving illegally, permit girl."

"N-no," I stutter. "I wasn't ho—" I can't finish the word or look at Kayla. Is this what she thinks about me? That I'm easy?

Kayla's feet hit the deck, and she leans forward in her rocker. "Lex, you were going to drive out of that parking lot. And I'm sure Hayden's 'attack'"—she makes air quotes—"was anything but. I doubt Mom and Dad will love hearing how their precious, perfect daughter almost *made it* in Hayden's pickup."

There it is. Kayla's still looking for Mom and Dad's approval, and shoving me under the semi is her method of rising to the top of the sibling heap.

I hate her for this. And hate gives me a voice.

"Kayla, I'm not getting in trouble for what you think I *might* have done." I look from Kayla to Craig. "And it's not like you're a couple of saints."

"We know that." Craig puts out his hand to stop Kayla from interrupting. "Look, forget about your parents. *I* was worried about you last night. You should never have left the dance with Hayden when he was drinking. What were you thinking, Lex? Guys misread all sorts of signals—especially *then*." He sighs. "That's the real issue. Right, Kay?"

"Yeah." Kayla actually sends me a kind of sincere look. "We're adults. We've both been stupid enough times to recognize what stupid looks like."

"You can say that again," I say, and hear the acid in my tone.

"Well, like it or hate it, I still think you owe Craig an apology for putting him in such a difficult position. For asking us both to cover for your little date malfunction," Kayla says.

Bodee looks at me. Apologize, his eyes plead. Make this go away. But I can't. I won't. Okay, I am a rat's ass for not stopping Hayden myself, but this is ridiculous.

"Hayden's normally a good guy, but he likes to celebrate. I guess most of my guys do. And I used to be one of them," Craig says. Another look passes between him and my sister. The way they're acting, it looks like their first time was in Craig's old pickup truck in the school parking lot. "But that doesn't mean I want you anywhere near him when it happens. That's why I ran his butt off last night."

"Hayden's the least of my concerns," I say. Oh, I'd like to push this. I really would. I'd like to point at a certain person who was way more out of control than a slightly tipsy Hayden Harper. But I don't. I'm not ready. I can't show my hurts—and look broken—in front of any of them. And all for different reasons.

"Alexi Austin Littrell, what's wrong with you?"

"Kayla Jane Littrell, none of your *friggin'* business."

I fight my need to tell Kayla her face might freeze in that indignant twist.

"Look," she says, "all I want is an apology. Either do it or I tell Mom and Dad about Hayden."

"Seriously? Are you still in elementary school? And just what are you going to tell them?" I ask.

There's usually a leverage game of some sort between Kayla and me, but this can't be one. Because Craig wouldn't demand an apology from me. He wouldn't say these things on his own. Not unless Kayla put him up to it. Maybe she has something on him, too.

My sister is silent for only a moment, and then she hits below the belt. In the one place she's gambling that I'll cave. "I'll tell Mom and Dad your date didn't go home sick after all. I'll say he went home because Bodee punched him."

I juggle fury, worry, and fear, and drop all the balls at once. "You wouldn't."

"You know I would."

"But that's not fair. Bodee only did it because he thought Hayden was . . ." I stop and take a breath. "You wouldn't punish him because of me, Kayla. He's apologized already and—"

Kayla's face hardens with determination. This is why she and Craig have broken up so many times. Why he just sits there sipping Sprite, letting her twist this. It's her way or else.

And this time she has me. I can't allow the *or else*, so I give in just as she knew I would. Refusing to let my voice quiver, I say, "Okay, you win. I'm sorry, Craig."

And then Kayla bursts out laughing and whips around to Craig, whose face is unreadable.

"Told you I could get her to do it. Told you Bodee was the key, didn't I? Did you see her face, Craig?"

Not the reaction I expect.

Kayla is in hysterics, bending over and holding her sides. She's laughing so hard, the rocker scoots around on the deck. "You should have *seen* the look on your face." She struggles to get the words out. "Priceless, Lex. Priceless."

No one else thinks it's funny. Not even Craig. I don't know what age you have to start worrying about blood pressure, but right now, I'm thinking it may be sixteen. "What's going on?" I demand.

Craig shakes his head, as if he can't believe he's participated in Kayla's little drama. "She bet me an hour-long massage that she could get you to apologize. I only went along with it because I really do want you to be more careful if Hayden's drinking."

"Well, thanks for that. I'll jot myself a little note. Stay away from assholes. Starting with the two of you." Craig hangs his head, but I don't care if he's sorry or ashamed or sad or disappointed in me. I feel boiling mad take over and I don't care what bridges I burn. "I'd rather be Janna Fields's maid of honor than yours. I'm out."

If this is half of what Bodee felt when he punched Hayden, then it's a wonder he didn't kill him.

Kayla stands and tries to lighten the mood by side-hugging me. I shove her away.

"Lex, come on, it was a joke."

"A joke? Craig's not laughing. I'm not laughing." I look at Bodee, and his eyes are wide with some emotion I can't read. "Bodee's not laughing either. Hey, Bodee, bet you one hundred dollars Kayla won't apologize to any of us."

And then I leave them standing there. Let her tell Mom I refuse to be in the wedding. Let her explain why.

I never have any trouble with words when it comes to Kayla.

The rest of the weekend is "pass the peas, share the hymnal, and play nice" in front of Mom and Dad. And ignore everybody else. "Homework," is the answer I offer as I shut my bedroom door and give them, even Bodee, the frozen shoulder.

Hiding out is easy because the text messages and phone calls I expect from Heather and Liz never come. The lack of curiosity about why Hayden and I left the dance so early, or why we never showed at Dane's, is strange. But no doubt I'll get interrogated on the way to school today.

"You're up early for a Monday," Mom says as I breeze into the kitchen before she even has to yell at me. When she sees my still-damp hair, she says, "Oh, Lex, I wish you'd dry your hair all the way. It's getting cool outside."

"Then you'd be telling me I'll be late," I say. Early as I am, Bodee is down before me.

Mom shakes her head. "I know a solution for that," she teases.

"Yeah. Yeah. I'll get up earlier tomorrow," I say. And we both laugh.

"Tonight"—Mom's tone is serious now—"I forbid you to disappear into your room again. No one has that much home-work. Right, Bodee?" Bodee's spoon stops midway between the cereal bowl and his mouth as he ducks his orange head. She continues, "I was thinking maybe the three of us could get a pizza and see a movie tonight."

"Sure, okay," I say. A little time spent with Mom goes a long way toward gaining me the space I need. As long as Kayla's not invited, I'm fine if Mom wants to spoil us with a pepperoni pizza and bags of movie popcorn. "Hey, come on, Bodee. I think I hear Heather."

Sure enough, the horn blares and Bodee dumps his bowl in the sink as I tell Mom good-bye.

Today's not just another Monday. This Monday has the potential to be very different. Hayden will be in the hallway and at the lunch table.

"You want me to walk?" Bodee asks once we're out the door.

"No."

"They mad at me?" he asks, jerking his head toward Heather's Malibu.

"Liz won't be. I've never seen her mad. But Heather's a different story. Depends on what tale Collie told her. And that depends on what Hayden told Collie. So who knows? I wouldn't worry about it."

"So that means you haven't talked to them," he whispers as he opens the car door and chucks his backpack to the middle of the seat.

I shake my head and slide in after him.

There's no music blaring from the radio.

But that's not the first thing I notice that's different in the Malibu this morning. Cocoa butter or suntan oil—something beachy-smelling—assaults my nose. "What's that smell?" I ask.

Liz taps a pair of scented cardboard flip-flops hanging from the rearview. "Terrible, huh? I already threatened to recycle the thing."

Heather stops the flops from swinging. "I like it."

Something's wrong. There's silence where there's normally chatty banter. Bodee notices it too. "I can walk," he whispers.

I shake him off. "So what'd y'all do the rest of the weekend?"

Liz shifts the seat belt so she can swivel toward the backseat. "ACT prep. What about you?" Her eyes are curious and careful all at the same time. "Where'd you and Hayden end up Friday night? Heather said you weren't at Dane's."

"Uh, no. Hayden . . ."—lying to Liz is hard because she'd never lie to me—"went home early," I say. "Bodee and I caught a ride with Kayla." Heather makes eye contact in the rearview, but I can't tell how much she knows.

"Did y'all have fun?" I ask before they can question me further.

"Not really," Liz says. "Ray and I are over."

"Again," Heather adds.

"Oh, Liz, I'm sorry," I say. Naked Ray isn't a bad guy.

"Don't be. I know it's the right thing. We both agree this time, but it's still hard to break a connection that's been so . . . He's practically a part of my family, you know? And now we have to find some way to act like it's normal not *being* together. So it's going to feel awful and klutzy."

Yeah, I do know.

"Because this time," she says with a firm look at Heather, "it really is over."

Looking at Liz more closely, I see the extra layer of foundation, the extra under-eye cream, that's fighting the puffiness. This decision cost her some tears. I want to reach out, but I don't.

"*I'll* believe it's over when I see it." Heather's tone is sharp.

"At least you and Collie are still together," I say for no particular reason except to make conversation and because I know they are.

"Nope," Heather says bitterly. "We are totally over too. Guess we all had Friday nights that sucked."

Liz doesn't react. This isn't new information to her. Collie tried to call me on Saturday and again on Sunday, but I rejected his calls. Guess I know the reason now. I'm glad I didn't pity him and pick up. These breakups are probably why I haven't heard from Liz or Heather this weekend. Splitsville requires phone time between best friends, with no time for second-best friends.

"What happened?" I ask as she catches my eye again in the rearview.

Bodee cracks his knuckles, and I silence him with a glance.

"I found out he slept with someone," she says.

Maybe I *should* call Collie. Oh God. This is a nightmare for Heather.

"One of my friends. Or at least that's what he said," she adds.

"Do you know, uh, *who*—," I ask. The words eke out past stiff lips and a sluggish tongue.

"She doesn't," Liz answers for Heather. "We spent half of last night trying to put the pieces together. Trying to figure out the one. I told her it wasn't *me*. And it definitely wasn't *you*. Who would do this to her?"

The car swings dangerously close to a car parked outside the bank. Heather corrects and the tires squeal. As she slows down she says, "Sorry. I'm just so pissed. Why would he even tell me? Bodee, you're a guy. Why do guys do that?" she demands in a brittle voice. "Spill their guts to their girlfriend that they screwed some girl, one who just happens to be my so-called friend. *Right*. And then refuse to tell who it was."

Bodee remains quiet. He looks at me for help, but all I can manage is a shrug. And then I stare out the opposite window. I know why guys screw other girls. Or at least I know why one of them did.

Because he told me why.

"I'm so lonely," he whispered as his mouth smothered mine. *Lonely*.

A reason to cheat. A reason to take.

I don't share this with Heather. She probably just needs to scream and throw things.

"Collie's a jerk," Liz says. "Thank goodness you didn't sleep with him. High school guys don't know what or who they want from one second to the next. No offense, Bodee."

"I'm not sure many of us know what we want from one moment to the next," I say, so Bodee doesn't feel obligated to defend his half of the population. "Not that I'm excusing Collie. He's an ass for doing this, Heather. And the girl he slept with is an ass too. But, well, maybe it's for the best that he finally told you."

Heather stays silent.

"While we're on *asses*." Liz looks pointedly at me, and my heart skips a beat. "Hayden. Lex, I hope you're not mad that I sent Coach Tanner after him when y'all left the gym. You don't *like* him like him, do you?"

So I have Liz to thank for Craig's timely appearance. "It's okay. I don't," I assure her.

"Good. That's one less thing to worry about," she says as we pull into the school. "After the way he was drinking, I don't want you with him anymore."

"Me either," Bodee says under his breath.

The space marked 164, the scene of Hayden's crime, is not visible from the underclassmen lot where we always park the Malibu. It's closer to the football field and we're on the cafeteria side, but my chest tightens all the same.

Heather opens the car door and slings her purse over her shoulder. "All right, girls, let's make a pact. No. More. Football. Players."

"No more football players," Liz and I say together.

"I like that rule," Bodee murmurs.

Of course he does.

It's been my rule. Heather's break with Collie means we're safe from whatever Hayden tells Collie about Friday night. It means that if there's a showdown between the football team and the Kool-Aid Kid, then Heather and Liz might side with us.

The real stress is at lunch, but I'm relieved when no clandestine Hayden meetings occur before then. I'm in fourth period before the question hits me.

What if Captain Lyric is a football player?

Does our rule apply to him?

"I know what you're thinking," Heather says as we walk toward our seats. "And he's not."

"What? Who's not what?"

"Captain Lyric. He's no football player. So it's safe to keep your little word-lover."

Safe is exactly how I like things, but I give Heather my best grin. "He's not my word-lover."

"What-*ever*."

"Okay, he is." And to my surprise, even though it's Monday, and he's never managed it before, I see a new set of lyrics printed on the desk.

I KNOW YOUR STORY
GOT ONE OF MY OWN
YEAH, I KNOW LONELY AND ALONE
HAPPEN IN A CROWD, HAPPEN IN A KISS
BUT I KNOW HOW TO CHANGE ALL THIS

And below the lyrics, a message.

YOU LOOKED HOT FRIDAY NIGHT

My heart beats a tattoo against my rib cage. Because . . . he knows who I am. I'm no random Desk Girl to Captain Lyric.

"Maybe it *is* a football player," Heather says. "Do you know the rest of the lyric?"

"That last part's not a song," I say, feeling like someone Tasered my brain.

"I know that. But dang, Captain sure made it one today."

I take out my pencil, control the quiver in my fingers, and print just below the actual lyrics:

And change is never a waste of time

I think for a moment and then erase his additional message. No need for another desk dweller to know the Captain raised the bar. I'm sure we're their own personal soap opera.

He knows who I am.

chapter 14

"LADIES, please. Your discussion doesn't sound like Maslow's Hierarchy of Needs," Mrs. Tindell says from her desk.

"Oh, it is," Heather murmurs without moving her lips. She's smirking like an elf at Christmas.

"Sorry, Mrs. Tindell," I say for the both of us, and nudge Heather with my elbow.

Heather manages to whisper, but I can almost hear the squeal she's muffling. "I can't take it anymore. You have *got* to arrange a meet."

I'd rather ride every roller coaster at Disney than meet the Captain face-to-face; and I'd rather peel my toenails off with a spoon than ride a roller coaster. "But that might ruin everything."

"Are you crazy? This guy's your own personal Romeo,"

she argues. "Not some Jack *A*. Like Collie."

"But what if he is?" This question escapes me as Hayden's meet-the-parents performance comes to mind. Because anybody can fool anybody for a while. Life—and love, if that's what this is—is easier to take when it's written on a desk.

I'd never have to tell a desk no. A desk would never *hurt* me. A desk would never . . . R . . . me. I exhale. The *R* word is abrasive, even in my mind.

"You'd rather have words on a desk than a Romeo in the flesh?" Heather asks.

She won't understand, and I can't explain why I'm afraid the mystery is better than the man, so I paste on a smile and lie. "Of course I'd rather have him."

"Well, then. I'm going to do you a favor and figure out who the Captain is."

"I'm surprised you haven't already," I say.

The bell rings, but not before I have cursed the minute hand for moving at the speed of a turtle in quicksand.

Bodee's not at his locker, so I dump my books and head to the cafeteria without enjoying one of his smiles. When I get into the cafeteria, I realize I'm batting 0 for 2. Hayden's sitting in my usual seat at our lunch table. I choose the longest line—nachos—and plant myself at the end.

Hayden stands and walks up to me. "Can we talk?"

"Rather not," I say.

"Well, you don't have to. But I gotta say this." He shoves

both hands in his back pockets and rocks from heel to toe, waiting for my permission.

I nod and look away. The quicker he talks, the quicker this is over.

"I was outta line. Way outta line on Friday," he says very fast.

"Did Craig tell you to say that?" I ask as we reach the lunch lady.

"Black beans?" she asks without looking up.

"No," Hayden and I say together.

"I want another chance," he demands.

The lunch lady nods and adds another layer of melted cheese to the nachos on Hayden's plate.

"You hear me?" he asks.

"Look, right there's your extra cheese," she says with a huff, and adjusts her hairnet with the back of her hand.

"I was talking to *her*, not you," Hayden says to the lunch lady.

"Well, of all the—," the lady says as her eyebrows disappear into the hairnet. "*Rude*," she mutters.

"Thank you, ma'am," I say for Hayden before I turn to him. "No way."

"Going to change your mind," he says with a patented smile, the kind arrogant guys use to impress girls. Apparently, he's dusted off his confidence and brought it with him to lunch.

Bodee would never say this to me. I can't believe Captain Lyric would either.

"Um." I stall, and take my nachos. I want to say, "You can't" or "My mind's made up," but those words don't come.

"Look, Alexi, I . . . well, all I'm saying is I'm sorry. . . . I plan to make it up to you."

The sudden lack of defensiveness in his voice catches me by surprise. There's fire in his cheeks and even a little drag to his step. I seize on the vulnerability. "Hayden, if you really want to make this up to me, then don't sic your football buddies on Bodee because of Friday night." Hayden stops. Liz and Heather are already at the table, and I get the feeling he doesn't want them to hear us. And I guess that's a good thing. Neither of us wants to know what they'd think.

"What is it with you and that Kool-Aid freak anyway?" he asks.

"You're lucky that 'Kool-Aid freak' stepped in." Repeating Hayden's words hurts on two levels. One, that Hayden sees Bodee as a freak. And two, this is too close to the way I used to see Bodee.

"If he hadn't stopped you . . ." I say it with hesitation, but I know exactly what would have happened.

"We'd have both been sorry. Sorrier," Hayden says.

Sweat beads on my upper lip. I nod.

"Tell you what, Lex, I'll forget about him and his Mike Tyson moves"—he tilts his nonbruised jaw toward me—"if you'll agree to give me another chance. Say you'll go out with me again."

I know this rock. And I'm intimately acquainted with this hard place.

"Why?" I manage.

"Is it so hard to believe that I like you?" When I don't answer, he pushes. "Look, you know the guys on the team aren't going to let Friday night go? Kool-Aid punched me. But if they saw us together, they might *forget*. I'll tell them to if you'll . . ." He hooks one finger around my pinkie, pulls me and my tray toward him.

"But . . ." I stare at our joined fingers. He apologizes one minute and threatens me the next. Do they teach this disarming tactic to boys at summer camp or in football practice?

"The guys should have already. It's practically a rule of the team," he says quickly. "So what do you say? Give me another chance to show you I'm not just a guy who likes to drink and take. I can be"—he leans in and whispers in my ear—"sweet."

Why can't I talk to him as if he were Kayla? It seems too simple to say, because he's a guy, and my "no" is broken, but it's the truth. I am powerless around men. Most men.

"Okay." I agree to a date, knowing that even if I could say no, I won't be able to take it if the football team, with Hayden in the lead, goes after Bodee the way his father did. I know Bodee won't understand when I go out with Hayden again.

Maybe he'll get angry or disappointed with me and I'll hate that, but that seems easier to take.

And all I want is for Bodee to stay safe.

I walk the five steps to our table and sit down. Instead of reaching for a nacho, my fingers fly to my neck, searching for the grooves. I force myself to relax. Will the scabs not to itch, not here at school. I can control myself for two and a half more hours, because even the promise of pain, where my fingers curl beneath the curtain of my hair, helps me cope with saying yes to Hayden when I wanted to say no. Again.

"Hey, you okay?" Liz asks.

"Just a headache," I say.

Heather shoves a french fry into her mouth and says, "Nope. It's the Captain. He knows who she is. Stressing her out."

"It's not the Captain." Liz puts her arm around my shoulders for a quick squeeze. "She was trapped over there with Hayden. You're pale, Lex. What'd he say to you?"

"That he wants a chance to make up Friday to me."

"Oh, Lex . . ."

"Don't 'Oh, Lex' her. I wish Collie would say that to me," Heather says. "The jerk."

"What happened to your No Football Players rule?" I ask.

Heather twists one of her braids into a circle and swipes at a tear. "Oh, I don't know what I want. I need him. I hate him. But I need him."

"You don't *need* him, you want him," I say.

"You've got the Captain. And evidently Hayden." She looks

at Liz. "And I give you a week, and Ray'll come back. And then what will I have? An ex-boyfriend who screwed somebody else and doesn't love me anymore. Nothing."

"You have us," Liz says.

"But that's hardly the same," Heather argues.

"I don't want Hayden, and I don't have the Captain," I remind her. "And I guarantee Collie still loves you; he's just being a stupid man about this."

"But at least you have Bodee. And he's not a stupid man."

"Don't have him like you think," I say.

"There's something about him, Lex," Liz says, searching the cafeteria for Bodee. He's not in sight, so she adds, "I think he's an old soul."

"He is," I agree. This doesn't give too much away.

"So you like him. But you probably don't know what to do with him. The guy's an oyster in the desert. Plenty of sand, but no water."

"What the hell does that fancy phrase mean?" Heather asks.

"She just means, I like him," I say. "And of course, I *can't*. So I . . . don't." Liz nods as if she understands. "So Bodee's a friend," I say firmly.

A *best* friend.

My honesty with the girls surprises me. But Bodee's right where I love him. In the room down the hall and up the stairs from mine. Dinner instead of a dinner date. A hand to hold instead of lips to kiss. He's my fort, my sanctuary. And I won't do anything to jeopardize this.

"So you have a friend, a lover, and a pursuer. You're a freaking diva."

"Hardly," I say, because it's far more complicated than Heather thinks. What I have is my secret, someone else's secret, and a . . . rapist (who I have trouble calling a rapist).

The rest of the day goes by in a haze, and little exchange of words. Except the ones from my iPod. Between classes, I forgo the grunge, letting James Taylor soothe my soul with his stories. Finally, the day ends, and we walk to the car. I go through the motions, putting one foot and one word in front of the other. How I manage to keep As is a mystery to me, when my mind is stuck in a purgatory of punishment and regret.

"I didn't see you much today," I say to Bodee as he climbs into the Malibu next to me.

"I saw you."

His words are almost lost as Heather punches play to turn the car into a karaoke session. Sad girls need happy music. We all join in, even Bodee. I'm not surprised he can sing after hearing Ben, but I'm surprised he'll sing along in a car with three girls.

"You want to go to the fort?" he asks after Heather drops us off.

"Sure." I can wait another hour to punish myself for telling Hayden yes. Dumping our stuff just inside the back door, I skirt around the pool toward the woods.

"You like having a pool?" he asks.

"I used to."

He doesn't ask for an explanation; he just falls into step beside me. We reach the fort's ladder in what feels like three steps. A spider has made a home in the space between the two bottom rungs. Bodee doesn't disturb it, but instead takes a high step above the eight legs. I want to squash it, but I climb over the spider too, since he worked so hard to avoid it.

"Lex"—he looks over his shoulder at me as we climb through the opening to the highest level—"your secrets are showing."

I am neither surprised nor horrified at the way he cuts right to my core. Maybe, in fact, I'm a little relieved. "I know. Weird day."

We plop down with our backs against the wall facing the big creek, and Bodee says, "You can let some of them go if you want."

For a moment, I am suspended in a vacuum where I'm blank with uncertainty; and then I hear the breeze rustling the leaves. The gurgle of the creek. Birdsong.

And Bodee's sigh releases me from the silence.

"I think I might be in love," I blurt out. It surprises him as much as it surprises me. "Well, maybe not, you know, *love*. But . . . there's someone I like."

Bodee doesn't pop his ring finger or his pinkie, but I watch him bend the other three until the joints *crack, crack, crack.* "I'm glad that you, well, have a good secret."

"But it's not. You'll laugh when I tell you the whole story."
I giggle. The nervous kind. Because I don't have to edit my
words before I speak. Bodee gets me raw. "The thing is, I don't
even know him."

I wait for Bodee's reaction, his disapproval or disbelief,
but he smiles. "So."

"It started on the first week of school in psych class. I'd
had a terrible day, but when I sat down in fourth period there
were lyrics written on my desk. Just printed in pencil. And
I know you've probably figured it out, but I love music. All
kinds of music."

Bodee reaches across and twists the cord of my ever-
present ear phones. His hand, brushing lightly against the side
of my neck, makes me shiver.

"I noticed," he says. "And you used to be in band."

Bodee notices everything. "Well, the first time it happened
was a fluke. He wrote something, I wrote something back and
thought it was over. But then he wrote back again. 'I'm okay.
Just like I am every day when you ask me what's wrong with
my smile.' On that day—a Thursday—the lyrics were just what
I needed. Because they're a lie. The name of the song is—"

"'If I Say I'm Okay, It's a Lie,'" he says. "My brother listens
to Fondue Fortunes."

"Yeah." Still, I'm surprised he knows this. "I never see you
with music."

"You didn't see me much before Mom died." He sighs.

"I'm sorry." The truth of his statement stings, but he shakes his head as if it's no big deal. "Well, that day, all I knew was somebody else out there understood me. Understands me. Because I was lying too, saying the same things and acting like everything's cool when it's not." Bodee squeezes my hand. "So I wrote back 'Trust me,' the words that come next in the song. And that's how it started. It's what gets me through the school day." I stop. "Stupid, huh?"

"No."

"You don't think it's crazy to think I'm in love with some guy who's never spoken a word to me?"

"Maybe he doesn't know how," Bodee says.

"You figured out how," I say.

"No, you did. You came after me during the funeral," he says. "Hey, what do you know; junior year and the Kool-Aid Kid gets a friend."

My head automatically cocks to the side as he uses his label.

"Hey," he adds with a crooked grin, "at least I'm not 'the kid who got beat up by the football team.' Yet."

"Yeah," I say, "at least," and grin back at him.

"So don't you want to know this guy who writes you lyrics?"

"Like you and I know each other? Or does 'know' mean have a face for that name?"

"Face."

"No, and I guess that's even crazier."

The left side of Bodee's face scrunches up; an expression I've never seen before, but that I take as curiosity.

"This thing with Captain Lyric is one of the few perfect things in my life. Sort of like you. I don't want to blow it. How awful would it be if the Captain is the kid who drives me crazy in English or the guy who always brings a liver sandwich every Thursday?"

Or a guy who would hurt me.

Bodee doesn't blush, but I can see that my comment about him being a perfect thing makes him happy. His voice is steady when he says, "Not crazy at all, Lex. Imagination is a powerful thing. I used to imagine . . . now you want to hear something nuts . . ."

I lean toward him until our shoulders almost touch.

"I used to imagine that my dad wasn't my dad. That my real dad was someone important like the president. Or someone nice like Vice Principal Oswald. Or a man like . . . your dad."

"That's not crazy. Sometimes I imagine Kayla is nicer, or at least less Queen of the Universe," I say with a laugh. Then I relent. "Okay. Sometimes she's cool. Just not lately."

"Yeah." Bodee wipes his palms on his jeans and then cracks his knuckles. "Point is, truth is a scary thing. Sometimes it's better not to know."

"I know, but how long can I love this guy?"

"Indefinitely," he says with a smile, and presses his thumb against his lips and then touches it to my forehead. "My mom used to do that with me," he explains. "And at night, before I'd leave for the tent, she'd hold her thumb up against the kitchen window until I was out of sight. It means . . ."

I realize I'm holding my breath as I wait for him to finish his sentence.

"I won't let anyone hurt you."

If a heart can smile, mine does.

"Bodee, thanks," I say, though I know he doesn't need it. "I'm sorry you lost her."

"At least I found you," he says.

chapter 15

BODEE and I sit in our contentedness until it's time to meet Mom.

She makes good on her promise to take us out to dinner and a movie. Bless her heart, she won't pry into Bodee's business, but I can tell how badly she wants to fill our casual silence with questions.

When we get back to the house, Kayla's waiting for me in my bedroom.

"Out," I say, and drop my purse onto my dressing table.

"This isn't about the wedding. I swear."

"Okay, talk fast. I've got homework." The kind that happens in the safety of my closet.

Kayla tugs on one of her huge loopy earrings, which tells me she's nervous as she says, "I know what you told Hayden."

Which thing I told Hayden? That I'd go out with him? Or that I didn't want him to send a football player after Bodee? Either way, I've been down this road with Kayla before, and I'd rather pedal a Big Wheel to and from school for a year than go down it again. "Kayla, don't start acting like Mom and Dad again." I rip my hoodie over my head.

"I'm not, and this is different. I think you have to tell someone." She twists an earring until her earlobe turns sideways.

"Why?" I say, stalling, because I still don't have a clue about what I'm supposed to tell.

"Because you *should.*" Kayla is impatient. "It's too important not to when a girl gets . . . hurt."

My heart nearly stops. "What exactly are you talking about?"

Kayla stops twisting and folds herself onto the edge of my bed. "You *know* what. Some guy on the football team raped a girl."

That is what Hayden told Craig? I never said football player.

Craig must have been totally out of it to let Kayla find out. He knows how she is when she gets onto something. I drop down beside her without bothering to pull my pajama top over my cami. "Maybe it was just a rumor, Kayla. I can't go stirring up—"

"But you know who it is."

I don't know if she's asking or telling, but I say, "No."

"You can't lie to me, Lex. Not about something like this."

Wrong. Wrong. Wrong.

"I know I was busting your chops about ho-ing it up with

Hayden, but if I thought for a second"—her hand makes a fist—"that he forced you—"

"Hayden didn't force me," I say in a level voice.

Kayla puts a hand on my shoulder, and I shrug it off. "You have to know more than Hayden told Craig," she continues. "And I think you need to do something about it."

"I. Don't. Know. Anything," I spit at her. "It was just something I overheard in the bathroom. Might be total crap made up by some freshman."

"Okay, look. I could see Craig doesn't think so. Because he's *worried*," Kayla says. "And I think he's afraid it might be Collie."

Oh, no. Oh, *no*. "Why does he think that?" I stammer, and shove my arms through my T-shirt so Kayla can't see my face.

"Because when I asked him who it could be, he finally said he'd caught Collie and Heather together in the locker room after he came back from running Hayden. And *she* was totally messed up. Crying and mascara running down to here, like, well, *you* know; he didn't go into much detail. So, I think you better do something; check on your friend, get her to *talk*." Kayla grabbed my hand. "I mean, to imagine this guy forcing himself on a girl. Like, what if that was you? That boy, *any* boy, lays one finger on *you* without you wanting it and I swear I'll tear him apart. And after that, I'll let Craig finish him off."

"Kayla—"

"You think I'm a self-centered bitch right now, but you're still my little sister. Nobody's going to hurt you."

Too late. But this declaration forces tears to my eyes. If things were different, I might release the lock on this dam and tell her everything. But that would change us forever, and I can't.

"If it's Heather, get her to tell someone. Okay?"

"Okay," I tell Kayla so she'll leave.

Once I'm behind two closed doors, I curl into a ball and suck in the familiar smell of the closet carpet. When I can't make myself smaller, I cry and pound my fist on the floor. There's an art to crying without a sound, and I'm a master.

But my silence only amplifies the quiet voice on the other side of my closet door.

"Lex."

Unable to answer and unable to uncoil my body, I stay silent.

"Lex," Bodee says again.

My toes start to cramp, and I have to stretch a little. "Yeah."

"I'm here."

"I can't come out," I say, which is better than "Go away."

"Must be nice in there."

If I wiggle a little, the night-light allows me to see the new pile of shredded football cards from the night before, and the discarded pj shirt I just barely managed to change before my fingernails went to town on my neck. I squeeze Binky to my chest and say, "Did anybody see you?"

"They're all in their rooms."

I exhale and realize Bodee's presence won't ruin my closet sanctuary any more than he ruined the fort. "Good."

"Don't want to barge in, but I know you're upset."

"How?" I push some of Binky's loose stuffing back inside him and wish it was as simple to fix me—that somebody could push all the loose stuff in me back inside.

"I saw Kayla leave," he says. "And I heard your voice. I could tell."

"Bodee," I start, but I don't know what to say.

"Because I know hurt when I hear it. I hurt too," he confesses.

"You sit in your closet?" I hear him rest his back against the closet door, and there's a pause.

"No. Mostly, I lie under the bed," he says.

"But . . ." In my mind I see Mom's extra Christmas decorations and a few rolls of wrapping paper stored under the antique bed Dad set up for Bodee. "Aren't there Christmas decorations and stuff under there?"

"Not anymore."

"What do you do under the bed?" I ask.

"Put my fingers between the slats and box springs and lift myself off the floor. I can do a whole bunch before I get tired enough to sleep."

He's not bragging; he's just saying it. But that explains why there are muscles beneath his loose white Hanes instead of the nonathletic flab I assumed would be there.

"Lex?"

"Yeah," I say.

"Stop scratching your neck."

"No." My hands have a brain of their own, and they're

disconnected from any logic. "I can't." But why is this *no* so easy to say?

"Yes. You can, Lex."

"Says the guy who does pull-ups under his bed," I say, but not cruelly.

"I'm not under there now."

Sitting up, I bury my nose in my T-shirt and consider his words.

"You don't have to come out," he says. "Just stop hurting yourself."

"Don't think I can."

"What would your Captain tell you if he were here?"

I think for a moment and talk-sing, *"What words are there to write? To describe this place in my life. It's a painful peaceful day."*

"What's next?" he asks.

"All in all. You have been. Redeemer. Pain Stealer. My best friend. Please hold my hand."

"That's nice. Well, then, imagine I'm him," he says, and sings the lines. *"All in all. You have been. Redeemer. Pain Stealer. My best friend. Please hold my hand."*

I can't smile, yet my body begins to relax. Like an involuntary reaction to Bodee and the Captain, it is a nice blend, and I am better. A little better.

Like fourth period in my bedroom.

"Bodee, can I tell you another secret?"

"I told you one of mine," he says.

"You see that vent above my bed?"

"Yeah," he answers.

"Tell me, how many slits are there in the vent?"

"One. Two. Three. Four . . ." He counts twenty before saying, "Not sure. I blinked and lost my place, but I think there are twenty-two or twenty-three."

"Twenty-two slits. I count them every night."

"Why?" He doesn't sound as if this is stupid.

"Because I need to focus on something," I explain.

"Guess it's tough to do in the dark."

"Actually, I count the metal strips instead of the spaces. Easier to see."

"So you try to count around all twenty-two to reach twenty-three?" he asks.

"Yeah, but I can't." He sighs his understanding, and I say, "It's impossible without blinking, so I have to keep starting over."

"It is hard," he says after several minutes pass, and I know he's tried it a few times. "If you come out, Lex, maybe . . . we could count them together."

Stay in here with the shredded pieces of football cards or count the vent slits with Bodee? Not a hard choice. "Okay."

He moves away from the door while I change into a fresh pj top that smells Mountain Spring clean. Arms crossed over my chest, I exit the closet and slide under the covers. Bodee is standing by the light switch. He's shirtless. His hair is sticking out everywhere. But there's something about seeing him this way that helps me understand how complex he is. More teenager than man on the outside; more man than teenager on the inside.

"In the dark?" he asks as his hand toggles the switch.

"Dark," I say, hoping this will ease me into dreamland.

After several seconds, my eyes adjust to the darkness, and I can see Bodee's silhouette. I wonder if he can see me under the mound of my comforter. Our quiet breaths are well under my parents' radar, but my heart races anyway. What would they say if they found us together in my dark bedroom? Would they send him back to live with Ben? No, I decide. My parents are not usually jump-to-conclusion people. But he'd never end up in my bedroom again if they found out.

"You okay?" Bodee asks.

"Yeah." Despite his words, he's calm, and so am I. No more heaving and sobbing. We're a duet of breaths as quiet as the whisper of butterfly wings.

Bodee eases into my dressing table chair and says, "If you count from the right and I count from the left . . ."

"We'll meet in the middle."

We both say, "One," and I can't tell my voice from his.

"Two."

"Three."

"Four." We are a chorus as sweet as any I've heard.

"Five."

"Six."

"Seven."

"Eight."

"Nine."

My eyes start to burn, but I stretch them wide, straining my muscles to keep them open.

"Ten."

"Eleven," we whisper together.

There is a satisfaction in my voice, because I know Bodee and I are staring at the same little sliver of dark in the middle of the vent. "We made it," I say.

"And *twelve*," he adds. "Twenty-three."

He is counting me past the dark. "It's not impossible," I say.

"Nothing is, Lex."

"Not even the deposition?" I ask.

"This is your twenty-three, not mine," he says. "We can tackle my demons another time."

Peace is a quirky thing. I feel it on Christmas Eve when my family takes communion at midnight. And when I get caught at the fort in a summer rain. Or on the rare occasions when Mom still calls me Boo-Boo. Peace invades me now at Bodee's twenty-three and fills me with calm exhaustion.

"Go to sleep. I'll be here," Bodee says.

In the moonlight that slips between the curtains at my window, I get a final look at Bodee before my eyes close.

His thumb is in the air.

chapter 16

SOMETHING is different Tuesday morning as I head to the
shower. For the first time in eighty-one days I am not tired
from a restless, dream-filled night. But I have to wonder: ten
years from now, will I still measure time by the number of
days since it happened or will I think in years?

"Morning," Bodee says as I enter the kitchen.

"Morning," I say to Bodee and Mom.

"You look cute," Mom says, and tugs on the tails of the
brown scarf I've tied around my neck.

"It's supposed to be cool today."

"Hmm. I love October." Mom sniffs the air as if the smell
of fall has invaded our kitchen.

"Me too," I say.

Heather honks and Mom says, "Have a good one, kiddos."

I wave bye since my mouth is full of toast.

In Heather's car, the music is up and the vanilla tree is on. Way on. Too bad it doesn't smell like fall in here.

"Back to red," Heather says to Bodee.

He runs a hand through his cherry hair, which he has a habit of doing if one of us says something about the color. There's still a touch of orange at the tips, and it reminds me of a rainbow.

Heather turns down the music a second before Liz stops singing, and we all laugh at her off-key note.

"So Bodee," Heather says. "You have any classes in East Wing?"

"Drama," he says.

"You're in *drama*?" How could I not know this about him? Come to think of it, I don't know much of anything he does at school that doesn't happen at the locker or in homeroom. After school I plan to find out more.

"I paint sets," he explains.

"Oh," I say. Even though this surprises me, it's nothing like imagining Bodee on a stage. Talk about an oyster in the desert.

"No classes with Mrs. Tindell?" Heather asks.

"Nope."

Liz and I roll our eyes at the same time, but before Heather can call "bitch-staring," Liz grins at her and says, "You didn't think it'd be that easy, did you?"

Bodee looks at me for a clue. "Captain search," I say.

"Had to start somewhere." Heather shrugs. "One down. I was pulling for you, Kool-Aid. I was pulling for you."

Liz wrinkles her nose and rips the dangling little vanilla tree off the rearview and shoves it into the glove box. "Last night she had a list of about twenty guys. Starting with—"

"Hey, hey. Don't tell Lex my possibles. She's not ready to know who her Romeo is yet. But I'm going to find him. You wanna help me, Kool-Aid?"

"Whatever," Bodee says without a hint of sarcasm.

"Careful, Lex, it's the quiet ones you have to watch." Liz rotates in her seat and reaches back to give Bodee a little pat on the knee.

My friends have officially adopted Bodee, and from the sweet smile on his face, he doesn't seem to mind.

"See you in fourth," Heather tells me as she and Liz split off from Bodee and me.

Fourth period arrives, but Heather doesn't. I take my seat and find the Captain's neat handwriting like a Happy Tuesday card written just for me.

THIS IS GONNA TAKE SOME THINKIN'
SOME MENTAL REARRANGIN'
I WANT YOU NOW, WITHOUT THE WAIT
   AND SEE

Giggling to myself, I write,

'Cause he's not right for you, so please choose me?

Whoever he is, the Captain has a way of choosing the right style of song to fit my mood. I don't know how he does it, but this one's subtle little message makes me laugh. He might as well have said, "Leave Hayden."

Mrs. Tindell babbles on about Axis I disorders as I try to think of new lyrics I might leave for him. He went old; I should bring it up a decade or two.

Hotwire a car, hijack a train
Get a map, steal a plane
Fly me to a lost little place
Where the water's not safe to drink
And all the people think

He gets that one right, and I'm going to be super impressed.

Mrs. Tindell is passing out homework by the time Heather steps through our open classroom door. She makes some excuse that causes Mrs. Tindell to pat her on the shoulder. But when Heather sits down next to me, she mutters, "Nobody we know is in the hallway for the first thirty minutes of class." She scowls at the worksheet before she adds, "There was some freshman who looked desperate for a bathroom, but I'm sure it's not him. He practically wet himself when

I asked where room 142 was."

"You cut class to spy on the Captain?"

"Seriously, you're worried I'm missing something?" She looks at our substitute, who is already settled back into her desk with a book. "But my conclusion: if the Captain's gauging your reaction, he's not doing it in the first thirty minutes."

"So you gonna skip the second half of class tomorrow?"

"I just might hang out in the hall all day if that's what it takes," she says, sliding my worksheet to her desk so she can read my first answer. "Or I could ask Mrs. Tindell who sits there the rest of the day."

"Heather, this is all crazy. Please don't talk to her." I nod toward Mrs. Tindell. "I'd rather not be the talk of the lounge."

"Okay. Told you I need a boyfriend," she whispers. "I'm reduced to working on your love life instead of mine."

"You know you can have your pick of boyfriends if you want one. Even Collie," I say, hoping to shift the focus off me.

"You think I should?" When I hesitate, she adds, "You know, forgive his ass?"

"It's your choice."

"Come *on*, tell me what you really think, Lex. Is he a terrible guy?"

Milking my scarf until the silk presses against the scabs on my neck, I say, "Good guys and terrible guys seem to be stupid at the same ratio."

"Bodee's not."

"Bodee doesn't count. He was raised by wolves on Neptune or something," I argue.

"Yeah. Back to Collie. Do I forgive him?" she tries again.

My handwriting on the worksheet is nearly illegible, so I take the time to rewrite the words before I fashion an answer I can live with. "Forgiving him and taking him back are two totally different things."

"What would you do?"

"Why are you asking me instead of Liz?" I say.

"I did already."

"And?"

Heather stares at Mrs. Tindell, who's grading worksheets, instead of me. "Liz doesn't trust Collie."

"There you have it," I say, as if this matter is now settled.

No matter what, I still have this soft place inside me for good guys who do stupid things, so I can't just say, "Don't date him; he's a dick." There's more to me than most guys understand, and I know there's more to him. Collie's not a devil. He's selfish. And stupid.

But so am I.

"You know what I need?" Heather whispers.

Parents who love you. An A in psych. Boys who don't cheat with friends. "No," I say.

"A campout."

"A what?" Unfortunately, I say this loud enough for the whole class to hear.

"Sorry, folks." Heather covers my startled question. "Back

to your worksheets. Just a little psychotic break."

Mrs. Tindell cracks a smile at Heather's joke, and everyone goes back to their page flips and pen scribbles.

"A campout," Heather says again. "And you need one too. At least, you need *something* to take your mind off whatever crap it's been fixated on."

"I doubt that," I say.

"Come on," Heather pleads. "It'll be fun. We can stay up all night and scare ourselves to death while we gorge on Sour Patch Kids and Dr Pepper."

Uh, minus the Sour Patch Kids and Dr Pepper, she's describing a typical night at my house. I'm about to say, *Absolutely not*, when she adds, "Please."

The brokenness behind that single word makes me say, "I'll think about it."

Liz is all about the idea when Heather approaches her on the ride home, but Liz is a sucker for Sour Patch Kids. And I have a sneaking suspicion she's worried how Heather is managing without Collie.

"There's no home football game Friday night. No cute boys to watch. What are we going to do if we don't do this?" Heather asks as she turns into my driveway.

"Whatever the two of you usually do on the weekend," I say.

"Bodee, tell her she needs to hang with us," Heather says.

"Um—," Bodee starts.

My hand grips his denim kneecap as if it's a lifeline. He lifts my hand, curls his around it, and presses his thumb against mine. It's my new universal sign for *You're safe*.

I'm glad neither Liz nor Heather notices.

"Convince me tomorrow," I say as I climb from the car and shut the door on the faint scent of Vanilla Paradise.

Bodee and I dump our books and head through the woods. After climbing to the top level, we don't talk about anything; instead, we relax and share the window view and just listen to the woods. The rain from last night, which I didn't hear because I *slept* through it, babbles over stones in the creek. And the drying leaves twirl upward in the breeze, rustling across our clearing and crackling under the feet of some out-of-sight creature. A couple of birds share a branch on the tree across from ours. "*Tika-tika-tika*," they warble, as if to remind us it's time to fly south.

Sometimes when he watches the clearing and I look as if I'm watching the clearing, I am watching him. He's still but leaning forward, like whatever is out there is better than what is behind him.

We squeeze out every moment of daylight in the fort. And arrive back at the house before anybody else gets home.

Bodee shoulders his pack and says, "Homework," as he disappears into the bonus room.

I prop my feet on the rails of the front porch and think how similar our porch is to the one at Bodee's house. Every time he climbs these steps, does it make him think of his house? Does he hurt for his mom? Or fear his dad? I wonder if he feels that our house is his sanctuary, or whether it is just another place that reminds him his mom is dead. I'm still trying to rid my mind of Mrs. Lennox's medicine cabinet, the disorder of the kitchen, and the pictures hanging crooked on the hallway wall, when Mom gets home with groceries.

Dinner is another opportunity to ignore Kayla and Craig. A side of resentment with my green beans and potatoes. I retreat at the first opportunity to sit at my desk and pretend I'm doing homework. The closet is just out of my vision. Teasing me with comfort; begging me to seek security. I delay the urge and finish the homework.

By ten thirty I turn off my light, finally obedient to the nagging inner voice telling me I have to climb in bed and at least try to sleep. I go through the ritual motions: the elaborate arranging of covers, turning my face into the pillow, Binky, closing my eyes. As usual, I end up flat on my back, tense, and miles from sleep. The ceiling draws my eyes like a powerful magnet.

I blink.

Squinting, eyes adjusting to the darkness, I don't *see* it. I fumble for the light beside my bed.

The vent is *gone*.

A cover from *Hatchet* conceals the vent's twenty-two lines and twenty-three spaces.

And I am smiling and wiping at sudden tears. Because he has stuck his one precious possession, using four pieces of tape, over the place I want to avoid.

A little while after I turn off the light, my door swings open on silent hinges, and Bodee takes his protective place in the chair at the window.

"I love it," I tell him.

"Figured Gary Paulsen wouldn't mind," he says.

"No, don't think he would. Thank you," I whisper, and wonder how many times I'll say those words to Bodee.

"Sleep, Lex."

"You'll stay?"

"For a little while."

Bodee is a dark silhouette against the window. He holds his thumb in the air, and for the second night in a row, I roll over, muscles relaxed and eyes heavy. And let sleep overtake me.

chapter 17

HEATHER is already chirping about the campout when Bodee and I join them in the car. "You check with your mom?" she says before I can buckle my seat belt.

"Not yet. Are you in on this?" I ask Liz.

"I wasn't as crazy about the idea, but . . ."

Liz leaves it hanging, and I know this means she has already given Heather a firm yes. The invite is tempting; a year ago this might have been something they'd have done without me. It's the lies (in bulk) I will have to tell during "Boy Talk," not the outdoor conditions, that drive me to say no.

"She's going. You're going. We're *all* going. Well, except Bodee. Because this is a no-guys-allowed thing. We can't exactly talk about you if you're there," Heather says, throwing a quick grin over her shoulder at Bodee.

Bodee pops the rest of his breakfast bar in his mouth, chews, and otherwise keeps his mouth shut. He stares out the window. No reaction to this information, not even a blush. But maybe he assumes they already talk about him. Maybe he's been talked about so often it doesn't bother him anymore.

"So. You're going," Heather says again.

Steamroller Heather flattens out my resolve like a pancake. "If I were to agree, where is this campout supposed to take place?" I ask.

"Can't be at *my* house," Heather says.

Considering there may be anything from a meth lab to a *pharmacy* in Heather's garage, we are all in total agreement.

"Hey, Lex, you're the one with the woods," Liz says.

"Oh, now that's a good idea," Heather says, and it's a little too rehearsed. "Come on, how about it? If your mom says it's okay."

Bodee is no longer staring out the window; he's looking at me. The question in my eyes is reflected in his: Should I share the fort with them?

"I guess we could set up a tent somewhere out back," I say.

"Don't you still have that tree-house-like thing in there?" Heather asks.

There are pictures at the house of me in the fort. Taken last year. "Yeah," I say.

"Perfect," Heather squeals. "For realsies, Lex, it's just what we need."

"Girls, it's a long way from the bathroom." Heather doesn't seem the kind to dig a hole, but just in case that's not a compelling reason, I add, "And if you get scared, you have to trek back through half the woods." Because Heather does seem the kind to freak herself out.

"You love that place, right?" Liz asks. "And it's safe?"

"I do, and yes."

"Hey, Bodee, help a girl out. Have you ever seen this fort?" Heather wants to know.

"Stop enlisting his help," I say, a little stronger than I mean to. "Every time he gets in the car, you try to get him to do this or that."

"Lex, this is really important and you listen to him," Heather pleads.

Bodee's lips twitch, but he says nothing.

Liz is the one who changes my mind.

"And you think it's sort of special," she says. "Like it's your little hideout, right? After last weekend, we could all use a hideout."

Liz is right. As she usually is. But I can't tell her it's okay until Bodee gives his approval. He smiles, and I pray that letting them into this space doesn't change what it means to us.

"Okay. Just this once," I say, and hope that satisfies them for the rest of the week.

I exist between the Captain's lyrics and Bodee's gentle presence until Friday. I haven't forgotten a single detail of what happened poolside in July, but with the cool air of fall signifying the change of seasons in Tennessee, I realize there is a change in me, too.

From sad to less sad.

The knock at the classroom door on Friday afternoon at one thirty brings another.

"Ms. Littrell, it appears you are needed in the office," Mr. Wingo announces to the room.

My classmates, including Hayden, who sits in the back corner of the class, snap to attention. They know, just as I know, that good students get called to the office for one of two reasons: a death or a delivery. In Algebra II last year, a girl found out her dad died when he fell into a vat of something at the paper mill. And my freshman year, they called the boy at my art table to the office because his grandfather died. It made me glad I was beside my granddad at the hospital when he died, and not at school hearing about it from the secretary.

"Should I take my books?" I ask. Translation: am I returning to poly-sci class?

"No, Ms. Littrell, I don't believe that's necessary," Mr. Wingo says with a smirk.

Leaving everything as is, I follow the office aide, a senior boy, to the front hall. We don't speak.

When we reach the secretary, the aide disappears into a back room and emerges with a clear vase filled with red roses. I don't count them, but the bouquet looks like the price tag equals one of Kayla's car payments.

"These are for you," the aide says, and hands over the vase as if he hears suspicious ticking inside. He thrusts it at me so that I almost drop it on us both.

"Careful," Mrs. Peggy, the secretary, says as I rest the vase on her desk.

Searching through the baby's breath and thorny foliage, I locate the white envelope just barely peeping out at the side of the arrangement. My name is scribbled in pen on the outside. Alexi Litrell, with a *T* missing from Littrell. The florist's mistake or the sender's? I hope it's the florist's. If you spend a car payment on something that dies in a week, the least you can do is learn how to spell the name of the girl you send it to.

My knees want to buckle with anticipation as I rip at the envelope. I take a breath before I am able to slide out the little white card and read:

I SAVE ALL MY SORRYS FOR YOU. —HAYDEN

The card falls from my hand and flutters to the office floor. Because the words in the apology aren't just words; they're lyrics.

Curse Hayden Harper . . . *and* CJ Schooler for writing that song.

Hayden Harper cannot be Captain Lyric.

But what if he is?

I can't love someone I don't trust. Can I?

And then I'm back with *him* again.

Summer humidity heating my skin and bats swooping over the pool in the moonlight. His hands sliding the strap of my one-piece to my elbows, his lips on my bare neck. "You're beautiful. Like her," he whispers. Trust. Friendship. A form of love that comes with day-in and day-out familiarity.

"Ms. Littrell, did you *hear* me?"

Mrs. Peggy's voice blanks out the nightmare, and I realize she's glaring at me over her computer screen.

"Huh?" I say.

"I *said*, no parking. Take your pretty little bunch and go back to fifth period."

"But I don't want them," I say.

I am either from Mars or Mrs. Peggy is having trouble imagining why a sixteen-year-old girl doesn't want roses.

"Well, you're *not* leaving them here. Now scoot," she says.

I've received flowers on my birthday from Dad, but never a dozen roses. Never this kind of extravagance. The vase ends up in the crook of my arm with some of the soft petals pressed against my cheek. They really are beautiful. Paler than the average rose; a soft faded red, like the American flag after it's been exposed to the elements. Or Bodee's cherry-flavored hair at the end of the day.

I thought Hayden was avoiding me after our showdown in the nacho line. But if he's the Captain, he wasn't avoiding me at all. He just kept on communicating in a way I obviously love. And giving me time. Which I appreciate.

And now he's buttering me up with flowers.

I think over what the Captain's written. Recall the lyrics from the first of the week from the Stonewalls and the Modern Beatniks. Then on Thursday he wrote

YOU'RE SHADOWS AND SNATCHES OF LIGHT, A DARK ROOM OF BLACK AND WHITES, AND YOU THINK I'M THE MYSTERY.

So today my response was

But you know every little thing about me. My real identity.

Oh my gosh. Was the timing deliberate? So I'd have to write *these* lyrics on the day I get roses?

By the time I reach Mr. Wingo's class, I've spent the entire time realizing Hayden is the Captain and no time considering the fact that he's in this class with me. I have to wonder if he tipped the florist to deliver my flowers during fifth period just so he could see my reaction.

So what do I do about his apology? And his generosity?

Find a trash can?

Rejection on that level is dangerous. If it pisses him off enough, he could still decide to take it out on Bodee. And if Hayden really *is* the Captain, it changes things. This cork-screw kind of thinking leads me to the only possible option. March back to my seat as if a dozen roses are something I get every day, and try to stall until I know what to do next.

I cause a scene.

Scattered clapping, a little foot stomping, some of the girls oohing and aahing.

Ray smacks Hayden on the back like a proud parent. So, is he in on this too? Hayden, on a Smug Scale of one to ten, is beaming at least one hundred. I send him a little smile, set the vase beside my desk, and take my seat.

Maggie taps me on the shoulder. "They're so pretty," she says, and I see she's fishing for the *who*. "Wish someone would send me flowers."

"Maybe someone will," I say, because it's too cruel to tell Maggie her dating practices don't lead to roses.

"Probably not," she says. "They from Dane?"

"Hayden."

"Whew, girl, you get *around*."

I'm thinking the same thing about her, but I don't say it.

Finally, Mr. Wingo restores order by waving write-up slips in the air as a threat.

And when class is over, the flowers and I bolt from the room before Hayden can reach me, but I know the time's coming to face the music.

Literally.

I make it through sixth period and the final bell. And find

Bodee waiting at the planter by the front doors.

His face does a curious thing when he sees me hauling the flower shop to the car.

"Nice," he says.

I shrug and wish we were walking home, even though Bodee is wearing only a T-shirt and would freeze.

Heather and Liz appear with linked arms and their heads tilted together as if they're conjoined at the brain. When they spot the flowers, squeals that put pigs to shame echo across the asphalt.

"O-M-*Gosh*," Heather says.

"I guess you knew about this."

"Are you kidding? Hayden told the whole lunch table," Liz says. "Not *why*," she assures me, "just that he was sending you flowers." She cups a particularly large bloom and inhales. "They're beautiful, but I'm not sure flowers make up for Friday night."

No, they don't. And she doesn't even know the whole story.

"Come on, Liz," Heather says, getting behind the wheel. "You're usually such a forgiveness freak. And everybody makes mistakes. It's how they make up for them that counts."

Says the girl who broke up with Collie for being honest about his.

"You're the one with a forgiveness problem," Liz says to Heather.

"With good reason," Heather says.

"Flowers won't make you forget," Bodee says as we balance

the vase between us on the backseat.

I think he's remembering all the arrangements from his mother's funeral, and I show him my thumb.

"What does the card say, Lex?" Heather asks.

"That he's sorry."

"That's all? I heard what he said to the florist, and it was supposed to be a song. I was standing right there when he placed the order," Heather says.

Crap. So Heather put him up to sending the flowers? What else did she put him up to?

"I think I've unraveled *a certain mystery*," Heather says, so delighted with herself that she slaps the steering wheel hard enough to honk the horn. And dashes my hopes.

"I don't believe it," Liz says.

"Believe it, baby. Pret-ty sure now. Hayden's the Captain," Heather says with a pat-herself-on-the-back grin in the rear-view.

I wish I could see Bodee's face, but the flowers are between us, and I can't sneak a peek without being obvious. I don't expect to find him looking happy.

"Do *you* think it's Hayden?" Bodee asks me.

"No," I say.

Bodee, being Bodee, is bound to hear the uncertainty in my voice, but he's nice enough not to point it out in front of Liz and Heather.

chapter 18

I put the flowers on the kitchen bar, and Bodee and I park ourselves in the front porch swing. We've got at least two hours together before Heather and Liz return to haul everything to the woods.

"It's chilly," I say.

"The good kind," Bodee says.

"You gonna call that lawyer about the deposition?" I ask.

He is quiet.

"If you push me, I push you," I say.

"Okay," he says, and chews on his collar. "But not today."

I accept this truce with a nod. Courage takes time. Which neither of us has had enough of.

Crisp fall air and the fading sunset raise goose bumps on my arms. I tuck into a tighter ball, thinking about Mrs. Lennox and how I wish I'd known her better, until I realize Bodee looks cold in his T-shirt. "I'll be right back," I say, and race to the bonus room to grab his flannel shirt from the closet. Doing something for him, after he's been so compassionate, is a treat for me.

His tent isn't where I stored it the night he moved in, but I see a neat stack of our Christmas boxes in the bottom of the closet. Except for the added bed and his mother's diamond stud sparkling on the desk, our bonus room looks unchanged; unlived in. There's something very military about the way Bodee lives, but I guess he's endured enough change without throwing his stuff around.

Controlled and quiet, like the guy himself.

My room—the loose hair clips, kicked-off shoes, and three days' worth of outfits that are not out of sight in the dirty clothes bin—must drive him crazy.

I'm prying into his space without meaning to, so I exit in a hurry and bound down the stairs and through the house to hand him his shirt. He goes a little pink at my thoughtfulness.

"Thanks, Alexi."

"Least I can do," I say.

Time whittles away. The first hour and then the second. Heather and Liz will arrive soon, and I've managed not to say anything important.

"Um, Bodee, what are you going to do tonight?"

"Ray asked me over to eat pizza and play Xbox."

"*Liz's* Ray? Liz's *ex*-Ray?"

"Yeah. You're surprised," he says.

"Well. A little. I wouldn't think you and Ray have much in common."

"We don't. I'm sure Liz put him up to it. She worries about me." He shrugs his shoulder and smiles all at the same time; a look I've come to understand. Translated, it means he is certain of something most people don't realize. "I make adults nervous, and Liz is sort of an adult. Comes down to it, guess it's not only adults."

"Not me."

"Not you."

Bodee with naked Ray makes me itch, but I'm not about to tell Bodee I don't want him to go. Especially not tonight. He can use a friend, and who am I to say it can't be Ray? Bodee has the intuition of a prophet; if Ray's bad news for him, he'll know.

"What about after Xbox?" I ask, wishing I'd stacked the Christmas boxes back under the bed. I don't want him under there. "You going to be okay up there by yourself?" The question sounds stupid the second it's out of my mouth.

"You worried about me or you?"

"Both," I admit.

"Follow me," Bodee says and stands, holding out his hand.

Our hands clasp, and his is warm, curling around my cold one. When we reach the den, he gives me a little pat and says, "I'll be right back."

From the top of the open landing near his room, he tosses me his sleeping bag. "I thought it might help."

It's down-soft and smelling of Bodee, which mostly means the scent of his soap and Kool-Aid powder. I squish the bag against my face and chest.

"You're worried about tonight," he says.

"I love them, but sometimes it's hard to—"

"Lie that often," he finishes.

"Yes. Not that I mean to or want to, but they can't know," I say.

"Why not?"

"It'll change everything."

Bodee walks down the steps until he is standing right in front of me. "Sometimes things *need* to change, Lex."

"Not like this."

He sits on the closest step, and the threadbare knees of his jeans rip as he rubs his palms down them. "If it were me . . ."

"It's not."

"But if it were"—Bodee widens the hole in the jeans—"would you want me to tell?"

I stop him from pulling on the threads, and he cracks his knuckles. "Yes," I say, because he's the one person I won't lie to. "But this is different. If I tell, a person's life is over; or at least it's radically changed, and I can't do it. And I don't need everybody feeling sorry for me."

"Oh, like they might say at school, there's the girl who . . ." He stands and backs up a step. And then another. And another.

"Like I'm the boy whose dad killed his mom? You know, Lex, I wouldn't be that boy if I'd told someone, *anyone*, a long time ago that my dad was hurting us."

Now I want to hand him back the sleeping bag and wrap him up. "I know it seems like it might be the same, but it's not," I say finally.

My abuser will never hurt anyone else. He's good and decent, and I was convenient comfort on what he thought was the worst night of his life. It doesn't make what happened to *me* any better, but I know it makes him different from Bodee's dad.

"You're wrong," he says. Bodee leans his weight on the stairway rails and ducks his head; his frame sags and fills the opening. He looks big, the way he did that night with Hayden, but even still, his burden eclipses him.

"Doesn't matter. I'm not talking."

"Lex, if he looks you in the eyes every day, the way I think he does, and he can't *see* what I'm seeing . . . then he's not that much different from my dad. Monsters aren't born; they become."

"And you're going to face *your* monster too?" I ask.

"This isn't about me," he says. Another step. Away from me.

"You said it was. You're the one who brought up your dad."

"Only because I think the way you're swallowing all this is working like a poison in you. One I've taste-tested."

"Well, we'll talk after you go to your deposition."

Bodee folds himself onto the top step, but now there are a hundred steps between us instead of ten. I regret pushing him, but he's no more ready to tell than I am.

If Bodee's angry, it only shows in the stiff line of his jaw as he stands again and cracks his knuckles. He turns toward his bedroom, but then pauses and says, "I'll be in the woods tonight if you need me."

"Near the fort?" Can he hear me hoping for this to be true?

"Within yelling distance."

Six hours, one large pizza, and two bags of Sour Patch Kids later, I have not yet needed to yell. Liz, Heather, and I are sitting cross-legged on Bodee's sleeping bag, and we have talked about everything . . . *except* the boys who drove us to the fort in the first place.

"Okay, then. Who's first?" asks Liz.

We know what she means, but I stand to swap the little propane fuel pack on our second lantern.

"I thought we decided we weren't talking about the scum of the earth until after midnight," Heather says. "You know, at the Bitching Hour."

Liz hits the indigo switch on her watch and smiles. "Close enough."

"Since you're so ready, let's start with Ray," Heather says.

The mention of Ray reminds me that Bodee spent the evening with him. Surely they are finished with Xbox by now, and since my parents are only semi–night owls on the weekend, they're sawing more logs by now than Currant Mill on Old 31, and Bodee has slipped into the night. Into the woods.

Dropping back into my place between them, I decide to test Bodee's theory about Liz. "Did you know Ray was hanging out with Bodee tonight?"

Liz lays her head on my shoulder. "I might have suggested it," she says.

"Why?"

"Away games have been really hard on Ray since his injury. Not traveling with the team and all. I thought this might get his mind off it. And I think Bodee's good for him."

"You can't get over him unless you stop protecting him," Heather says, and pops another Sour Patch into her mouth.

"We broke up. I don't hate him," Liz says. "He's a good guy, Heather; we're just not right for each other."

Naked Ray Johnson. I'm in the middle of telling my brain to shut it, when Heather says, "Not according to Alexi. She gets a little hemorrhoid-looking twist every time he's around."

"Do not," I say.

"You definitely scrunch your nose."

"Do *not*," I say, but know I'm doing it as I speak.

"You kind of do," Liz says. "So spill, what is it about Ray you don't like?"

I laugh and say, "I like Ray just fine."

I can't tell them that every time I think about Ray, a little chorus plays in my head: I've seen him naked. I've seen him naked.

And Liz hasn't.

"What about Collie?" Heather asks me. "You guys used to be close, and now you do that hemorrhoid thing with him, too."

"I do not have a hemorrhoid thing. And Collie and I are still friends."

"Not like you were. Heck, Lex, I spent most of our relationship thinking the two of you might get together. I was afraid he'd ditch me and go for you."

"What*ever*," I say, shaking my head. I am really surprised Heather thought there was something between Collie and me. Other than her, that is. Because the big deal during my friendship with Collie, minus elementary school, was helping him plan how to make Heather fall for him and how not to act anything like her loser dad.

"Lex, do you know who he slept with? If he told anyone, it would have been you," Liz says.

"Sorry." I shake my head and praise God for my perfected lying skills; a trait I'm sure He doesn't appreciate. I hope He doesn't pay me back for them in one lump sum, because I know exactly who Collie slept with and when. I've known since the night of the alumni football scrimmage.

"Nothing? He told you nothing?" Heather says.

"I know he's really sorry, and he wants you back," I say.

"Don't you take him back, Heather. At least not until he proves he's different," Liz pleads. "You don't want to be with some guy who could end up just like your daddy. A washed-out football quarterback, drugged up or drunk all the time. You need someone who is . . ." There's a list, like a high school yearbook, that I can almost see Liz scroll through, and then she says, "A guy like Bodee."

I swallow the Sour Patch Kid in my mouth without chewing. Heather doesn't laugh the way I thought she might. "You're not interested in Bodee," I tell her.

"Hmm, well. I like his smile, and that hair's crazy-cute. You gotta admit, he's got some boy-next-door looks going for him."

"Well, you don't live next door," I say, trying to keep my tone even.

"It's not like *you* want him," Heather argues. "You're just friends, as you keep telling us all the time. And besides, you just got a hundred-dollar bouquet from Hayden that says he wants you."

"Lex, you've got to admit: Bodee's a lot better for her than Collie."

"Well, yeah, but so are a bunch of guys at school. And Collie's not like her dad. He just made a mistake."

"A mistake." Heather's off the sleeping bag now. She paces the fort like a lawyer waiting for the judge's decision. "He *screwed* someone else."

"Guys are like that," I argue. "And he was probably drunk." Tipsy, as I remember. Very tipsy. Very sad.

"That's as big a problem as the mistake," Liz says. "I was actually relieved when Ray couldn't play football this season. Some of those guys party too much."

Heather hasn't returned to the sleeping bag, but she's still and listening.

"And that's why I don't want Hayden," I say. "Number one, he's a football player. *Player*. Think I'll learn on your dime. Number two, he drinks. Think I'll learn on your quarter."

"True," Liz says, looking back and forth between Heather and me. "But it's not because they play football. Not really. I mean, Ray's a good guy. Just not for me."

"And Hayden's different," Heather says, and sits back down. "He's not as sweet as Bodee, but he *is* a great guy. Neither of our boyfriends—*ex*-boyfriends—ever even considered sending a hundred dollars' worth of roses to us."

"So? It just means his daddy gave him a credit card," I say.

Liz puts a hand on Heather's knee and then on mine. "But you're leaving out an important fact."

"What's that?" Heather and I say together.

"He's probably your Captain Lyric. Assuming Heather's right."

Heather nods as if this one is a done deal.

"Why are you both so hell-bent on thinking he's the Captain? Somehow, I can't see Hayden Harper jamming to Midsouth Hyatt."

"Me either," Heather agrees, "but all I know is that he called the florist, and when she asked him what to put on the card, he turned around to me and said, 'I have to use a song.'"

"You told him what to put?" Liz asks.

"Are you kidding? The lady at the shop suggested it," Heather explains.

Great. Some thirty-year-old picked out Hayden's apology. So romantic.

"Hayden as the Captain. It's not a total stretch. When did he break up with Janna?"

"Last week of summer," I say quietly.

"And when did you start getting the lyrics?"

"First week of school," I answer. I've already done this math. Already arrived at these conclusions.

"He told me at your party after the alumni game, before everything went to hell with Collie, that you were one of his goals for the year," says Heather.

If this is true, a lot happened at that party. A lot.

"But why'd you set me up with Dane first? If Hayden liked me the way you say?"

Heather chews her bottom lip and then gives me a sympathetic grin. "Okay, well. Maybe it won't hurt to tell you now. Hayden lost a coin toss. Some football thing they do if two guys like the same girl."

"They flipped a *coin*," I say, as my agitation switches to anger. "I decide who I date."

Liz, always sensible, usually correct, says, "But Lex, you never tell anyone *no*. Take this Heather-Bodee thing. You could be head-over-toenails for the guy, but you'd go along with it for Heather's sake, or maybe Bodee's."

I'd expected aloe, but instead Liz uses rubbing alcohol and steel wool. Chewing the inside of my cheek, I question if she realizes how often I lie to hide my feelings, and find I am speechless.

"But you're not, are you?" Heather asks.

"Not what?" I say.

"Head-over-toenails for Bodee."

"Um, no." We share a platonic bedroom, an air vent, and a beat-up book cover. That's not love, not in the head-over-toenails sense.

"Then I think . . . I'm going to ask him to sit in the front seat on Monday and see what happens," Heather says.

Liz fakes being appalled and fans her face.

I say, "Go right ahead. And if *Collie* sends you a hundred-dollar bouquet one day, what happens to Bodee?"

"Oh," Heather says.

"She's right," Liz says. "Bodee's not a plaything. He's not some rebound kind of guy. He's too nice to hurt."

"But I wouldn't do it on purpose." Heather fidgets and says, "Where are the gummy bears?" She rummages through our supply sack, pulling things out left and right, while I imagine Bodee attached to Heather by the lips.

I cringe at this. Name-brand Heather and simple, generic Bodee. Speak-her-mind Heather with speak-only-truth Bodee.

Touching.

Kissing.

I could see Bodee with Liz before I could see him with Heather.

But kissing one of them? I don't want to think about how Bodee kisses a girl. Or what *Heather* might think about the way he kisses.

But I do. Would he be tentative? Strong and passionate?

Maybe a combination of all three.

"Okay, which one of you ate all the yellow ones?" Heather grumbles, holding up the bag of gummy bears to show us the leftovers. Green. Orange. Red. The colors of Bodee's hair. She bites the head off a green bear and says, "You're right about Collie. I'll never get over him."

"If he apologized, would you take him back?" I ask, and steal a red gummy bear.

"Lex, he *apologized* when he told me. Hell, he even . . . *cried*. But . . ."

Liz reaches out and grabs Heather's hand as Heather's voice starts to shake. "He told me his big *secret* after . . . after we *slept* together. In my car. So romantic, huh?"

Heather's head hangs; tears slip down her cheeks, while she chews the remnant of the gummy bear so slowly I can barely see her jaw moving. Liz's jaw, on the other hand, doesn't drop open the way I thought it would. She just nods at this secret bomb Heather's dropped on us.

I know what Heather needs, so I pull her to me until my

chin rests on her hair. She cries, but there are recognizable phrases that emerge through her sobs. Phrases I could have written.

"I'm such an idiot," and "It hurt," and "I thought he cared about me."

Liz huddles around us, her arms snaking around the two of us. And then she says the one thing I never expected to hear.

"I *know*, Heather. I slept with Ray."

We are a tangle of broken hearts.

chapter 19

WHEN we break apart, Heather asks, "Lizzie, when?"

"Last year. After that little boy died. You remember—"

Heather covers her mouth with her hand, but she doesn't berate her best friend for concealing the truth for a year and some change.

"It's why I tried so hard to warn you against sleeping with Collie," she explains. "God, I've felt so guilty. So you slept with him after the homecoming dance?"

Heather shuts her eyes to answer. "He'd been acting so strange. So I thought, well, I thought if we did it, finally, after all this time of waiting, everything would be . . . okay again, you know. But then, right after, he told me I wasn't his first. That this summer he'd slept with . . . with some girl."

"Honey, I'm so sorry." Liz strokes Heather's back.

It shocks me to find myself in this new hug-and-share friend mode with Heather and Liz.

But they don't ask about my sex life, and I don't volunteer. Let them keep their assumptions.

"Oh, Lex; you must think we're awful," Liz says. "That I'm such a hypocrite."

"No," I say. *She's* not the hypocrite.

"We're stupid. That's what we are," Heather says.

"No, *not* stupid. Just normal. Unfortunately, lots of girls sleep with guys and wish they hadn't," I say. It is unfortunate, but at least it's their choice, not something they were forced to do.

"True, and it sucks. Royally sucks. I'm glad you're smarter than us," Heather says.

Yeah. These lies, while they are too easy to tell, are hard to live with. "I don't have a boyfriend," I say, "so I'm not dealing with the same pressures."

"But you will. Hayden starts *singing* to you in person, instead of writing on your desk, then it might be you crying in the fort," Heather says. "If you aren't careful."

I prefer to do my crying in the closet. "Not to worry, *Hayden's* not singing to me."

"Look, Lex, I really think he is. The Captain, I mean. Maybe you just need to come right out and ask him."

Liz scrubs at her mascara with the inside of her T-shirt. It looks like black watercolor on her pale cheeks. She says,

"Uh-*uh*, Heather, she can't do that. It's not romantic enough. We might've had jocks without a romantic bone in their bodies, but they weren't the Captain. If Hayden *is*, then it's one of those truths she just has to discover."

"And how would I do that?"

Heather looks at Liz like this is a no-brainer. "We could plan something. A meet or something."

"*Party*," Liz corrects. "Let's make it a party."

"I hate parties," I say, and shudder at the thought of the one in July.

"But you couldn't hate a costume party," Liz says, and she's on a roll. "Halloween is around the corner."

"Oh, *yeah*," Heather adds, getting onboard.

Evidently, the gestation period for a bad idea is about ten seconds. As soon as a glimmer is conceived, it's a full-grown, star-crossed-lover-and-costume-magic *plan*. My head is still turning side to side, saying no, but they don't seem to notice. Or care.

A noise. A crunching noise. In the distance.

I put a finger over my lips to shush Heather and Liz. And listen.

Another crunching noise.

Something or someone is nearby. Betrayed by dead leaves that crackle in the silence. And sound too loud for an animal.

Careful not to make a noise, I dim the lantern nearest me and stand to one side of the window to peer out. It could be

Bodee, but I don't tell Heather and Liz that.

Then I hear a giggle.

Bodee doesn't giggle.

Heather scoots closer to Liz. "What is it?" she whispers.

"Someone's out there."

When I'm quiet, totally quiet, I hear everything in the woods. Even something that's usually inaudible, I notice. Like soil as it crumbles under a shoe. But I can barely hear anything now except Heather's raspy breathing.

"Shhh," I whisper, flapping my hand at them.

Heather and Liz pull Bodee's sleeping bag up to their chins. "It's okay," I tell them, but they don't buy it until we hear a slightly intoxicated, masculine voice.

"Oh, fair *Juliets* . . ."—giggle—"come down. Your Romeos *await*."

More giggles.

"That's Collie," Heather and Liz say together.

"I swear to God, if they were listening," Heather says.

Oh, *no*. This cannot be good. The guys, the *sex* guys, have invaded.

I grab the lantern and Liz takes Bodee's sleeping bag, as we scramble, hand-under-hand, following Heather to the ground. Lifting the lantern for a better look, I see four familiar faces. One with a beaming smile, and two who look fairly nervous. Hayden, Ray, and Collie. And a half step behind the Rickman High "offensive" line, Bodee stands; his face is unreadable as he looks at me.

Like a face-off, with the three of us lined up at the foot of the ladder.

"And how are you ladies this fine fall evening?" Hayden asks in a ridiculously jovial tone.

"We were good," I say, when Heather and Liz are silent. *Were.*

"What are y'all doing out here?" Liz asks, cutting to the chase, and I can see she is more uncomfortable than excited.

"Our ladies . . . ," Collie says.

"That's *ex*-ladies," I say.

"Our *ladies*," Hayden continues Collie's sentence, and even in the minimal light and shadows, I can see the grin, "were hosting a campout, and we wanted to . . . make sure you were all safe."

Safe. Right.

From what I can see, Collie's blood alcohol level might be off the charts, the way it has been since Heather broke it off.

Why is Bodee with this group?

"We're fine," I say.

"We're not," Collie says. "We got"—giggle—"lost."

Hayden looks at me as if he can use a little help controlling his drunken buddy. "Look, Lex, can we stay awhile?" He jerks a thumb at Collie, who is swaying on his feet. "He hasn't shut up about Heather and the fort since he found out from Ray that you girls were camping tonight."

"Well, um," I say, but Hayden's already got his foot on the ladder, leading the way.

Ray is on his heels, and Liz looks at me with a shrug, as if we may as well just endure this little raid. I stand there like a chopped-off pine while Heather and Liz head toward the ladder after them.

"Will you make sure they don't tear the place down?" I ask Bodee, since Hayden's already hanging half out of the window, and Ray's howling at the moon like a wolf.

Under his breath, Bodee says, "Sorry. It was a keep-your-enemies-closer thing."

This leaves Collie, the lantern, and me still on the ground. I'm not sure what to do about Collie, who is in no condition to climb twenty feet.

In an alcohol-induced haze, he stumbles toward the ladder, tripping over his feet. Before I can get out of his way, all six-feet-two, 195 pounds of him crashes into me. The lantern flies from my hand, and off balance, I slam into the ground.

His body, like a dead weight, falls on top of me, pressing me down, choking the breath out of me. I am crushed and blinded by Collie and the dark shadows cast by the fort. Every part of him touches me. Accidentally, and then with purpose. His hands, his hot breath, his lips against my neck . . . I am frozen. A scream catches in my windpipe and has no release.

I have no voice.

"Heather," Collie mumbles. "I *love* you," he says, and starts kissing me. *"Heather."*

I'm dimly aware of raised voices as the lantern from upstairs casts a dim glow on our entwined limbs.

The sound of Heather's name frees me from my panic.

"*I'm not Heather*," I whimper, struggling to push Collie away. He rolls off me as the rest of them reach the ground, scrambling like firemen on their way to a blaze.

Collie shakes his head to clear it, and looks from me to Heather, who's standing stiffly by the ladder, hands on her hips. And realizes his mistake.

"Baby"—he's still on his knees—"thought she was you. I thought she was *you*." He blinks at Heather's stormy face. "Love you. Came to tell you I *love* you," he pleads.

"He did," Ray agrees.

I struggle to a sitting position, elbows on my knees, while I hold back a fountain of tears. *Crack. Crack. Crack.* Bodee's cracking his knuckles to keep from slamming his fists into Collie's face. He steps forward and helps me up.

"I'm okay," I tell him. "He just tripped and fell on me."

"With his damn lips?" Heather spits out the words.

I can't tell who Heather's accusing. Collie. Or me.

"Heather, he's pretty drunk," Liz says. "And in the dark, you and Lexi sort of favor each other."

Heather glares at me. Definitely, a *glare*. "We don't," she says, "look *that* much alike."

But Collie's nodding his head like an idiot.

"Hey, now wait a minute!" Hayden's voice interrupts the escalating tension. "We came out here so he could apologize, not make things worse. Just because the dumb-ass can't stay on his feet and tell the difference between you two when he's drunk, well, that doesn't mean things have to get complicated. If anybody should be mad, it's me. None of y'all are even going out right now."

"Neither are we," I mumble.

I feel Bodee's reaction, every flexed muscle, and wonder what he's thinking.

"I'm the one who's going to complicate things," a new voice booms across the clearing. "Get over here, all of you," he shouts at the boys. "You three. Out here. Right. NOW."

"*Coach*," all three football players yelp at the same time.

chapter 20

CRAIG still has on his Rickman pullover and khakis from the game. I've seen him dressed this way more times than I can count, but I've never quite seen this expression. Anger and sympathy for his players, neither emotion trumping the other.

"Coach," Ray says. "We were just—"

"Leaving," Craig says for them.

"But Coach, *you* got a girl," Hayden says.

And Collie whines, "You know what it's like when you screw up."

Does he ever, I think. Craig is so acquainted with the doghouse, he's added a second floor to make the place more comfortable.

"Yeah." Craig repositions his visor so it shadows his eyes and walks close enough to Collie to grip his shoulder. "And

I also know intoxication at one in the morning isn't a good way to fix it."

Hayden. Ray. Collie. Craig. The four of them together in a perfect little line. The sight causes me to sway. Bodee's hand is an anchor. He finds my elbow in the dark, as an undertow of fear threatens to rip my legs out from under me. All my anxieties, all my silence, all my secrets are standing right there in that line of men.

Craig's saying something, but I don't hear him at first. Bodee squeezes my elbow, and I try to focus.

"Lex, you okay?" Craig's asking.

But my head pounds and my lungs burn from holding everything inside. I manage a nod.

"Mr. Tanner, I'll take care of everything here," Bodee says.

Craig must have agreed, because he marches the boys away from our clearing in single-file silence. There's no vent, but I start to count. One, two, three, four, and repeating again, until I can't see them anymore. They're gone, but I can still feel him, the *ghost* of him, pressing his body over mine, apologizing while he kisses me, crying while he thrusts.

Bodee releases my elbow as Liz comes to check on me. I dust off my jeans so I don't have to look at her. Instead, my eyes follow Heather back up the ladder. Though she's using my sanctuary, right this minute she hates me.

She can't hate me worse than I hate myself.

You let him. You let him. *You let him.*

Liz takes my hand; the compulsive dusting off my jeans and the *You let him* fade.

She removes a leaf from my hair and tucks the loose strand behind my ears. Quietly she asks, "What really happened with Collie?"

I untuck the hair immediately, covering my neck with my palm, although there is no way she can make out scratches in the dark. "Nothing, Liz. He tripped and fell on me. Then he called me Heather and kissed me." My answer is mechanical.

"Are you hurt?"

YES, my heart shouts.

"No," I say, and turn away from her.

"But you're still upset," Liz says. "Collie's not exactly small."

"I'm fine. But Heather's not. You should check on her," I say.

The working of Liz's brain is so visible, it's as if I can clearly see the gears grind into understanding: Something happened. Not what we think. But Alexi can't talk about it now.

"I'll explain it to her; don't worry, Lex. Why don't you let Bodee take you home?" she suggests.

"You still want to stay out here?" I ask. "By yourself?"

Liz hands Bodee his sleeping bag. "Yeah. I think she'll need to talk about all this. Don't worry," she says again.

Bodee nods for both of us, and Liz climbs back up the ladder.

"Follow me," he says.

And I do. The path he takes does not lead to my house.

There is the heat of Bodee's body and his fingers curling around my icy ones. I don't remember taking his hand or him taking mine, only that it feels good and safe and right. He knows where we're going, and each step is deliberate. My numbness ekes away. The ice that's been packed around my heart since July starts to melt as Bodee's warmth cauterizes the wounds.

"It was . . . one of them," I say.

"I know."

I'm thankful he doesn't ask which one, because those words are stuck in my throat. By the time he stops, my eyes have adjusted to the dark well enough to see the dome shape of his tent.

His fort on the ground.

Bodee unzips the flap and guides me inside. "You're cold," he says, tucking the sleeping bag around my shoulders. "Now tell me what he did to you."

He just waits for me to speak. And I can.

"It was a couple of weeks before school started, and everybody got together at my house after the has-beens game, as Craig called it. It was just a normal, fun, summer night; a moment between sophomore and junior year where you really feel you're different and grown-up. Closer to becoming a senior. Closer to feeling like real life is happening. You know?"

Bodee nods.

"God, it was hot; and the pool felt amazing, and we were all laughing and yelling. Of course, some of the guys had alcohol, but little enough that my parents couldn't see the difference between crazy, hyped-up teenagers and intoxicated ones."

"I remember how hot it was that night." Bodee touches the wall of the tent. "I didn't even set this up. Just slept outside. Go on," he says softly.

"All the guys were diving. We hadn't heard yet that Ray's injury during the game was bad enough to keep him out the whole season. I remember Liz sat watching her phone instead of swimming, waiting to hear. We were listening to some dance music, and the guys lowered the water in the pool by a foot doing cannonballs. I thought everyone was having a good time."

"Sounds fun," Bodee says.

"It was. Except over in the glider, Heather and Collie started arguing. And then Kayla got miffed at Craig, because he was spending time with the guys after the game instead of her. I didn't know their lives were falling apart; I was just thinking that Dane had been awfully flirty with me and wondering what that meant."

"You liked Dane?" Bodee asks.

"I liked the idea of him. At the time," I say.

"Then almost at the same time, Heather slaps Collie, and there's this huge scene. And then *Kayla* starts yelling at Craig, and she drives off in a huff to some girl's house for the night. Craig is pissed, super pissed, that Kayla broke up with him in front of his guys, and Heather tells everyone she never wants to speak to Collie again. Selfish *asshole*, she calls him; and *she* leaves. That kills the party. Kills it. And then before I know it . . ."

"You're alone with a rapi—," Bodee says, after I can't finish the sentence.

"Yes." I cut him off before he can finish the *R* word. "Mom and Dad had gone on to bed because Kayla and Craig were there." Bodee can't see my eyes, or the tears that don't fall, but he puts an arm around my shoulders.

"But we'd been alone tons of times. He was hurting, and I hated to see him hurt like that. So I pulled up a chair next to his. We talked about the game, and girls, and why girls are so complicated and guys are so simple. And I said she'd forgive him."

"Did you believe it?"

"She always had before," I say. "But *he* didn't think so. 'This is the end. The real end,' he said over and over. And he was so upset. I couldn't convince him."

As I talk and remember his words and his rawness, the gap between the story I'm telling and the story I lived narrows. "He stands up behind me, and I hear the metal legs of the chair scrape on the concrete, and then he's gripping my shoulders, massaging them. The music is still on. "

"Did that worry you?" Bodee asks.

"No. We were comfortable with each other. Honestly, I didn't think much about it."

Not at first.

I remember his strong, tense hands gripping my shoulders, and the memory pulls me back into the smell and feel of July. He's kneading my muscles and dipping lower. Lower than is comfortable for me, but he's not thinking of me. He's just distracted from the pain of losing her, and I don't tell him it hurts a little.

But then his hands aren't just on my shoulders.

"He started touching me. Lower. Not my shoulders. And then he pulled me out of my chair," I say. Beside me, Bodee twitches, and I'm conscious of his tension.

That night I feel *his* tension. Shock holds me in place, and I don't move away. I'm still wet from my last dip in the pool; my hair sprays droplets of water, my feet leave wet footprints as he spins me around to face him.

"'You look alike,' he tells me. I tell him my hair's longer than hers. That she's prettier."

"Can't be," Bodee says.

"It's all so weird, so impossible, I can't speak when he touches me. We've always been friends. Always." Past and present blur as I say, "But tonight he can't wait to be okay; he kisses me. My neck. My cheeks. My mouth. I struggle a little and try to say she'll come back, but I can't."

"She didn't come back," Bodee says.

"Not that night," I say.

Not when he guides me to the back corner of the deck. Not when he slips my one-piece down and lays me back.

And I let him. Allowed him. We weren't drunk, and I didn't

want him. So why? That question won't go away.

Bodee squeezes my hand and lets me know I can finish. And I want to. This telling—every word of it—is like tearing a strip of duct tape from my skin. "When I hear him rip the plastic of the condom wrapper, that's when I'm aware, that's when I really understand what he wants." The tears I've tried so hard to hold back flood my cheeks. "I'm not that girl, but I can't tell him no. The why of it doesn't make sense now, but I couldn't. I just couldn't stop him. And I hate that I didn't. Bodee, I let him."

"Lex, this is not your fault. He took advantage of you, of your vulnerability."

"I appreciate you . . . defending me, but . . . I was there."

And I'm there again. This is the reality of my world: the scent, the tearing cellophane, the snap as the condom stretches into 3-D protection. Not bought for me; not *meant* for me, but at that moment it doesn't matter to him. His eyes are closed, his breath is in my face, his arms strain to hold his weight, and he forces himself inside me.

And he doesn't fit. Even after he moves, he doesn't fit.

"Sex hurts," I say to Bodee. "I hated it. Hated it even more that it meant nothing. *Nothing*. And I . . . cried."

"Did he not even *look* at you?" Bodee asks, and I know my pain is mirrored on his face.

"No. He's crying too, saying he's sorry and that I'm beautiful. And I don't know if it's for him . . . or because of her. But his eyes are closed, and he doesn't stop pushing or . . ."

The noises *he* makes can't rival the ones I keep inside me. The outraged consonants and guttural screams, like dueling lions clawing and clashing in my throat.

"Lex, you can let it out. Let it go." Bodee buries my face in his chest. "Say the words," he says.

"It hurts."

"Not those words. Tell me what he did to you."

"He hurt me," I say again.

Bodee holds me tighter, his breastbone firm against my jaw. "What did he do to you, Lex?"

These words are a peep of a peep. "He raped me."

"What?"

"He raped me." These words are less peep, more whisper.

"What? Say it, Lex. Stop blaming yourself. Blame *him*. *SAY* it."

"HE RAPED ME!" I scream. And scream and scream. Bodee muffles my cries into the plaid of his shirt; and lets me sob and clench my fists. And he holds me as I hit and hit until my muscles ache; until I am quiet and limp and out of tears.

And the dueling lions are silent.

chapter 21

THE plaid of Bodee's shirt is wet, but softer because of it.

He doesn't shush me or say I'm okay. He knows I'm not. There's none of the pacifying I feared. Bodee is all arms and heartbeat. All unflustered feelings and fail-safe strength. A kiss breezes the top of my head, but he's so gentle. As if no part of him would steal my security. Ever.

"You're safe now. You're safe," he murmurs, stroking my face.

I sag and curl up, and my cheek rests on the rough texture of the tent floor. Bodee lays a hand on my hair and remains upright.

"Will you hold me?" I ask.

Bodee moves to his knees and reaches across me. A flashlight blazes orange as he cups it in his palm. Slowly, he lets the light grow until our eyes adjust. Then he says, "Lex, look at me."

He palms my face, a bare touch of hands. His eyes wait for mine to meet his, and then he asks, "Who am I?"

"Bodee," I answer.

"Okay, then. Remember who I am. I'm going to hold you now," he warns.

And he does. The sleeping bag cuddles us closer when he pulls it up around us. My back rests against his chest, and he is careful to position his arm around me in such a way that I can feel his warmth but am not threatened.

Tonight, there's no oyster; he is all pearl.

We stay this way, awake and quiet and warm and relaxed, until dawn cracks the horizon and filters through the tent in a light blue.

"Guess you'd better head back before they do," Bodee whispers.

"They aren't up yet," I say with certainty.

Carefully, I roll over and face him. We are burritoed in the sleeping bag, me against the zipper and Bodee against the seam. I know my breath is rank, and my mouth tastes like day-old pepperoni pizza. His mouth is closed, so maybe he's thinking about what he had to eat last night too.

This close, every line of his face is mine to peruse. The blond facial hair that's a little bristly and barely shows on his strong jaw. Curly eyelashes and red-tinted hair. His roots are visible, and I can see little-kid-at-the-beach blond at his temples.

Vibrant eyes, chocolate brown, kind.

The mosaic of Bodee Lennox.

But in this early light filtering through the aqua tent, what does he see in me? Boring light-brown hair, wild and messy at this hour. Raccoon circles beneath my eyes, worsened by running mascara. Cracked lips.

A night of tears and emotional baggage visible in my face.

I am just the broken girl Bodee held through the night. In the tent that used to be his bedroom. The rape has devastated places in me that even Bodee's magic can't fix. If he were to put his heart in my hand, he might never find it again. And I'm not cruel enough to let him break while he tries to heal the impossible.

"Where's your mind?" he asks.

But I can't tell him that. "I guess, Captain Lyric. I want to know who he is."

"And if he's Hayden?" Bodee asks in guard-dog mode.

"I don't know. I've got a lot of stupid in me. Maybe I should give him another chance." This is a "signal" sentence. The type of sentence a girl says to a boy in order to create distance between them; a way to send the message about where she thinks the relationship is going. We have to be the couple who shared a sleeping bag, but not a kiss.

The side of Bodee's mouth twitches, and beneath the down fabric, I hear his knuckles crack.

"I have to know. Hayden's not *him*, is he?"

My rapist, he means. "No, it's not Hayden."

Relief dawns, but he closes his eyes as he follows up. "And he wasn't hurting you the night of the dance, was he?"

"No. But *I* hurt me by not telling him to stop."

"Why didn't you?"

"That's the thing. It was like the pool all over again, like a flashback. I wanted Hayden to stop, but I couldn't say the words."

Bodee puts a finger over my lips as more explanations tumble out. "You don't have to say more; I only need to know it wasn't him."

"Heather sort of likes you," I say, changing the subject.

Bodee withdraws his hand and says dismissively, "That's nice."

"She'll take Collie back, so . . . be careful."

"Thanks, Lex, but my sights aren't on Heather."

"You have sights?"

"Every guy with a heartbeat has sights," he says.

"Who's in yours?" My heartbeat betrays my calm voice, and this close, I know Bodee can feel it spike.

"Well, now"—he flashes me the coy grin that I love and rarely see—"you have your secrets, and I have mine."

I figure since we're sharing the same sleeping bag, we're close enough for me to press him for information. "Do I know her?"

"Not yet," he says.

Biting back a sour taste, I say, "Will I ever?"

"I think so," he says.

It's six fifteen, I realize, as I check my watch, squirming and fidgeting to have something else to look at besides him. Now I know he likes someone. "I better go," I tell him.

"Let me unzip us," he says. "Scoot toward me."

I wiggle closer, and he toggles the zipper behind me. It slides down and cool air hits my back. Inches from his heart, from his mouth. I feel his breath near my ear.

"Uh, Lex, forgive me if . . . I shouldn't ask, but may I . . ." He hesitates, then says, "May I kiss you? Before you go off chasing the Captain," he adds.

Now my heart's at jackhammer speed.

"Before Heather starts chasing you?" I ask, and nod. Saying yes. Because he's Bodee enough to give me the chance to decide.

And because there are few things I'd rather do more than kiss Bodee Lennox right now. To find out if what I feel when he kisses me is the same as how I feel when his hand is in mine. I can put the distance back between us, I tell myself, just as soon as we're out of the tent.

"Um, I've never kissed anyone before," he says.

"Well, just so you know, girls don't usually taste like day-old pizza," I say.

"Oh, and guys don't always taste like bologna sandwiches."

We both laugh a little, then tilt our chins until our lips meet. I lead, he follows. Which has never happened before. It doesn't last long. And it's definitely his first kiss.

But not many first kisses can be this sweet.

"We . . . we can't do that again," I say when we break apart.

"Of course not," he says, and for the first time, I think Bodee is lying to me.

There is a pause as we stare at each other.

"See you at the house," I say, and back out of the sleeping bag and crawl from the tent. I zip up the flap, leaving Bodee in his paradise.

Even though I'm familiar with the woods, I am not sure what direction the fort is from the tent until I reach the creek. Following along the bank, I cry a little and tell myself it's just one kiss and I can't be sorry. I *won't* be sorry.

But the facts are simple.

I am broken and Bodee knows, because I haven't hidden it from him.

I'm not sorry he knows.

I want him, but I can't have him. Not because he's not right for me, but because I can't expose him to any more of my baggage. He deserves so much more.

And, anyway, he says there's some other girl in his sights.

I will pursue the Captain and move on. And Bodee will too.

The girls are zipped in their bags—a pile of down in the middle of the fort. They don't hear me climb the steps or pad across to the little table. Using gummy bears, I spell out *I'm sorry* on the floor by their overnight bags. If I hear from Heather before Monday morning, I'll know Liz convinced her that what happened with Collie was a fluke. If Heather's still in a pissy mood, which usually lasts several days, I'll ask Mom for a ride.

By the end of the weekend, Liz has checked on me and Hayden's left ten messages on my phone. Before he can send the eleventh, I text him a thank-you for the flowers. This starts a conversation and a loosening of the vise grip around my heart toward him. Better to be more open to him or I'll end up wanting to kiss Bodee every night.

U forgive me? Hayden texts.

Will u stop partying?

I'll try, he responds.

See u on Monday.

By the front door, he says.

I don't text him back, and he doesn't text me.

When I ask Mom to drop us at school, she pats my shoulder and says, "You and Heather have a tiff?"

"Something like that," I answer.

Heather's car horn is more the sound of school than the bell. I miss it on this rainy Monday, the way I'd miss the Kool-Aid if Bodee's hair wasn't blackberry today.

"Drama girls. Bodee, don't you let them get to you," Mom says as she gathers a stack of picture books, her glasses, and a bottle of water.

"No, ma'am."

In the car, Mom quizzes me about the campout and the flowers, something she would have done Saturday night or Sunday lunch if she and Dad hadn't gone on an overnight event with their church group. I leave out some details: the desk mystery, the guys' arrival, Heather's anger, the, er, *sleeping* arrangements.

"Craig said while y'all were camping out, his boys played a terrible game against Saint X."

"That's what I heard."

"Shame to break their streak. Thought they might have a perfect year."

"Too late for that," I say. I'm not talking about football.

The circle drive at school is congested, so Bodee and I climb out across the street and walk.

"She talks a lot," Bodee says.

"You think?" I joke. Mom never met a stranger.

"I like it," he says. "I like *her*."

I know he's remembering his mother. I want to take his hand, but Hayden appears. I have to remember Hayden, not Bodee. I'm not hurting Bodee.

"Walk you to homeroom?" Hayden asks.

"Um," I say, hesitating. "Sure." And decide not to go to my locker. No need to flaunt him in front of Bodee.

Heather is not in fourth period, and I'm sure she's not spying on the Captain this time. No more need for that, according to her. The desk, blank, as it typically is on Monday, takes most of my worksheet time to complete. Even though Heather is convinced Hayden is Captain Lyric, I don't have him in mind when I pencil in these words:

> There's a house in the trees
> There's a tent on the ground
> These are the safe places
> Where I lay myself down

Heather's a no-show at lunch, and I wonder if she even made it to school today. Liz is sitting with a freshman from the Science Club, but she waves at me across the lunchroom.

Hayden is there, waiting to capitalize on the absence of my friends.

"Wanna eat outside? It's not too cold today." He points to a table outside the window, where a group of art students usually congregates.

"Sure."

"You a fan of one-word answers?" he teases as he snags us both some pizza.

"Nah," I reply, and get a laugh.

He chatters in a constant stream, mostly about football, until we walk to fifth period. Of course, he moves into Maggie's seat behind me, and Maggie takes another desk across the room. She gives me a discreet thumbs-up.

Which only reminds me of Bodee.

After school, Hayden offers us both a ride home, but I turn him down and wait for Bodee by the planter.

"Eventful day?" he asks, and slings his pack onto his back.

"Not really. For you?"

Rumbling thunder interrupts his answer. We both look at the sky. Lightning. Rain, the gully-washing kind, is less than a mile away. We're going to get a bath before we make it home.

"No. Just long," he says as the first drop of rain plops on my head.

"Which class do you have with your girl?"

The sky opens up and he says, "Fourth."

While I'm reading and writing lyrics, Bodee's checking out some girl. It's okay. *It's okay,* I tell myself. We kissed once, but I resolve to be happy. For him to be happy.

But the rain echoes my mood. A downpour of gray emotions. Bodee walks close to me, and I wish us back in the Malibu, to the time before I knew Bodee had his *sights* on someone else.

I don't hear the truck slow down until it's rolling along beside us at five miles an hour, kicking up a small puddle that sprays the sidewalk.

"Hey, hop in," Craig yells across the front seat through the lowering window.

Bodee opens the truck door, which almost gets away from him in the wind, and I slide onto the bench next to Craig.

We're already dripping. My jeans are plastered to my legs, and my hair is slicked back from my face.

"Thanks," I say, and dry my hands on the cloth bench.

"Yeah, thanks, Mr. Tanner," Bodee echoes.

"No problem. I need to talk to Alexi anyway."

Bodee's thumb presses my thigh where Craig can't see. Does he think being alone with any guy but him makes me nervous? Probably, since I know he likes Craig. His thumb stays glued to me until we're in the driveway, and Craig makes it clear he's waiting for Bodee to exit the truck. And leave he does, but he goes only as far as the front porch.

I slide over against the passenger door. "Please don't start with me about the boys," I say, anticipating a discussion about the campout. "I didn't know they were coming."

Craig swivels the dial on the radio until the only thing we hear is the rain on the cab roof. I look toward the porch; my breath fogs a small square on the window that I dot the center of with my nose.

"It's not about the boys. They celebrate and commiserate too much, but they're pretty good kids."

"Oh." This makes me nervous. Craig and I haven't *talk*-talked in a long time. It always makes Kayla jealous when anyone else besides her gets face-to-face time with her man. Even her little sister. *Especially* her little sister.

"This is about the wedding."

"What about it?" I snap.

"Talk to Kayla. Please!"

"Look, Craig, I love Kayla, but I'm not playing her games anymore. I know you love her, but she needs to grow up."

"Maybe," he concedes. "But Lex, she wants you to be in our wedding. That's not really too much to ask, is it?"

Oh, yes. It definitely *is*.

"She better get over it," I say. "Mom and Dad have already said they'll honor my decision."

"Please, Lex. Even if you won't do it for her, will you do it for me?"

"What did you say?"

"Will you do it for me? For your *best* buddy's sake? Come on, say you will, Lex."

I can't look at him. He'll see the knowledge in my eyes.

This phrase. *Will you do it for me?* I've heard it before. Years ago. In the den. And the *best buddy* is what seals my memory. Swiping my hand across the fog cloud on the glass, I stall and try to decide what to do.

Craig's hand finds the back of my head. He touches my hair. My eyes stare at the glove box. And see nothing.

Oh God. I am still. Completely.

Slowly, he parts the dark strands until my hair is divided on my shoulders. What is he thinking while his eyes bore through the back of my head?

"Lex, my God, what's *happened* to your neck?"

chapter 22

SCRAMBLING away from Craig, I throw myself out of the cab and run. Rain thwacks at me, every drop an icy sting. As if God is playing paintball with crystal bullets.

But it's remembering that sends me flying to Bodee.

Bodee meets me halfway to the porch. He umbrellas his shirt over me and doesn't ask questions.

"I know *why*, Bodee. Why I didn't stop him." I gasp out the words.

"Fort," he says.

I don't have breath to say yes or no, but we race toward the woods like a pair of figure skaters who perform together so often that they move in perfect union. We have to slow down once we're under the trees. The path is sloppy, and mud kicks up as we run slapdash toward the creek. Wet leaves stick to my shoes, and I slide. Bodee keeps us upright; not that his traction is better than mine, but because it's what he does. He planks the creek with the board, and tests his weight and balance against the slickness of the wood. Always checking, always careful. And protective. If I'd befriended Bodee years ago, maybe I would have found my voice. Maybe I'd be with him now as his girl, instead of his patient. He holds my hand as we cross the narrow ribbon of raging creek, and he doesn't release it until we reach the fort's ladder.

"What happened?" he asks, after we climb to the top.

There are gummy bears and ants on the table. I stare at them and squeeze the water from my hair.

"What happened?" he repeats. His hair is dripping black-berry rain.

"Craig begged me to change my mind about being in the wedding. And he said, 'Will you do it for me?'"

Bodee watches my face. "And?"

"Oh God, it was years ago. I was probably six years old. Or seven. No, I must have been six because Craig started really hanging out with us after Granddad died. Anyway, Craig and Kayla were babysitting me. They did that on the nights Mom and Dad had meetings at church."

"My mom went to that some," Bodee says.

"I was already in bed after juice and my story. I always made Craig read 'just *one* more.' He had the best voices. That night he read *Mrs. Frisby and the Rats of NIMH*, and we were almost to the part where Mrs. Frisby goes to the rosebush to meet the rats. Have you read it?" I ask.

Bodee shakes his head.

"Anyway, I couldn't fall asleep because Dad had a pot of those miniature roses in the den. And I got it in my head that *we* had a Nicodemus—that's the head rat—living in Dad's little rosebush. I had to check."

As I pause at the stupidity of this idea from an adult perspective, Bodee helps me pull off my soaked hoodie and hangs it on a peg.

"But when I got to the den"—I cover my eyes as if this will stop the image from coming—"Kayla and Craig were on the couch. And Kayla was on top . . . I thought she was *hurting* him. You know? I was just six."

I don't say that Kayla came up off the couch naked when I screamed.

"What did she do?"

"They both scrambled for their clothes. Then she grabbed me and yelled that if I *told*, Mom and Dad would make Craig go away. He'd *never* read me stories or take me to Chuck E. Cheese's or watch the Ewoks with me again. He'd go and never come back."

"You really cared about him."

"More than Kayla," I admit. "I cried that Mom and Dad loved Craig and they were good and they didn't make people go away. But she said *this* was different."

"And it probably would have been. How old was Kayla?"

"She's eight years older than me, so fourteen. Too young

for that," I agree. "She pinned me in the chair, the ugly blue one in the corner, and I said Mom and Dad would probably get rid of her and keep Craig. She smacked me and I cried, but she didn't care. She forced me to look at Craig and said, 'You will never, ever, *ever* see him again if you tell Mom and Dad what you saw. When they ask you tomorrow about tonight, you say we read you a story and you went to sleep. And that's *all*.'"

I'm shivering from the memory. And the rain. And Bodee looks lost as to how to help me.

"Craig took me from Kayla, held me and wiped the tears from my face and told me he was my buddy. *Best* buddy, I said, and we did our special high five." I show Bodee the behind the back, spinning high five Craig taught me to do. "So he asked me if I wanted to keep hanging out with him."

"Of course you said yes."

"Of course." In my memory, Craig was smiling the whole time. Now, I realize he was tense and nervous, faking calm. "He said it was okay, but we needed to keep what I saw a secret. That best buddies keep each other's secrets."

I hear my six-year-old voice say, "They do?" and sixteen-year-old Craig repeat, "They do."

Bodee's head flops backward instead of its usual forward, and he sighs.

"'You just need to forget, Lexi. Not for Kayla, but will you do it for me? For your best buddy?'" I say in Craig's voice.

"Yea-uh," I told him then, not realizing I'd actually forget. That I'd bury it until Craig himself excavated the truth today.

"They made me repeat what they told me to say. *Good,* they said, and then Craig read to me until I went to sleep."

"Not good," Bodee says.

"No. They taught me to lie. Taught me to forget. And this summer, when Craig . . . when he led me to the back corner of the pool, I was still thinking what he taught me to think. That best buddies keep each other's secrets."

chapter 23

BODEE breathes. Breathes again. All while I hold my breath.

"Mr. Tanner?" he says through his fingers. "It was Mr. *Tanner?*"

I hear the total shock in Bodee's voice, and I realize the truth is out there and there's no calling it back.

Bodee knows. *He knows.*

That terrifies me, but mostly because it's no longer all mine. Not within my control anymore. My hands are on my neck, scratching and tearing and ripping, even before I know they aren't in my pockets.

"Lex, stop. *Stop.*"

But I don't.

Skin wedges under my nails on the first dig—microscopic particles and blood—as easy as raking them in sand. I go for round two and scrape more skin, and I'm frantic. I'm tearing and bleeding. Faster and faster in a rage, where Bodee's voice can't reach me.

I struggle and flail and fight him, desperate to contain my secret, to go backward in time. Where I haven't told Bodee about Craig. Haven't tattled on my best buddy.

Rapist.

Craig raped me. He raped me. I scream into the flannel of Bodee's shirt, and I cry and moan and curl into the pain.

I don't want it to be true. I want to count to twenty-three and pretend it never happened and make the shadows go away.

But darkness conquers me.

All this time, I watched him and Kayla and their stupid roller-coaster relationship. Break up. Get back together. Break up. Get engaged. They always ended up together. Always. Like Craig was already family. Unavoidable. Permanent. So I made excuses and tried to put it out of my mind. But it happened. It's real. Like my heartbeat. Like breathing. Like Bodee's knowledge of it now.

Oh God, if I could only take those words back.

It was *my* secret. *Mine.*

But it's ours now.

And Bodee holds me. He's panting, too, trying to stay calm and calm me at the same time. But I hear it in his voice, his soothing, comforting voice, long before I hear the words. This knowledge—the *who*—surprises him the way it still surprises me.

"I thought it was Collie."

"It's Craig," I cry.

"And that's why you wouldn't tell. He's been your buddy."

"My *best* buddy." I sound as if I'm six, and for the moment I am. "He didn't mean to hurt me. He's not like your dad." I stop fighting. "I can't ruin his life."

"But you're letting him ruin yours."

At least we agree it's ruined.

Since it happened, I've lived a phantom life. Like an amputee patient who can still feel the missing limb where there is only a nub. I am a nub, and Bodee and high school and the Captain and Sunday dinner are only phantoms.

I try to scratch again, but Bodee is stronger.

"You may think Craig is a good guy," he says.

The fact that he no longer says *Mr. Tanner* isn't lost on me.

"But that doesn't change the fact that he took advantage of you, *hurt* you. No wonder you couldn't stop him. He's a man. You were only sixteen."

"Fifteen. My birthday's July thirtieth," I say in a daze.

"Exactly. He had no right to do that to you at fifteen or sixteen. Or anytime. To ever put you in a position to have to tell him no. Besides, if he marries Kayla, you can never get away from this."

"But he'll lose his job. Football. Kayla. Everything," I sob.

"That's not your problem, Alexi."

"It is. He's family," I say.

"No. Family is my mom. Your mom and dad. And Kayla.

It is not Craig. Not the guy who raped you."

"The guy who ruined me. That's what you said," I say, turning his words on him. "And if I tell, not only does my family fall apart and Kayla hates me forever and ever, but everyone will know I'm ruined."

"You're not ruined, and Kayla won't hate you. My God, Lexi, he's a *teacher*. What if he does it to some other girl?"

"He won't," I argue. "But you already said it: he's ruined my life. And you obviously don't know Kayla."

"Lex, I'm not saying it wouldn't be tough; I'm saying you can take it. You've already been so brave." He sighs. "I can't undo things you know with . . . Mom"—there's a catch in his voice—"but I can't help them either. Besides, what happened to my family didn't keep you from being my friend. You can move on from this and not let it define you. If you decide to."

"That's what you're doing?"

"Yes. I'm choosing to move forward. To be here with you instead of back there on the porch with a broom in my hands. Helpless."

This is all logical, but I don't want logic. Don't want a survival story that works for someone else. And I could never survive my dad killing my mom like Bodee has; I'd still be in a deep hole.

All I want is to keep life the way it *is*.

Kayla's difficult. Craig's a hero. Mom and Dad are in the dark. And I am a *normal*, untouched virgin. I've kept it that way for three months.

I can keep doing it. And I will unless Bodee talks.

"I can handle this," I tell Bodee.

"Lex, you're ripping the skin off your neck. You're lying to everyone, including yourself. You're *not* handling it. You'll barely even call it what it is. That man *raped* you."

I push my hands, which are still in his grasp, between us and show him the skin under my nails. "I choose this pain over the pain of—"

"*Healing?*"

"You won't tell," I say. I am adamant.

This close, I feel him stiffen with indecision. Betrayal.

I jerk from his hold and put a foot of space between us.

"You will not," I say.

"I'd rather you tell," Bodee says, finally.

"This is exactly why I kept this to myself," I say. "I trusted you."

"You still can."

"No. Not if you're going to tell someone," I say.

"I don't know what I'm going to do, Lex. I didn't think, really didn't think, it could be him. It complicates something that's already complicated."

I know this burden he asked to share is heavier than he realized. He likes Craig too.

Liked.

"You see. That's the way it's been. Every time I think about that night, I blur out his face and wish he was someone else. *Anyone* else. But he isn't. He read me stories and he . . . hurt me."

"What did he say afterward?"

Like it matters. "That he was sorry. That I could understand. That I looked like Kayla looked when he knew for sure she loved him. And he meant it. I felt sorry for him and told him I was fine."

"And he believes you?"

"No. Of course not. I'd bet he's dropped twenty pounds since then. And every time he looks at me, it's there in his eyes. But I know the game. I know he's doing what I'm doing when he looks at me and then whips his head toward Kayla. He's trying to pretend it never happened."

"His regret doesn't change things," Bodee says.

"It does for me."

"Well, it doesn't for me. For God's sake, Lex, he used a condom. There was plenty of time for him to think about what he was doing." The rage that sent Bodee's fist into Hayden's jaw is in his voice. "Oh, I'd like to . . ."

Crack. Crack. Crack.

"What?" I say.

"Hurt him. Punish him. Pay him back."

"You can't," I say, knowing clearly that he can. A mere accusation of this nature is as life-changing as proving it. "And you can't just put your thumb in the air and fix this for me any more than I can bring your mom back."

"I can't just . . ." Bodee rakes a hand through his hair. "I need some time, Lex."

And for the first time since Bodee came, he walks away from me.

Craig and Kayla aren't at dinner that night. I entertain Mom and Dad with made-up stories of a high school that is closer to what they remember than what it's like. School spirit, lunch ladies with hairnets, and too much pepperoni. Even Mrs. Tindell's corrections. Overdoing it, so they'll hear my tone but not look at my eyes. But after a few minutes, thank the good Lord, they are immersed in their own little world of bank loans and elementary students. Bodee says nothing more than "please pass the biscuits" and "thank you, sir."

He hasn't told. They still don't have a clue.

From the moment Mom asked if I'd like sweet tea or lemonade, I could tell. There was no shame when she looked at me. No pity or internal volleying of what do I say and how to say it, the way she always is with Kayla. Mom has a look when she's walking on eggshells; she doesn't have that look tonight.

We all hear Kayla come home. Heck, our next-door neighbors, so far away that I'd have to have an arm like a center fielder to hit their house with a baseball, probably heard Kayla come home.

"The wedding is *off*," she announces defiantly.

Mom stands at this news. "Off?" she asks. "Oh, honey."

Bodee's fork stops midway between his plate and mouth.

"It's not really over," I say to him, rolling my eyes.

"Honey, what happened?" Dad asks.

"He wants to move the wedding back. And do some thinking. *Move it back*," she says indignantly. "We've been together ten years. What else is there to think about?"

"Then . . . he didn't really call it off," Mom says, trying to pacify. "When does he want it to be?"

"Wouldn't say." Kayla twists the brand-new engagement ring off her finger and slams it on the kitchen counter. "He *said* he had some stuff to work through. My God, I've put my whole *life* on hold for him. Didn't go away to college. Stayed at the bank. I didn't even move *out* because of him."

"Honey, Craig will come around. And you've broken up with him at times. This will work itself out."

Dad's reasoning just makes Kayla slam her fist into the counter. The ring bounces at this earthquake.

"You want him to be sure," Mom says.

"He should already be sure."

"With these tantrums? I highly doubt it," I say to Bodee.

Mom shoots daggers in my direction before she asks Kayla, "Do you know what brought this on?"

"I know he talked to Alexi this afternoon." She points at me, and I stop eating. "What did he tell you?" she shouts. "What did you tell him? You did something, didn't you?"

Bodee nudges my foot under the table. How the tip of his sneaker can say *The opportunity is here*, I don't know, but it does. I could tell her, tell them all, and I'd never have to worry again. At least not about Craig. Bodee nudges me again. *Tell them.*

"Nothing. He didn't tell me anything," I say. "I don't know what you're talking about."

Bodee sighs. A deep sigh that we all notice.

"Were you there?" Kayla asks him.

"Yes," Bodee says.

Now I kick Bodee. Does he not read foot language as well as I do?

"It was raining and Craig"—he pauses—"gave us a ride home."

"And that's it?"

"I didn't hear him say much of anything," Bodee says. "But . . ."

"But what?"

"I wasn't there the whole time," he says.

"Lex?" Kayla says. "I wanna know what he said."

"Nothing," I repeat.

"I don't believe you. You're lying. There's always been something between you."

"Honey, there is absolutely nothing between Lex and Craig." Mom's appalled even at the idea; she slams her plate into the sink, and Mom doesn't slam things. "He's ten years older than Alexi. You're being ridiculous."

See, this is what I was talking about, my foot says to Bodee's.

"Kayla, control yourself," my dad says firmly. "Stop blaming your sister. You and Craig will work this out. Or you won't. But that's between the two of you."

"You always take her side," Kayla screams, and runs out of the kitchen, slamming things as she goes. Leaving behind an avalanche of emotions.

"May I be excused?" Bodee asks.

"Of course," Mom says, and looks as if she wishes *she* could be excused. "She needs to move out and grow up," she tells Dad as she clears the table. "I've about had it with her."

I listen as a glass bowl rattles around in the sink, and as my parents take their frustration out on the china instead of on Kayla. When everything is back in its place and the dishwasher is humming, Mom apologizes to me. "I shouldn't have shown my frustration with Kayla to you, Lex. I'm going to go try and fix things with her."

"Let her be," Dad says.

"I can't. She's my baby."

He smiles. "I know." He squeezes Mom's hand before she leaves the kitchen.

Kayla's mad at me. Mom and Dad don't know me. Bodee's hiding in his room, disappointed with me.

So I text Hayden.

R u who I think u r?

Who do u think I am? he texts back.

Someone w the right words, I hint.

Sure hope so, he says.

See u tomorrow.

K.

Retreating to my room, I am surprised to find Bodee there already, doing homework at my table.

"You want me to leave?" he asks.

"No."

We work until Mom comes to the door several hours later. "Oh, hey, Bodee. Y'all working hard?"

"Yes, ma'am."

Her face apologizes. "You mind if I talk to Lex?"

"No, ma'am." As Bodee gathers his books, I wonder if he'll be back, or if we're both upset enough that it's an under-the-bed-instead-of-on-it night.

"You okay?" Mom asks, referring to Kayla's rant.

"She's always mad about something."

"It *is* hard. Craig's been a part of this family for a long time. I'll hate to see him go, and I know you will too. The two of you have always had a special relationship, but Lex, you can't fix this."

"I won't."

"Good. There's no need for you to feel guilty or responsible or to think Craig will listen to you. If they're supposed to be together, then they'll have to learn how to fight."

"You and Dad don't fight."

Mom pats me and tsk-tsks. "Of course we do. We just know that when we do, we still love each other more than we love having our own way. We don't agree on everything."

They probably disagree on vacation destinations or colors for the bathroom remodel, I think, as she leaves the room.

They don't fight over telling her parents she was raped by that guy who's *been a part of this family for a long time.*

Down the hall, Mom's door clicks shut, and I slip up to Bodee's room. There's no proof he's there, but I have a hunch I know where he is. Bending over, I lift the bed skirt.

"Can I join you?" I ask.

He squints against the light. "Sure."

I lie flat and shuffle sideways, my nose just inches from the frame, until I'm hip to hip with Bodee.

"Nice place," I say.

"Thanks."

I angle my head and shoulders toward him, until my cheek is against his shoulder; I am diagonal and he is straight. "What are you thinking about?"

"My mom," he says.

I take his hand.

"I've been wondering what she would tell me to do if she were still alive."

"And?" I ask.

"She'd say to get out from under this hot ol' bed and go sit in Lexi's room until she can fall asleep," he says.

"Wise woman."

"The very best," he says.

And we scoot out of there quicker than I scooted in and follow Bodee's mom's advice.

chapter 24

THE next morning I remember that my cell phone vibrated on the nightstand right before I fell asleep. I ignored it, thinking it was Hayden. But as I check it now, I see it was Heather. She's back from Madsville one day earlier than I predicted.

Pick you up in the a.m.

I choose another outfit I can match a scarf to, strip my bed, and gather the little pile of neck-scratching clothes from the closet. Jamming them in the washer before anyone notices I'm in the laundry room, I pray the blood comes out of the sheets.

"You need a ride?" Mom yells while I'm still putting on makeup.

"No," I yell back.

I add mascara, snatch my book bag from my bedroom, and join Mom and Bodee in the kitchen. "Heather's coming," I say.

Mom breaks the seal on a package of muffins and slides them across the bar toward me. "Crisis over, huh?"

I nod, toss Bodee a muffin, and peel the bottom from mine while Mom waxes on.

"Forty-eight hours. Bodee, just a little fact for you, most things with girls can be fixed in forty-eight hours."

"That's why there's no hope for me and Kayla," I say.

"Alexi," Mom says, her chirpy mood disappearing. "Don't say that."

"Truth. I speak the truth," I say, and toss the muffin paper in the garbage. "Let's go," I say to Bodee before Mom can offer any more commentary.

"How will she be?" Bodee asks as Heather pulls in the drive.

"No idea."

The front seat is empty, and Liz is in the back.

I hear Heather say, "Cold out there, Bodee. You riding with us or not?"

I growl a little as I get in beside Liz. Out of politeness, I hope, Bodee climbs in beside Heather.

And Heather acts fine. Like the campout is forgotten, the seat-switch topic is taboo, and she's got nothing to say about any of the other stuff. And I don't bring them up or mention Collie or the fact that she is actually following through with hitting on Bodee.

Liz throws out a conversational bone. "Mom says we can have the Halloween party at my house. She's already figured out a menu."

"Uh-huh." My eyes are on Heather. I stare with intent at the back of her head and wish I knew steps one through three on how to do a lobotomy. "What"—I mouth and point at Heather—"is she *doing*?"

This begins the dual conversation. The one for the whole car. The one for only the backseat.

"Experimenting," Liz mouths back, then says, "I already have a basic guest list, but I'll need you two to see if I'm leaving anyone out."

"Hurting Collie," I whisper.

"He hurt her. Couldn't reason with her about . . ." She points silently at Bodee and then says, "The decorations are going to be awesome."

"Everything you do is awesome," Heather says. "So, Bodee . . ."

(I hate the way she says his name.)

"Would you wanna go to Liz's party with me?"

"I'm not much of a party guy," he says after a moment.

"That sounds just like something Alexi'd say. *Boring* to stay home all the time. Come on, it's just for one night. We'll have fun."

And if you don't, she'll shift you to the backseat before you can blink.

"When is it?" Bodee asks.

Heather puts the car in park and says, "Next Friday night."

"I'm supposed to visit my brother. Ben."

I hold back a sigh of relief.

"But maybe I can come by after," Bodee adds.

Dull knitting needle. He is supposed to tell her *no*.

"It's not perfect," Heather says, and smacks his thigh. "But it'll do. Maybe I'll color my hair like yours. What color do you think suits me?"

"Cherry might be nice," he says.

"What flavor is this?" She tugs on the little lock of hair behind his ear.

"Tropical Punch."

"We're late," I announce, and vault from the car. I tell myself it's his life. Her life. If they want to have Kool-Aid dates, they can. But *not* at my house.

Hayden's waiting at the door. "Guy with the right words at your service."

"Sounds good," I say, and wish I meant it.

He smiles, and I spread one on too, but I don't forget Bodee said yes to Heather.

And I keep not forgetting about it. When he sits in my room at night. Or when we stick to the agreement not to kiss again. Or when he rides in the front seat with Heather every day for a week and a half. Or when Craig avoids me in the hall at school. Or when I tell Hayden I'll see him at Liz's party.

I don't forget.

I can't.

On the desk this week, we worked our way through Joni Mitchell, a rap song I almost couldn't remember, and the Beatles. Yesterday, Thursday, at Heather's insistence, I added:

If you'd like to meet, come to Liz Pullman's house tomorrow night. Wear all black.

"It's going to be Hayden," Heather says.

"You know or you guess?" I ask.

"Gut feeling."

"He sure hasn't said anything to let me know it's him," I say. She twirls a braid, and I know we're shifting from me to her. "You think there's any chance Bodee likes me?"

"Sure," I say, but he hasn't said a word about her. Or the girl from fourth period.

"Does he talk about me?"

"We don't talk much at home."

At least not lately. We spend no less time together; in fact, we spend more. Nearly every minute at the house. He makes sure I don't take pain out on my neck, and I haven't for six days. I make sure he doesn't end up doing pull-ups under the bed.

But there was a brief relapse last night following another tough conversation.

"You thought any more about telling?" he asked.

"No. You thought any more about your deposition?"

"Stop making them the same," he argued. "They're not."

"No, because Craig won't try to kill me."

My cruelty doesn't push him away, but it does silence him. And send him under the bed.

In one way, I'm better. Telling Bodee has released some of the pressure. But in another way, I'm worse, because I can't tell him I'm better. We define "better" differently.

Better is a day I don't think about digging at my neck, not a day I think of telling on Craig.

There's a cold war between Bodee and me, with no hope of tearing down the wall. Lately, the only thing that sends me to the closet is when I see him with Heather. Granted, I don't think he's interested, but he indulges her.

"You and Bodee, you're thick as thieves," Heather says once she signs her name to the worksheet. "If you don't talk about me, who or what do you talk about?"

"His mom. Mostly."

"Oh, that makes sense. You're like his antidepressant or something," she says.

"Sure."

"I talk to Hayden about you."

"And I still talk to Collie about you." Okay, only once. But once counts. After the campout fiasco, I finally took his call, and he apologized for kissing me. He babbled on about how weird it was and that he never meant for it to happen. And how he wishes I would stop closing him out. He misses our friendship.

And I do too. Damn collateral damage of July. Maybe, over time, we'll heal.

She flinches at the mention of his name. "Liz says she invited him." She lowers her voice. "I heard he's going with Maggie."

My eyes widen, but I recover before she notices. "You're going with Bodee."

"Weird, weird *year*. If you'd told me last October that Collie would kiss you and I'd invite Bodee Lennox anywhere, I'd have said you were crazy."

The bell rings, and I say, "And I'd have said you were right."

Friday, the day of the party, there are only four words on the desk.

I WILL BE THERE

"You're not wearing a costume," Bodee says when he sees me waiting for Heather at the kitchen table.

I avoided him this afternoon, and he knows it, because he's walking on the balls of his feet. He does that when he's nervous.

"What you see is what you get," I say.

He laughs at the irony. "See you later."

Heather doesn't hide her disappointment at my non-costume when she picks me up thirty minutes later than we planned. She's an Egyptian queen, but all I notice is her hair, which is still natural and not the cherry-red color of Kool-Aid.

"You like?" she asks, shaking her bare belly and her hips, which are clad in pants that are more old-school MC Hammer than the Queen of Sheba.

"You'll freeze," I tell her.

"Not if someone shows up to keep me warm," she says.

Gritting my teeth, I say, "Yeah."

My heart thuds around in my chest, the way loose two-liters rattle around in the trunk of the car, as we drive to Liz's. Cars line both sides of the street, and I wish I'd done more looking at the guest list and less brooding. Cobwebs stretch from one magnolia to another, and there are neat rows of tombstones in the front yard. Just to get in the front door I have to wedge between a vampire, Michael Jackson, and one of those counting sheep from the mattress commercials.

"There's a guy in all black on the back patio," Liz whispers as she hugs me.

"Is it Hayden?" I ask.

"Not sure." And she's not. "Could be; he's big enough."

"Go on," Liz says, and pushes me out the door. "Check him out."

"Nice costume," I say, and sit. The plastic love seat wobbles as the all-black dementor slides over to make room for me.

He holds up a finger, which he has trouble unearthing from the folds of his black sheets, and indicates I should wait. The Captain bends to his left and lifts a small whiteboard from under the bench. At the top, he's scrawled *DESK* and underlined it in a heavy marker.

I laugh at this quirky idea and take the marker from him. Our handwriting looks funky as I write my name to the left of *DESK*, a question mark to the right, and hand the marker back, hoping he'll write his name, too. He shoves it back.

Thanks for meeting me, I write.

THAT'S NOT A SONG, he writes back.

I made you a mix tape
That I worried you'd hate
But you called me at three a.m.
With it playing
Softly saying
Song number three
Is about you and me
And I've felt the same way for a while

CLEVER . . . WRITE ANOTHER.

I've been saving this lyric since September, but now seems
the right time to use it.

I want to know who you are
A name and a face
A heart to unbreak
I want to know who you are

Laughter from beneath the sheet, and I know this is the reveal.
Time.
Stands.
Still.

It's Hayden. Hayden Harper dressed like a dementor and laughing like a clown. Enjoying every minute of this charade.

I laugh with my mouth too, but my heart cries. So gullible. The lies I tell myself are the ones that really sting. Only now, while I'm looking at a football player, do I realize how much I thought I'd be staring at Bodee.

"You surprised?" he says, and takes my hand.

"No. Heather's been saying it was you for weeks."

He puts on a grin. "Disappointed?" he asks. But the way he asks it shows me he believes that's not possible. Who wouldn't be thrilled to see his now-sweaty dirty-blond hair and steel-gray eyes?

"Only that the mystery is over," I lie.

"I'll still write you songs. Like that Cameron Roots one you just wrote down. That was great," he says.

I correct him. "Bandana Rhoades."

"Thank God for Google," he says with a laugh.

The lyrics aren't inside him.

They are only words. I knew this about him already.

But Captain Hayden is my reality. He's here in front of me, and he's the blank slate I need. He doesn't know about Craig, or the closet or my neck. He knows nothing about me, and he never will.

Damaged. Broken. Ruined. If I can hide these things from my family, how much easier they'll be to hide from Hayden. We can glide right through junior year with pictures and desk songs, and a pile of group memories. Liz will get back with Ray, probably tonight. And Heather will eventually forgive Collie. And then it will be three girls and their three football players.

Take it. Take it, I tell myself. But this fits like a discounted pair of jeans with IRREGULAR written on the tag: you search and can find nothing wrong with them.

Take it.

So I do.

Kissing Hayden is different this time. It's not awkward and it's not saturated in whiskey. All I need to make my life normal is in this kiss. Deep, penetrating. I only come out of the kiss-trance as he tries to touch my neck. I shimmy a little, and he pulls me into his lap and forgets all about my neck.

I try to forget he is not Bodee, so I kiss him harder.

Which he likes.

He's in the middle of liking it when the screen door slams, and I know we aren't alone.

"I was hoping that would happen," Hayden whispers as I shift from his lap.

Bodee. Not in black. Not coming for me. Not Captain Lyric. Not happy.

"Hey, Kool-Aid," Hayden says.

"Don't call him that," I say, and stand up.

"Last time I kissed you, he punched me. So I'm thinking, 'Hey, Kool-Aid' is pretty mild."

"Bodee," I say as apologetically as I know how.

But Bodee turns and leaves.

Hayden tugs me back into his lap. "Let him go," he says, and kisses my cheek.

"You don't understand."

"Oh, I think I do." There's a cleft in Hayden's chin that I've never noticed before, and it bobs arrogantly in front of me. "He likes you, and you feel sorry for him. So you accidentally encourage him. But trust me, you're not doing Kool-Aid any favors by giving him your I'm-so-sorry-you're-sad eyes. Girls like you don't go with guys like him."

"He's important to me," I say, and ignore the rest.

"Okay. Go on. Talk to him." He releases me. "But come right back, Alexi. I've got another game we can play with the marker board."

The crowd in the house has increased since I went to the patio. I shove Marilyn Monroe into Elvis, and then Captain America into Betty Boop (Maggie) to get to the front door.

Bodee's almost to Ben's truck down the street when I catch up to him.

"Wait. Please wait," I yell.

Please and Bodee are peanut butter and jelly. He stops.

"He's the Captain," I say, hoping this will explain my actions.

"I'm sure he is."

I kick at the reflector embedded in the road. "Why are you so mad at me? You came to this party to be with Heather."

Crack. Crack. Crack.

"Do you like him?" he asks.

"Do you like her?" I fire back.

"No, you know that," he says.

"What about fourth-period girl? Do you like her?"

Now it's his turn to kick something. Ben's truck tire. "Yes," he says.

"Well, then, we're even."

"I can't believe you'd choose him. Him, Lex. He's a . . ."

. . . normal life, I think. My chance at a normal life is on the patio, not here in the middle of the street. Besides, it's better for Bodee. He needs his fourth-period girl, uncomplicated, unruined, unbroken.

Not me.

These scrolling thoughts burn like rubbing alcohol, but I pour another bottle on my festering heart and raise my chin. "I'm choosing him," I say.

And this time, Bodee believes the lie and leaves me standing on the dotted line.

chapter 25

HEATHER drives me home in time for curfew. Twelve thirty a.m.

She says nothing about Bodee's quick appearance and disappearance at the party. He's only a garnish to Collie's caviar, anyway. And Collie, who came with Maggie, ditched Maggie and hung with Heather. And Heather let him.

Things between Bodee and me are still messy like pumpkin guts, but things between Heather and Collie don't have to end up gutted and scattered to hell on yesterday's newspaper.

"Do you want to know what really happened with Collie?" I ask her.

"He told you about . . . the girl."

"Yes." That boy's told me everything since kindergarten. Up until the alumni game. But this time, when our lives are falling apart at the same time and mine with a misery I could not share, I avoid him. Because his tale comes too close for comfort to mine. Sex. Mistakes. Apologies. "And I said I wouldn't tell," I explain. "But I couldn't look at him for what he did to you."

"So why are you telling me now?" she asks.

"Because I'm tired." Too tired. "And because of the other night, Heather. The mess at the fort. You need to know there's nothing between Collie and me."

"I do. I do. Just sucks to know he told you and not me."

"That's different. I'm just his friend." I don't remind her that Collie did tell her. But with such incredibly poor, *guy-stupid* timing that it canceled out his honesty. "It happened the night of the alumni game. At my house," I say.

Heather works the steering wheel with her fist. "Oh God, we were into it that night," she remembers. "We got into a huge fight about his drinking so much with the guys. I told him if he was going to act like my father, he could get lost. That I had plenty of losers in my life, and I didn't need another."

"And after you left he was distraught."

"Who was it? Julie Raimer? She's always had a thing for him."

I shake my head.

"Tanya?"

"Heather, it was Maggie," I say, before she can guess every girl who's ever sat with us at lunch.

"Maggie. But she . . . why would he do that?"

I give her a look. "Maggie, Heather. She was *there*," I say.

Sort of like Hayden.

Now Heather pounds the steering wheel, and I don't stop her. "We waited. We waited all that time, and then he slept with *her*."

"He was drunk. You know he doesn't care about Maggie."

"But that just makes it worse. Why do guys sleep with girls they don't love?"

"'Cause . . ." I don't have an answer. "I'm sorry I didn't tell you," I say.

"Lex, I doubt you lied to me because you promised him. So why?"

I take a deep breath, because she's gone right to the heart of it. "Because Collie is one of the few constants in your life. With your family and all." As I pause and look at her, she nods. "And if you didn't need to experience this pain, I wasn't going to give it to you." I lay my hand on hers, and she doesn't jerk away. "I'm really sorry."

She nods her understanding. "If I knew something like this about you, I wouldn't tell you, either. And Lex . . . whatever you've got going on, I hope . . . I hope it gets better soon. I miss your smile."

I smile.

"Your real one," she says.

"See you Monday," I say.

There are snores coming from the den. I lock the kitchen

door behind me and tiptoe to the couch and nudge Mom awake.

"I'm home," I say. "You can go on to bed."

She rubs her eyes and closes the book tented on her chest. "You have fun?"

"Yeah." Maybe someday I'll stop lying to her, too.

"That's good, honey." She pecks me on the cheek and cinches her robe for the walk to the bedroom. "See you in the morning."

My heart is doughy, as if it's being pummeled and kneaded as I head upstairs and open the door to my room.

It's empty.

I try the closet, thinking I should polish off this crappy day on the floor, but the closet door is closed. There's a Post-it Note over the knob that says, *Locked.*

Bodee. Always a step ahead of my pain.

So I crawl into the bed, not bothering with pajamas or darkness, and make a cave of my covers. I bury myself in them, and the words that tumble out are muffled by my pillow: all pleas and prayers.

"Why am I so stupid—things are always wrong—no matter what I do—how hard I try—what am I supposed to do—oh Bodee—will you ever forgive me for this—please—Bodee—please—Bodee— please—you have to."

"I forgive you, Lex," says a voice from under the bed.

It's embarrassing to know you've said things you never intended anyone to hear. I wipe my face on the pillow and flop over to hang my head off the bed and peer underneath.

"Hey," I say.

"You look funny upside down," he says.

"I look funny right side up. Why are you under my bed?"

"'Cause someone put the boxes back under mine." It's too dark to see him smile, but it's not too hard to hear him.

I smile too, because for once I was ahead of his pain.

"You wanna come out?" I ask.

He doesn't answer, but stuff crinkles and rattles and slides, and he emerges.

Sneakers and all, he lies down on my bed.

"Who am I, Lex?" he asks.

"Bodee," I say.

"Remember that," he says, and puts a careful arm around me as I snuggle against his chest.

Even when I choose Hayden, Bodee's still here. Constant. And we fall asleep in our clothes. It's more accurate to say we fall awake in our clothes, because neither of us closes our eyes for a long time.

Bodee doesn't bring up Craig again until Tuesday morning. It's early. Maybe four thirty. The pressure has been building for this conversation ever since Craig showed up at church Sunday and sat in our pew and proceeded to eat pot roast and potatoes at our table. He and Kayla were tense, but civil. Mom and Dad were oddly reticent. And Bodee and I . . . well, we got through it.

And now Bodee and I are horn-locked and stubborn.

"Lex, you have to tell her before they work things out," he says. "Don't let him back in."

"I can't." I roll away from the cave of his arms.

"Well, I can't keep doing this."

I prop up on one elbow and say, "Doing what?"

"Staying in your room."

"Sorry it's such a burden."

"Shhh. Someone will hear us."

He's right, but shushing gets on my nerves. "So," I say sarcastically. "You can't keep doing *this* anymore."

"Don't be that way. You know I only—"

"What if I said the same thing to you? What if I said, 'You're broken, and I don't want you in my life unless you testify against your dad'?" He has no defense except to roll away from me.

"See, Bodee. It's not that easy."

"Nothing's easy. And I *am* broken. The difference between us isn't the brokenness; it's what we're going to do about it."

"Bodee, this is bullshit. We can't keep having this same conversation. You already know my mind is made up; I don't *want* anyone to know. I have to deal with Craig in private."

He faces me again, and the nightlight puts the planes of his face in sharp relief. Lock-jawed and unyielding, he says, "I can't let you do that."

"You're going to *tell*."

"Yes. I've made up my mind. If you don't, I will."

"Then whatever this is, whatever we are, is *over*," I say.

"I didn't know it ever started."

"You *kissed* me." The words bring the memory of the two of us in his sleeping bag.

"You kissed Hayden," he says back. "You chose him."

"And I'll do it again. I'll lie my face off if you tell Kayla or my parents about Craig."

Bodee rolls off the bed; his sneakers make a soft thud against the carpet. "No, Lex. You'll tear your neck apart and then look back ten years from now and realize you're stuck in the same closet tearing up football cards."

While I'm still gasping, he opens the door to leave and then stops short with a little yelp.

I am shushing him as Bodee backs into my room.

Followed by Kayla.

"Well, well. Isn't this interesting?" Kayla says snidely, and shuts the bedroom door behind her.

"Oh, don't start. We were only talking," I say.

"Craig and I used to *talk*."

Bodee turns his face toward me and mumbles, "I don't doubt it."

"Move on, Kayla, we weren't doing anything."

"At five a.m.? In your bedroom? Right. Nothing about you is as innocent as Mom and Dad think."

"Believe what you want. We were just talking."

All I see of Bodee is his back, but he's cracking his knuckles like walnuts.

Kayla advances farther into the room, and our whispers rise in volume. "Here's what I think. You are going to tell me exactly what you said to Craig the other day that made him leave me. *Or* I'll make sure your little bedroom buddy here is thrown out of our house."

I don't react to her kidney punch. "Do they teach you to make threats at the bank or something? I didn't tell Craig anything."

"You told him to leave me," she says.

"I did not. Why would I do that?" *Besides the obvious.*

"Because you hate me and you're jealous and can't stand for me to be happy."

"Kayla, I don't hate you. You're my sister."

"Craig's always been your little hero, and I've always been the witch," she says.

"He is *not* her hero."

Kayla must have forgotten that Bodee was in the room, because she whips around at the sound of his voice.

"What would you know? You've been here a month."

"Thirty-four days, and I know more than you," he says, and leaves his perch on the edge of my bed.

I know that tone. He's going to make good on his threat to tell her right now. "No, Bodee," I say, trying to calm the storm.

"Yes, Alexi," he says back.

"I'm not stupid. You're both hiding something, and I'm going to find out what it is."

"You won't."

"I'll do whatever it takes to keep Craig."

Bodee is between Kayla and me. "No, you won't."

She smacks his chest. *Thwack. Thwack.* "You don't get a say in this."

He catches her wrist, and though he's gentle with her, she tries to jerk away as if he wants to beat her.

"Too bad, because I'm going to have my say," he says.

Oh shit. Oh shit. "Bodee."

"I know all about you and Craig *talking* while you were supposed to babysit Alexi," he says in her face. *Crack. Crack. Crack.* He's winding up. "You know what I mean, Kayla," he says in disgust. "What kind of person threatens a six-year-old? And you've been making these threats all her life. Well, you're done. You've threatened Alexi for the last time. And I swear, you try me, you'll find this is no bluff. I'm the one who will make sure Craig never comes back."

I take a breath when he's finished. Partly because he hasn't told, and partly because I've never heard him talk this firmly.

"You'll regret this," Kayla hisses, her face ugly with fury. "You're going to be so sorry."

"Oh, trust me, I already am," Bodee says. "Lex, just tell her."

"Nothing to tell," I insist.

"Fine," he says, and goes to the door. "You're on your own. I'm through."

"He's as crazy as his father," Kayla says when Bodee has gone.

"Don't. You. *Ever*. Say. That."

"Now who's making threats? What did all that mean anyway?"

"Nothing. Nothing." *Everything.*

Kayla is half in my room, half in the hall; her knuckles wrap the door facing. "I want him gone, Lex. I want him out of this family. And I'm going to make sure of it."

She leaves before I can say, "He already is."

chapter 26

THE towels in the bathroom aren't wet when I drag myself to the shower. There's no half-torn Kool-Aid package in the trash. And no wet toothbrush at the sink.

Remnants of Bodee.

Gone.

And there's no Bodee, sitting, legs crossed at the kitchen bar, waiting to see what boxed breakfast food we will split today.

Mom's head is in the fridge. "You hungry?"

"Not this morning."

"Bodee left you half of his granola bar."

"Left me?"

"Yeah." She slides a box of apple juice across the bar toward me like she's working downtown at a honky-tonk. "Ben picked him up today. He didn't tell you?"

"No."

I drift out of the kitchen and up to the bonus room. *Ben picked him up,* I hear my mother say. Is he moving out? Going away? Not coming back?

He can't keep doing this, he said.

Proof. I want proof that he's staying. Proof I didn't see in the bathroom.

But the first thing I see is Cinderella. Faceup in her yellow dress. Smiling across the bed like she has no idea I'd rather never see her again. The little stack of whites, the underwear that made him blush in front of me the first time, is gone. Three plaid shirts that usually hang on plastic suit hangers instead of the old wire ones: gone. And Mrs. Lennox's diamond earring is gone too.

I lift the bed skirt, wondering how I can face the final nail in this coffin.

The boxes are stacked under the bed.

My whole world rocks and sways, as if I'm standing up on a raft in the pool. My knees sag and I sit, and then stretch out facedown on his bed.

I can't keep doing this.

I push the decorative pillows to the floor and . . . my hand touches what I was afraid I wouldn't find.

Hatchet. The worn cover is back on.

I open the book with its Scotch-taped spine and read:

To Bodee,
My brave little Brian. I love you.
                                        Mom

He took everything else and left this behind.

For me.

"Lex," Mom calls from the kitchen. I let her yell. Even when I hear her on the steps, and the landing. I lie on the bed, running over those words from his mother with my thumb.

"Heather's here," Mom says.

"Did he say when he'd be back?" I ask.

"No. He said he needed some time with his brother." She pats my leg. "You worried about him?"

I nod and sit up, letting Mom see my tears, but not the book and the note from his mother. She assumes these tears are for Bodee, instead of for her daughter.

"It'll be good for him to be with Ben. They need some time too. Maybe he'll talk to his brother." She looks away and gives me space to wipe my face. "Heather's waiting," she reminds me.

I love this about her. That she is like me. Emotional, and embarrassed about being emotional.

I tuck *Hatchet* into my bag and walk like a zombie to Heather's car. Liz is back in the front seat.

"You had one more minute," Heather says. "Where's Bodee?"

"With his brother."

"He's not moving out, is he?" Liz asks. "'Cause he doesn't normally go see his brother, right?"

"I don't know. Maybe."

Our threesome, turned foursome, turned threesome again, is quiet. Thinking of Bodee.

Heather says, "Well, huh," and Liz sighs, eye-checking me in the mirror. I shift and turn my face to the window where she can't see me. And cry slow, silent tears.

Hayden takes my hand at the front door and leads me, like a limp doll, to homeroom. He kisses my cheek, as if his reveal of Captain Lyric allows him this new license to touch on school grounds.

Bodee is not in homeroom.

And not at his locker afterward.

When Hayden realizes I have spun the dial on my combination lock twice without opening the locker, he asks for the combination and takes over. For the first time, he notices my glazed-over state.

"You okay, Lex?"

"Not really," I say as my locker swings open.

"Can I do anything?"

"Not really."

Hayden hands me the two books I point to and says, "I'd ask you what's wrong, but you probably won't tell me."

He's right. So I say, "Thanks," and walk away, with my locker still open and the lock still in Hayden's hand.

I don't take my book to third period, and we have an open-book test. My name is the only thing I write.

I realize something as I walk through the hall.

Any ability I have to move forward—even stupid moves like choosing Hayden because he doesn't *know*, or thinking I could have a normal relationship and forget all about Craig— is all because of Bodee's strength. I don't know how to do it without him.

I lay my head on the desk in fourth period, the blank desk, and close my eyes.

"You aren't going to write?" Heather asks.

"I'm out of words," I tell her.

When the bell finally rings, I check myself out of school under the guise of a migraine, and walk home and straight to the fort.

When I reach the top I see a bird, no bigger than a minute, land on my window—the one where Bodee and I brush shoulders as we look out over the woods.

"*Chirp*," the bird says to me, twitching his wings.

"It's October, buddy. Your friends are halfway down I-65 by now," I tell him.

He chirps again.

"Sucks, huh?"

The bird plucks his gunmetal-gray tail feathers, and one

floats to the open sill. *"Chirp. Chirp,"* he says.

"Be that way. Probably why they left you behind."

"CHIRP." He flies away, leaving his feather.

This morning, for one second between my pain and the fear that Bodee would tell, I imagined what it would be like to be free.

That's what Bodee is imagining for me, I think. What he wants for me.

Freedom.

This choice is mine, I realize. I can be the bird clinging to a windowsill in Tennessee when all my friends are in Florida, or I can be the bird who flies away.

I can be free.

I decided to keep my secret, and now, I decide to let it go.

I want my life back. Want the lies and the loneliness to end. I don't want to settle for cute-boy Hayden just because he doesn't know about me. Hayden, who Googles his lyrics and drinks his whiskey. I'll never fall in love with him.

But right now, if I don't take a risk, I'll fall into a breathing-next-to-each-other relationship because it's easy. Easy is empty.

Hayden's good on a desk, but he isn't good for me. And I already have a boy who knows me.

If he'll forgive me. Trust me. After I turn the lies to truth.

Bodee once told me—the one time he sat in the closet with me—that what I couldn't say, I should write down. "Words will lead to voice," he said.

Careful not to damage the book, I untape the cover and dig a pen from the pocket of my backpack. The inside of the cover is blank, waiting for my words.

It takes courage to write the obvious.

Craiq raped me.

I chew my pen cap and let the words come. At first, they are summer rain on the beach, making tiny dents in the sand that the wind will smooth away.

I didn't call it rape, because I didn't actually say no. But he knew. He KNOWS he was wrong. That a twenty-six-year-old man doesn't have sex with a fifteen-year-old girl. He used a condom, so he had time to think and to stop. And he's had time to set this right. To tell. Which can never set everything right, but it helps. Instead, he wants me to pretend that it never happened, to stay in his life so he can kiss my sister and feed her lies. That he is still a good guy. He may be again, someday, but not to me.

Then my anger becomes rage, and I bear down with the pen to write the words I should have said to Craig.

> *Your hurt is not an excuse to take.*
> *Your loneliness is not an excuse to cheat.*
> *Your desire is not a reason to rape.*
> *You raped me, and now, I'm going to rape you.*

Of Kayla, of our house as your second home, of your job, of me as your sister-in-law.

And it will hurt, but it won't hurt the way you hurt me.

I won't be sorry for this. You are not my BEST BUDDY, you are a selfish asshole, and I hate what you did to me!

chapter 27

WHEN I get back to the house, Kayla and Craig are in the den. They aren't touching, but they're on the same couch, and they're sitting close together. My manifesto, the end of Craig's normal and the beginning of mine, burns inside me.

Craig raped me. I hate what you did to me. And all the words in between.

But Bodee isn't here, and I want him to be.

He's mad at me, but I know him. If I say please, he will come, and forgive me long enough to stand beside me and hold my hand, while I tell Craig to go to hell. The boy who taught me to stand up should be here for the standing.

So I will wait.

But Bodee doesn't magically appear. I can't wish him here

the way I wished his hand in mine the day we kicked acorns on the way home.

Dinner comes, and I pass Craig a slice of pizza, barely able to contain the fury in me, now that it's at the surface. And then I pass the celery and then the ranch dressing and then more Sprite. I want to dump the Sprite over him and scream like a two-year-old.

There is a change in Craig. The camouflage and the lies aren't working for him, either. He doesn't look at me like we're best buddies anymore. He doesn't eat any of the things I pass him at dinner. He doesn't eat much at all, I notice. His weight loss, my neck; we've blown each other's covers.

But I won't feel sorry for him. The way I used to.

"Where's your *boy*friend?" Kayla asks.

"He's not my boyfriend," I say without looking at her. "He's gone. With his brother, Ben."

She says, *"Good."* And ignores the disapproving looks she gets from Mom and Dad.

In moments like this, I can almost lump her into KaylaCraig. One word, one being, one person, to despise for what they do to me. But they aren't the same, and she is my sister. Sorrow for her quenches my anger, because I can't ruin Craig's life without ruining hers.

She might not forgive me for this.

She might hate me for what I take from her the way I hate Craig for what he took from me.

She might tell Mom before I'm ready.

On the surface this is a normal meal. We eat, we talk, and we pass the food and clean up the kitchen. But in my brain, the lists of "mights" concerning Mom and Dad have started. They might make me see a counselor. Might watch me too closely. Might pity me. Might treat me like I am an antique heirloom that can be seen but not touched.

"It might break," I hear them say of my great-grandmother's lamp. "She might break," I hear them say of me.

And Mom and Dad won't press legal charges against Craig. They don't believe in retaliation.

That idea is ingrained in me. Another reason it has taken so long to get to this point with Craig. To understand that telling what has already happened is not retaliation. To see the difference between suffering the consequences and taking an eye for an eye.

But they do believe in honesty, my parents. If they were in my head and could see this warped process, they'd say, "Honey, we have to be honest, even when it's hard."

I'm going to be honest.

Even if it's hard.

And I'm going to heal.

Tonight I throw away my neck-scratching shirts. If I need another one, and I probably will, I'll cross that bridge later. For tonight, I will not give Craig more than he's already taken.

I miss Bodee the way I miss my virginity. Like he's gone

forever, and I'll never get him back. In bed, I can't sleep, but I refuse to look at the vent. I try flipping one way and flopping another. Pillow poofed; pillow flat. Knees up; knees down. Curled up and snow-angeled out.

Counting doesn't bring him back.

The later it gets, the more honest I get. *Hatchet* isn't all he left me. He left me . . . *me*. Me. Myself.

And more than that, Bodee left me with hope. For love. For wanting someone to touch me again and to lie with me without fear as my first response. Because Bodee slept in his sneakers, because Bodee asked for a kiss instead of just taking it, and because he kept space between us. And he danced with two fingers until I asked for three or four . . . and his hand on my hip.

I know we're still broken. *Both* of us. But Bodee's got the glue to make us whole.

He is love.

I wait for the alarm to go off.

Heather and Liz don't ask about Bodee in the car. They don't even say "Happy Halloween." For the first time during our junior year we don't speak on the way to school. I have the torn copy of *Hatchet* in my hand, and whether Bodee is kiwi, or blueberry, or cherry, or tropical punch or any flavor of Bodee, I will give it to him at the locker. If he's there.

I walk by Hayden's outstretched hand, and though I see his raised eyebrows and the questioning look he sends Heather, I don't stop. Maybe Heather shrugs to tell him she doesn't know, but I'm not sure, because I don't turn around.

Bodee's not at his locker.

There are no lyrics on the desk, which causes Heather to say, "You were sort of rude to him this morning."

"Yeah," I say. "Hey, tell him I'm sorry."

I don't write any lyrics either, because now I know who he really is, and the magic has gone.

The two forty-five bell rings, and I walk out the front door. Foolishly, I look toward the planter where Bodee often waits for me. A snatch of plaid forces me to do a double take, and I get plowed by a boy on his way to a tuba lesson. Stumbling, I look again.

He's there, he's really there, and I run to him.

His arms open and fold around me. He spins me around until I'm dizzy.

"I missed you."

"You must have, you're hugging me at school," he says.

"I *missed* you," I repeat. More like I had trouble breathing without you.

"I've been with Ben," he says.

He tosses his hair, which is shorter and blond. *Just* blond, I realize; the same as it was at his mom's funeral. Back when there was a mile between us.

"Mom told me you were with him."

"Lex, I did it." He is smiling. His teeth smile, all of them gleaming for me to see.

"Did what?"

"Gave my deposition."

We spin again, and I squeeze him. "You really did?"

"I did," he says. "And I feel different." *Crack. Crack. Crack.*

"You don't *sound* different," I tease him, taking his hands in mine.

"You're different too." Bodee straightens my hair out behind me and smiles as his hand brushes my neck. Smiles when he sees that there are no fresh scratches.

I hand him the book cover.

He reads it through once, twice, maybe even a third time. "When did you write this?"

"Yesterday."

"Are you going to—?"

"I'm going to shove it up his ass."

It's not funny, but we both laugh. Maybe with wonder; maybe with nervousness.

"You sure you're ready?" he asks.

"No," I say. "But it doesn't matter. I have to do it, even though it's hard."

Liz spots us on her way to Heather's car. "You coming?" she yells, a curious expression on her face.

"No. We're walking," Bodee yells back, and says to me, "You don't mind, do you?"

I shake my head, and we walk. "You know they're going to talk about us," I say.

"Won't be the first time."

"And it won't be the last," I say. And we both smile again.

"You okay if we stop in here?" Bodee points past the wrought-iron gates of Pleasant Grove Cemetery to the neat rows of stones beyond. "Kind of want to tell her about today."

"You think she knows about me?"

He points upward and says, "Pretty sure she's watching. Probably up there pulling strings with the angels."

"Maybe she sent me a little bird. If it was her, you tell her thanks."

"Wouldn't put anything past her."

He talks while the sun sinks, and I watch him. And think about what I'll say to Craig.

Little kids in costumes share the sidewalk with us. A dachshund outfitted like a hot dog trots beside a little boy who is Batman for the night. I don't remember Batman with a hot dog, but it makes me laugh to watch them take on the neighborhood.

Dusk has just dimmed the color of autumn when we arrive at the driveway. A group of trick-or-treaters ring our doorbell as we walk up behind them. "Hang on," I tell them, and slip inside for the bowl of candy Mom has prepared.

"Thank you," they chorus, hopping down the steps and heading on to the next house.

"Where're your parents?" Bodee asks.

"Mom and Dad always help with a Harvest Fest in the church parking lot." I light the candles in the jack-o'-lanterns and put the candy bowl by the door. "This is what I usually do. We don't get that many trick-or-treaters at the end of the street."

When Craig pulls into the driveway, he and Kayla both climb out of the cab on the driver's side. If she's sitting in the middle seat, *riding hump* as they call it, they must be back together.

"You ready?" Bodee asks.

"Uh-uh."

Bodee pulls me under his shoulder. "It won't come with a bow on it, but God'll tie it up," he says.

"What does that mean?"

"Just something Mom used to say when she knew something hard was coming on," he says.

"Look who's back," Kayla says.

"Hi, Kayla," Bodee says, ignoring her sarcasm.

"We need to talk," I tell my sister before she can start in on Bodee.

"Finally going to come clean?" she asks. "Need your bedroom buddy to hold your hand?"

I don't answer, and we wait while Craig rummages around in the fridge. Every sound is amplified, even the little *thwew* noise the refrigerator door makes when it closes. This is the last time he gets anything out of our kitchen, I think, to amp myself up.

Craig walks through the door and takes one look at me.

And *knows*.

He squeezes the can of Sprite in his hand like it's his weapon of defense.

"Kayla wants to know what's going on." The first words

are the hardest. "Do you want to tell her, Craig, or do you want it to come from me?"

There is a quality of silence, of stillness, that I will always associate with this moment. As if time loses its breath and has to gasp to get it back again.

Kayla looks from Craig to me, and now she is terrified. As if nothing she imagined could be as bad as this moment before she *knows*. She's right. And it's about to get worse.

"Lex, don't," Craig says, putting out a hand. "Don't do this. Please."

"Please" doesn't work on me the way it does with Bodee. The way it did with me when Craig and I were best buddies. "Me or you? Decide now."

Craig sinks to the couch and covers his face with his hands, and I watch him shake. I'm shaking too, but Bodee keeps an arm around me.

"Craig, what *is* this? What's going on? Tell me," she demands, and sits down as if her legs won't hold her. She leaves a cushion between her and Craig, pushing against the armrest, as if she can get away from the shit storm that's about to take place.

"I can't," he says, his voice muffled by his hands.

"Have it your way." I pass *Hatchet* to Kayla with the cover open.

"A book? What the hell is this? What . . . ?"

She screams as her eyes fall on the words, as she absorbs what she sees.

"No. No. *No*," she cries, at me, at him, at both of us. She reads on—the soul I've laid bare—the lies I've stopped telling.

And she stumbles out of the room.

Bodee looks Craig square in the eyes and says, "If you touch her while I'm out there, I'll kill you," and then he goes after her. He pauses for a second at the door frame to make sure Craig believes him, then he goes where I can't go to say what I can't say.

I don't know what Bodee is saying to Kayla. Maybe, yes, it happened. Yes, Craig's a bastard. Yes, Lexi's been hiding it. Yes, Lexi needs your support. Yes, I know it hurts you.

Or maybe he's just silent, standing beside her. Because even his silence is brilliant.

Regardless, while Bodee soothes and Kayla cries, I watch the life drain from Craig's expression. He knows, as I do, there's no going back.

Nothing's been said between us when Bodee and Kayla return. Bodee has an arm around her as he guides her to my side. Tears stream down her cheeks.

She believes me.

Today, she isn't Craig's girlfriend; she's my sister, and she whisks me into her arms.

We cry together, but her tears come harder than mine.

Because I've already cried.

"He did this to you?" It's not a question, but she has to confirm it.

My head moves against her shoulder.

"He did this to you." No hope left, no doubt that she's wrong. "Oh God, I'm so sorry, Alexi. I'm so sorry."

To make her stop, I say, "I'm okay."

"No, you're not. You can't be. Because he's still here. How can you be better?"

"Because you know. You finally know." Tears gather and fall and puddle on the hardwood. "That he raped me," I say. Not to Kayla; I say it for me, out loud, in my house. To hear it echo back. To know the lie, like a spreading cancer, is dying. The relief is unmatched, even greater than the first time I said it to Bodee.

Of all the reactions I imagined, this was not one of them. Kayla protective; Craig deflated, a wet noodle on our couch. She dries her tears, which are partially for her and the changes this means, but mostly for me. Then she turns and faces Craig.

"You did this?" she yells, and slaps the book with my words at him. *You did this to her.*

Craig cries in earnest, looking up from the book through eyes filled with guilt and regret and fear. "I'm sorry. I'm so sorry."

Who is he apologizing to? Kayla or me? Bodee's arm tightens around me as Kayla rises.

"Why are you still here?" she screams at him.

He doesn't answer.

"You effing . . . ," Kayla starts in on him, reeling off her pain, letting it fly, inventing cuss words as she goes. "To just sit there and *cry*. I'd like to rip off your balls!"

"I'm so sorry, Kayla. I'm so *sorry*."

And he is. Sorry covers him like a pall.

"What do you want, Lex? What do you want me to tell him?" Kayla asks.

"I just want him gone."

"One week," Kayla says. "I'll give you one week to turn in your resignation and get the hell out of Rickman. Or I tell everyone what you did to Alexi."

"Oh, *no*, Kayla. Baby, you don't mean that!"

He focuses on her now. He's horrified, as if this is beyond what he can take. Not the punishment he expected.

I see his *I'm so lonely* face, but it's as if I'm still hearing the condom package tear, the image is so intense in my head. I will not look at his broken heart or listen to his sorrys. Not any longer.

"Don't you dare act like this is okay," Kayla says through gritted teeth. "Don't you dare think you can just—"

"But . . . but Alexi will be fine. I mean, now that we all *know*. We can work this out, Kayla. We can—"

"Are you serious? Are you totally out of your mind? You're really thinking that's an option? You're lucky I don't call the cops right now and have you arrested for statutory rape."

Bodee nods, and I amp up on Kayla's rage.

There's no dignity in him when he cries, "But Kayla,

I . . . I don't know where to go. What to do."

"Not my problem."

"But you love me," he says.

"Yeah," she says honestly. "But there has to be someone out there who is . . . *better* to love . . . than a guy who rapes my little sister."

"Kayla," he pleads.

Kayla's finished, but I finally find my voice, *my* words. "Don't you Kayla her, Craig. Don't you ever Kayla her again, you son of a bitch." Bodee reaches for my hand as I catch my breath. He squeezes, and I know the rage I feel is on my face. "There's no coming back, Craig. There's no making this right. There's only you resigning from your job and moving away from Rickman. There's just you, out of this house. Out of our lives."

Craig sits there, speechless and shell-shocked.

"You heard Alexi, get up," Kayla says, and kicks his leg to jar him from the couch.

My tears dry as I watch the full realization pass over Craig's features. "Leave. *Now*," I say, and my voice is calm and strong and determined. At last.

Craig rises then and stumbles out the front door, and as I stare at the unopened Sprite on our hardwood floor, I hear his truck start up.

And I think: The Littrells don't have to buy Sprites anymore.

Craig's the only one who ever drank them.

He's gone.

There's no spoken agreement to keep this between us, but when Mom and Dad get home from Harvest Fest, Kayla says, "I broke up with Craig tonight, and it's over. I'm finished with him for good. It's time for me to . . . to get on with my life."

Mom starts to say, "Oh, honey," but Kayla throws out a hand, cuts off the sympathy.

"He won't be around anymore. Dad, there are a couple of boxes of his crap at the back door. Will you burn them?"

Mom and Dad exchange a look. I can see they think this is Kayla being Kayla.

Dad says, "What if you change your mind tomorrow?"

"I won't," she says, and looks at me.

"Okay," he says, and gives her a long squeeze. I imagine he's thinking, She *will* be sorry, but this will teach her a good lesson.

Mom and Dad will probably cry when they realize their almost son-in-law is really gone, but for now they give all their support to Kayla. As tough as she is, when she's under the crook of Mom's arm, she sobs. I know there will be a day when I'm in this same safe place, telling Mom the real story.

Mom told Bodee most girl things could be fixed inside forty-eight hours. It's taken Kayla and me about ten years to even get started.

I hug Kayla too. "You'll tell Mom, right?" she asks in my ear.

I can't imagine how, but I know I have to. I nod. "Over the weekend."

"I'll help you," Kayla says.

In the shelter of our family circle, I look over at Bodee and think about what his mom said.

Because she was right. *It doesn't come with a bow on it.*

I think God's going to be tying this one up for a long time to come.

chapter 28

"MOM, Bodee and I are going to walk to the fort."

"School night," she reminds us.

"We won't be long."

Bodee and I need to talk. Away from closets and air vents and bed slats. This afternoon was a roller coaster, from the planter at school to all the family hugs. We haven't said much about the deposition, or Bodee leaving, or what I did when he left, or even the way things happened with Kayla and Craig.

"I thought you'd left for good," I say, once we are in the woods.

"I thought about it," he says.

"I know."

"Because I thought you'd given up. And I didn't think I

could stand to watch it happen. But then I started to realize I wasn't much better. Blasting you about not talking, when I wasn't talking either. As you told me."

"I'm not sure you're capable of blasting," I say, letting him know I've forgiven him for his harshest words.

He thanks me with *that* smile. "I decided if I couldn't change you, maybe I could inspire you. What was it? What made you decide to tell?"

"You," I say.

"But you didn't know about the deposition."

"No." Sometime maybe I'll find the words to explain. "But it was you."

"Well, I wish you'd done it for yourself," he says. "Because I did the deposition for me." He thinks for a moment and then adds, "Well. For us."

"Sort of blurry thinking, huh? Me. You. Us," I say, releasing his hand so I can climb the ladder. In the fort, we share our window, bumping shoulders, staring down at the clearing even though it's almost completely dark. As if it's one of those 3-D graphics where some new image emerges if you stare long enough.

Something has.

Me: a girl who was raped. Him: a boy whose dad killed his mom.

Us: a girl and boy who survive.

"I did it for me. Us," I say, using his words.

"Not for Hayden?" he says.

"No," I say. "I don't think there'll be any more Hayden."

"Why not?"

"You," I say, and take his hand.

"Me?"

"You. I choose you."

I turn from the window, and Bodee turns with me. He doesn't seem to mind when I loop my arms around his back and lay my cheek on his shirt. "Bodee, who am I?" I ask, from the circle of his arms.

"Alexi."

"Wrong," I say, and look up to meet his eyes.

He has a curious expression, and I wonder what it looks like under a mop of kiwi green instead of just plain lemonade.

"Well, who are you then?"

"I think I'm somebody new. I'm not sure yet. That okay with you?"

Bodee lifts my hair and kisses my neck, and then my forehead, and my cheek. His lips part and I anticipate his question.

"You don't have to ask for a kiss," I tell him.

And he doesn't. That kiss is the best one of my life.

Maybe it's because Craig's gone.

But probably it's just because it's Bodee, and he's here.

When we finally break apart, he says, "Lex, who am I?" A smile, not the full one, curves his mouth.

"I'm not sure," I say, knowing the answer is not as simple as saying his name.

"Name?" he says playfully.

"Bodee," I answer.

"Another?" he says.

"The Kool-Aid Kid?" I ask, touching the undyed blond hair and twirling a length of it around my finger.

"Another?"

"I . . . don't know another."

"You want to know a secret?" he asks.

I nod.

"You're the girl from fourth period."

"I am?" I say, not understanding what this means. "But . . ."

"Alone. Before this crowd. Alone, in this terrible dream. Who am I in this visible silence? Can they hear me scream?" he sings very softly without taking his eyes off mine. The very first lyrics the Captain left for me.

I stare at him blankly for a second, and then I get it.

"You're Captain Lyric?" It's too storybook to be true. "But why? How?"

"Because you were hurting, and I didn't have the words. That first day of school by our lockers, I saw your neck. I know about things like that from my mom. I wanted to do something, but I didn't know what." He brushes his thumb over my lips. "You always have your earphones in, so I took a chance."

We sit on the floor of the fort, and he tells me how sometimes he wanders the hallways during lunch. And how that first week, Heather and I sat there talking in fourth period after the bell rang, and he saw me. That's how he knew which desk was mine. How he wrote those first words in the empty classroom after we'd gone, and then waited to see if I would write back.

"But you told me you had a girl in your sights."

Bodee grins. "I didn't mean she was in *my* fourth-period class."

"And I asked you if I knew her and you—"

"Lex, I just hoped you could look at yourself one day and understand what I see when I look at you."

"But the party?" I say. "When I asked to meet?"

"I went there that night to tell you."

"But you weren't wearing black," I say.

"Lex, you've seen everything I own. I didn't think you'd mind."

"I don't. But . . . oh." I remember the kiss with Hayden. "I wanted it to be you. I wish I'd known."

"Yeah. Me too." He's thinking about that kiss he witnessed too.

"But why was Hayden even there? Why was *he* dressed in black?" I have so many questions. But I want this to be true so badly that I have to check and recheck everything.

"Heather," he says simply. "But don't be mad at her; she wanted to fix things for you so much that she told Hayden about Captain Lyric. The desk, the meeting, everything."

"And Heather told you?"

"Yes," he says, and takes my hands loosely in his. "Eventually."

"Bodee, why didn't you tell me before now?" I ask. There have been so many opportunities.

He sighs. "The first time you mentioned the lyrics you were so happy." He looks away. Then down at his feet. "I wasn't sure that you'd be as happy if you knew it was me. We promised—"

"No skipping ahead," I say, remembering our walk home from school the day of the dance.

"No skipping ahead," he repeats.

"For what it's worth, I'm glad I fell for you instead of just your words."

"Me too." He surveys me, weighs me, it seems, and then says, "While I'm confessing, you need to know something else. I told someone about Craig."

My limbs turn to jelly. *"Who?"* Honest Bodee. He said he would tell, and he did.

"Liz." He grits his teeth and waits, but then he can't wait. "You mad?"

I think for another long moment. "No." Liz is the perfect person to know.

"You need a friend."

"I have you," I say, giving him a hug.

"You need more than me. There's still a long way to go, Lex. For you. And for me. For Kayla. With your parents, when they learn the real reason Craig is leaving Rickman. It's not going to be easy. And what if I spend the night with Ben or you go on another campout? You need someone else who knows. Who loves you."

I think about this all the way to the house, zooming in

on the subtle way Bodee said he loves me without saying it. I think about how wise he is. He never rushes. And I won't either. There's plenty of time for saying those words and many others in our future.

And he's right about Liz, and I'm glad I don't have to retell the story for her to understand. Because when I think of Craig, I still want to tear things apart.

But today is better than yesterday. And this hurt is still a hole in me, but it's a shrinking hole.

Tonight, I'm in bed and Bodee is lying beside me with his sneakers on. And it's late and we're so tired. And completely talked out.

I have the urge to count.

The compulsion is overwhelming. Even now, one hundred and three days after . . .

One.

Two.

Three.

Four . . .

We'll keep on *counting* until we get up to twenty-three . . .

Five . . .

But now I don't have to worry about blinking . . .

Six . . .

Because . . . *seven* . . . I can count Bodee's kisses with my eyes closed.

Dear Reader,

Thank you so much for reading *Faking Normal*. As you can probably guess, this project is very near to my heart. While it is a work of fiction, the pain expressed in these pages is one I understand. Alexi's story is not my story, but I have a story.

Do you have a story?

If so, I want to talk to you for a minute. Not because I'm an expert. (I'm not.) Not because I'm an advocate on a soapbox. (I'm too new to healing to be that, either.) Not because I'm an author who has more to say. (I'm wordy, but not about this. This is *hard*.)

I'm just another human who has been there. I'm channeling brave right now, too, because I'm worried that you might be hurting. And I hate that. The only way I know how to help is to offer a few dimes of truth that amazing people have given to me over the years. These are the lessons I continue to learn myself:

1. **WHAT HAPPENED TO YOU IS NOT YOUR FAULT.** I don't care what you were wearing, or what you said or didn't say, or if you took a drink or a hit that day. No one is allowed to take from you. Maybe you don't believe me yet, but this is the truth. You didn't make this happen. Self-blame is not the answer.

2. **YOU ARE NOT STUCK IN A NEVER-ENDING CYCLE OF PAIN.** I know it feels that way. I know you wonder if the way you

hurt right now is the way you will always hurt. It doesn't have to be. You can choose to start walking down the wonderful, terrifying, life-altering path of healing. Every path looks different, but here are a few starting places:

- *Reach out to a counselor or a rape crisis center.* There are national resources for this, and probably one in your town. The laws and definitions of sexual abuse vary from state to state, but you can reach out to RAINN, the Rape, Abuse & Incest National Network, through their website at www.rainn.org. They even have an instant messaging system. You can also reach the National Sexual Assault Hotline by dialing 1-800-656-HOPE (1-800-656-4673) twenty-four hours a day.

- *Please talk to a professional who understands the way you are hurting and who can help you plan a strategy for healing.* I know this is scary, but speaking with a professional is a gateway to healing. It's confidential, and it will get the words out of your soul and your mouth. It will give a safe voice to your pain and help you gain some necessary perspective on your situation.

- *Tell someone trustworthy in your life who loves you.* If you are like Alexi, right now you're thinking, *No. I can't. Courtney, you don't understand. If they know, I'll always be "that girl" or "that guy."* But I do understand, and the only way you'll stay *that girl* or *that guy* is by keeping it all locked inside. Pain has a way of working its way out even if we try to keep it in. Channel brave: Tell someone who loves you the truth.

- *Examine your coping mechanisms.* Alexi has several coping mechanisms: scratching her neck, counting the holes in the vent, and hiding in her closet. These things tell us she is not okay. One of my favorite parts of *Faking Normal* is the way Bodee helps Alexi count past the darkness to twenty-three. *Twenty-Three* was the original title of this manuscript because the number represented a place Alexi couldn't reach without help. What are your coping mechanisms? Are they dangerous? Are you trying to control pain with pain? Please don't hurt yourself anymore. Try to find healthy coping mechanisms.

3. **IT IS NOT YOUR JOB TO PROTECT YOUR ABUSER FROM THE CONSEQUENCES.** Craig's punishment isn't included in *Faking Normal* because it's a story of its own. For Alexi, for that day, getting him out of the house was the initial victory. There will be many choices for Alexi in the days to come. I believe she will face them all with waves of bravery. Will she and her family seek legal action? Will they make sure Craig never teaches again? Will she tell anyone beyond her family?

Bravery comes one day at a time. Seeking justice is a legal

right and privilege in our nation, and I hope as many of you who can, will. There need to be harsher consequences for abusers, and we need to do everything we can to end the prevalence of rape and rape culture. I wrote *Faking Normal* to (hopefully) inspire the first step, but I pray we all keep walking toward a safer world.

4. **THERE ARE BODEES IN THE WORLD.** This may be a hard truth to believe, but I promise you, there are guys and girls out there who are not takers. There are guys and girls who will keep the inch between you, who will dance with only two fingers on your hips, who will sleep in their tennis shoes if that's what it takes. *Trust* is such a difficult word if sexual abuse has been part of your story. I'm not suggesting that you trust everyone; I am reminding you that there *are* trustworthy people out there who do not want to hurt you. Try to find a way to keep your heart open. I know doing this changed my life in so many ways. I had a friend who patiently loved me from pain to less pain, from fear to trust, from "everyone takes" to "there are good guys."

5. **GRIEVE YOUR LOSSES, BUT REMEMBER THIS MOMENT DOES NOT DEFINE YOU.** Don't give your abuser more power than he or she already has. You were a beautiful human being before this happened to you, and nothing has changed. Whoever took from you didn't steal your future, your ability to love, your ability to move on, your ability to see yourself as

a wonderful, beautiful soul on our planet. Grieve what he or she took, but don't give him or her one bit more than that. You are more than a victim; you are a survivor.

6. **WRITE IT DOWN.** Alexi's bravery begins when she writes what happened to her on the back cover of *Hatchet*. Writing has been pivotal to healing for me. Writing could be a good starting place for you, too. Use a journal. Use a book cover. Use a scrap of paper. This is a simple outlet for channeling your own brave.

I know a book like *Faking Normal* doesn't fix a pain that is abuse-size, but I pray that it feels like a hug, some love, and a shared dose of bravery. You are loved and cherished and you can make it. Keep counting beyond the darkness!

—*Court*

acknowledgments

I tried this once and it was too long. I'm streamlining for space, but please know, I would go on about all of you for the length of this book if they'd let me.

First, to God. He is the boy who loves me anyway (like Bodee is for Alexi) and He is the reason I understand there is peace and love after pain.

Thanks, shout-outs, praises, blessings, and love:

To Kelly Sonnack. She's amazing, and tough, and brilliant, and I trust her to the moon and back.

To Rosemary Brosnan. You gave me the best birthday present of my life. You are a treasure of knowledge, encouragement, honesty, and belief, and *all* the words of praise don't fit here, but please know, from the bottom of my toes, I thank you for letting me be on your team.

To Andrea Martin. I feel like if we were in the FBI (don't you wish we were?), you would be the best handler in the world.

To the entire team at Harper: Brenna Franzitta, Valerie Shea, Cara Petrus, Laura Lyn DiSiena, Kim VandeWater, Patty Rosati, Olivia deLeon, Susan Katz, Kate Jackson, and all the people I don't know yet but who work so hard. Thank you for being in my corner and making this experience amazing. I owe you all Goo-Goos.

To Ruta Sepetys and Sharon Cameron. There would be no book without those "You have to write this" conversations in L.A. xoxo.

To my village: Erica Rodgers, Kristin O'Donnell Tubb (long live Annie and Eve), Rae Ann Parker, Hannah Dills, Jessica Young, Genetta Adair, Patricia Nesbitt, Janice Erbach, Alina Klein, Kate Dopirak, Jolene Perry, Tricia Lawrence, Sarah Davies, Tiffany Russell, Taryn Fagerness, SCBWI, every English teacher I ever had, SSUMC kiddos and families, BUMC families, LWC students, Portia Pennington, Susan Eaddy, Katie McGarry, David Arnold, Ashley Schwartau, Cassie Frye, Lauren Thoman, Tracy Barrett, Jennifer Jabaley, S. R. Johannes, CJ Redwine, Myra McEntire, Katie and Matt Corbin, Leah Spurlin, Brooke Buckley, Jami Unland, Dr. Bruce Harris, T, Sarah Elizabeth, CJ Schooler (#007), and Victoria Schwab. You read. You listen. You love. (Some of you even laser tag.) You're there. Always. I'm forever in your debt. Your fingerprints are all over the story and my life.

To Adam. Be the crash. Rhinos forever.

To my Stevens, Ledbetter, and Potter family—I love you. Thank you for loving me.

Finally, to all you readers. Of the two of us, you are my better half.

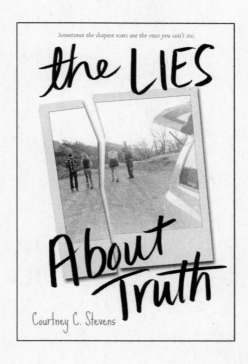

CHAPTER ONE

Night was like Christmas. There wasn't nearly enough of it to go around, especially in June. At 8:55, I walked down our little bayside street, crossed the road, and wound through the lot of the Worthy Wayfarer toward what I hoped was an empty shore. My company consisted of sand, circular thoughts, and a wretched pair of shorts.

Fletcher, my therapist, thought getting me back in clothes that didn't cover my whole body, even at night, was a step in the right direction. I'd agreed to try, and this was my first attempt at bare legs. It was dark, I was in my favorite place on the planet, and I was fine. Showing scars to no one *was fine*. That's what I told myself as I reached the dune walk.

I loved the abandoned beach. Loved the sound of sloshing tide. Loved when the Florida sand was neither hot nor cold, but perfectly warm between my painted toes. Over the last year, I'd forgotten the glorious *swish-swish* sound athletic fabric made during a run. That was the one thing about Fletcher's challenge I was looking forward to. Six miles of *swish-swish*. I pressed pause on my playlist and listened deeply: gulf breeze, ocean, my heartbeat, *swish-swish*, and . . . dang it.

There were people on *my* beach.

Ducking into the sea grass, I watched the scene—a graduation party. I'd gotten an invite—a pity nod, I'm sure—and I'd deleted the message. The smoky smell of bonfire flames licking wood tempted me to join the party. But wearing shorts, with this many people around . . . I couldn't think of anything worse.

This was Gray and Trent's class get-together, not mine, but a few of my former classmates sat on towels. A group of seniors danced and lifted Solo cups and sang off-key verses. Others sat on driftwood logs talking and laughing. Graduation had been two nights ago, and they all seemed to be sucking the last of high school through a tiny straw.

Good for them.

The fire and moonlight made slipping through the dunes seem unlikely, but I needed to run. And I wanted to keep my word about the shorts. The moment I stepped out of the shadows to dart toward the empty coastline owned by the military, Gina yelled my name.

"Sadie." The wave that came with her greeting was shallow and tentative, but her smile was canyon-deep.

She was genuinely happy to see me. If only I could recip-rocate.

I froze on the spot and waited, standing between two tow-ering dunes. There was something about being with an old friend that brought back old habits, good and bad. Even after eleven months of awkward interactions.

"Hey, Gina," I said when she was still a few steps away.

She wove her windblown mane into a tight knot as she approached, and I envied the casual way she put her cheek-bones on display. "You got my text," she said. "I hoped you'd come, but I can't believe you're here."

I tugged on the edge of my shorts and pointed to my shoes. "Actually, I was out for a run."

She didn't comment on the shorts, but her gaze lingered on my thigh and a long triangular scar I called Pink Floyd.

"You could come say hi," she suggested.

I backed away a few steps. "I don't think so."

Best friends, even former ones, were supposed to under-stand crap like social anxiety and scar exposure. All of my previous explanations had failed to register—or Gina couldn't accept that sometimes when things changed, they didn't change back. Even if we both wanted them to.

Gina's response was to rocket-launch me into another lion's den. "Um . . . Gray's here. I know he'd love to see you."

Every time we were together, she tried to sell me the same story. I didn't know whether it was supposed to lessen her guilt or increase mine for avoiding him.

"Please stop trying to fix—"

"I'm just saying you should hear him out. He's still not over you." Gina toed the sand and made a concerted effort to lift her eyes to mine. "Six years is a lot to throw away."

Gray Garrison and I were once comasters of the swings, sworn Potterheads, fellow indie band enthusiasts, and in some variation of young love, cooties and all, for every minute we'd known each other. A year ago, the high school halls had felt like a really long wedding aisle. A lot can change in a year.

"I'm sort of with Max now," I told her.

Yes, Max was in another country, and yes, *with* was a relationship of emails, but we were our version of together. And maybe if I admitted that now, she'd stop pushing Gray at me.

Gina's pretty, scarless face—whose only technical imperfection was a smattering of adorable freckles—froze in surprise. "Um, that's great, Sadie." She shoved her hands into her pockets and shifted her weight back and forth before adding, "I just want to remind you there's *nothing*, still nothing, between me and Gray."

Except that one little bit of sex or something I'd interrupted.

"Not that it makes it okay, but we were all pretty messed up back then."

Back then wasn't that long ago.

"Neither of us ever meant"—she held up empty hands and gestured toward my face, toward the scar I called Idaho—"to hurt anyone."

I knew that.

Knowing something wasn't worth shit sometimes. This was exactly why I avoided talking to Gina. She always brought this up. Always told me she was so, so sorry. Always shoved me toward the past. And here we were back on that same treadmill.

The thing was, I believed her. Gray, too, for that matter. Neither made idle apologies or hurt people, especially me, intentionally. But they had, and I still couldn't muster up an *It's no big deal.* Or even an *It's a huge deal and I can't forgive you.* So she went on apologizing, and I went on keeping grudges.

Thank God for home school. At least I hadn't heard this every day.

Gina continued her babble. "Wouldn't it be nice to hang out again? You could walk over there with me, sit down, have a drink, ignore Gray if you want, tell me about running or surgeries or how Max is or . . . anything. I . . . miss you."

I missed her, too. The words wouldn't come out. I was immediately glad they hadn't, because Gray's hands landed on my shoulders, soft and gentle, interrupting everything. I knew they were his without spinning around. Body movements were like fingerprints; they were all unique. His was a choreography I used to dance to.

"Hey, you," he said.

How did a voice hovering over an ear have that much power?

"Hey, you," I said, and turned to face him.

Gray, with his boyish face and perfectly kissable nose. No

scars, no imperfections, except a right ear the tiniest bit lower than the left. He spread out his arms—a clear invitation—and out of either obligation or habit, I hugged him. His chin landed on top of my head, my face smooshed against his chest, his hands crisscrossed against my back.

Rubbing alcohol on open wounds hurt less.

One, we weren't a couple anymore. Two, once you've been held, you know what it feels like when there's no one to hold you. And three, he was Gray, both the guy and the color of this situation. Max and I emailed, but a computer couldn't whisper in my ear. A computer didn't have arms.

Gray let me go. "I'm glad you're out of the house," he said.

Not only was I out of the house, I was having a conversation with two—count them—people. Other than my parents, that didn't happen very often. I wasn't exactly scared of people, but people seemed scared of me.

"I was out for a run," I explained again, taking several steps back.

"Oh. I thought maybe . . ." His words trailed away, but the implication was clear. He thought I had come to see him or Gina. They'd both texted me about this party earlier in the week.

On a whim, I tested a theory. More to remind myself I was right than because I believed he'd changed.

I looked Gray straight in the eyes.

He looked away.

That didn't make him a monster, but it sure made me feel like one. Friendship, much less a relationship, was impossible when he couldn't stand the sight of me. So I was the one who had officially broken it off.

"Still can't do it," I said.

He knew *it* meant to look at me, because he sighed. Gina reined us in, placing her hands on our shoulders. Always the peacemaker.

"I need to go," I said.

Before I sprinted away, Gina stopped me with a question. "Is Max coming back for the . . . anniversary?"

I nodded. If some people are knotted in friendship, we were all one big tangle. Gray and me. Gina and Trent. Max, Trent's tagalong little brother. Our foursome, occasionally fivesome, used to be inseparable. Neighbors, couples, and the second generation of friends in our families.

Our parents had stuck together over the past year.

We hadn't followed in their footsteps.

The wreck happened June 29. We were twenty-two days away from the one-year anniversary of Trent's death.

"I need to go," I said, more urgently than before.

"What about school? Are you coming back in the fall?"

I didn't want to talk about school or the anniversary. I wanted to run.

"Sorry. I gotta go," I said, in full retreat mode.

"I'll check in later," she said.

Gray just stood there sighing with his fingers laced behind his head. I'd heard him sigh more in the past year than in all the time we were a couple.

As I took off, my eyes drifted in the direction of the party. My old classmates were probably sighing too. Everyone out there knew about Trent, knew I'd gone through the window of his Yaris, knew why Gray and I broke up. They probably assumed I blamed Gina and Gray for more than cheating. (Fair assumption, as she was driving the car that caused my face to have a scar named Idaho. And he was right beside her.)

Maybe I did. Maybe I didn't. Blame was crazy complicated. Some days, everything—Trent's death, my face, all the break-ups, Max leaving the country—was Gina and Gray's fault. Some days, God was the fall guy. Some days, blame never entered my mind. I liked those days best. I didn't want to be an angry jerk who sat around reminiscing about old grievances and pointing fingers, but I couldn't seem to control the emotion with any accuracy.

All I knew was that the farther I got from the party, the more I wished Gina or Gray would come after me. Neither of them did, so I cranked up my music and ran. I wasn't a sprinter, and after a mile, my lungs reminded me of that.

I slowed to a stop, put my hands on my knees, and took a deep breath. In front of me, five concrete pylons rose out of the water like a broken-down gate. "The Wall," as we all called it, was once a military building on the shore. Now, thanks to a hurricane, it was a gull stoop at the one-mile mark. This was where I wrote my list in the sand.

Because it was damaged.

Because what it once was didn't matter to the birds.

Because I understood "the Wall" and "the Wall" understood me.

It was nice to have friendship with a place.

In the company of moonlight and Coldplay, I wrote the things I wanted from life this year.

1. Wear a tank top in public
2. Walk the line at graduation
3. Forgive Gina and Gray
4. Stop following. Start leading.
5. Drive a car again
6. Kiss someone without flinching
7. Visit the Fountain of Youth

Beneath the list, I scrawled the only Latin phrase I knew. *A posse ad esse.* It means . . . "from possibility to actuality."

Apart from the Fountain of Youth, these were simple, achievable things, in concept. Hell, some of them I could do in a day. But I'd had many days, many opportunities, many lists in the sand, and no progress. Nearly every night I wrote these things.

And every night the ocean washed them away.

Tonight—probably because I'd seen Gina and Gray, or maybe because I felt like that old broken-down wall—I added one thing beside number three.

And tell them the truth.

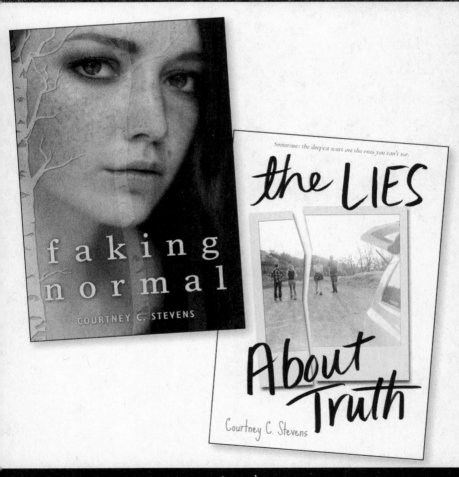

JOIN THE

Epic Reads
COMMUNITY

THE ULTIMATE YA DESTINATION

◀ **DISCOVER** ▶
your next favorite read

◀ **MEET** ▶
new authors to love

◀ **WIN** ▶
free books

◀ **SHARE** ▶
infographics, playlists, quizzes, and more

◀ **WATCH** ▶
the latest videos

◀ **TUNE IN** ▶
to Tea Time with Team Epic Reads

   Find us at **www.epicreads.com**
and **@epicreads**